Fall

Fall
By
Melyssa & Joey Winchester

This book is dedicated to the people who believe true love never really dies, no matter the distance, time and circumstances.

Second chances are not given to make things right. But are given to prove that we could be better even after we fall. – Unknown

Prologue
All That You Can't Leave Behind

Joshua

Alyssa Jeffries.

The girl who changed my world the second I laid eyes on her.

Known as Aly to a select few she was close to, always known as AJ to me.

A woman that no matter how far or fast I run, I can't seem to escape.

Also, the woman who's going to bed tonight with one less parent.

"Did you hear me, Josh?" My buddy Kevin's voice calls over the line, his annoyance evident in his clipped tone.

"Yeah, I heard you. It's just a shock."

Wayne Jeffries is a legend in my hometown. Some would even go so far as to call him a saint.

The way he'd reach out to the neighborhood kids, bringing us in for a hot meal, while at the same time giving us the obvious attention we were lacking at home.

He filled our heads at the same time as our stomachs while most of us sat immersed in a hockey game on television.

Wayne was the epitome of good.

He's also the man who saved my butt more times than I can count, and who I owe most for being the man I am today.

Well, maybe not *exactly* the way I am now.

Knowing he's gone—suffering a stroke at the age of sixty-six—when the last time I laid eyes on him, he looked like he would outlive us all, it's exactly like I told Kevin.

It's a shock.

"She's not doing so well, man. I know how you are about any mention of coming back here, but I think in this case, you might want to make an exception."

If there's anyone who can change my mind about going back to Toronto, it's her, but it still isn't a guarantee. The reasons I left town haven't changed, even if my situation has.

"Kev, I feel bad for her; I do, but me coming back isn't going to alleviate that. If anything, seeing me will just make it worse."

Alyssa and me, we've got history. It's historical shit, and not something I'm eager to go back and confront. Call me a wuss, but the girl's better off not having me there. She's safer that way.

We both are.

"Not really seeing how it could be worse than losing her dad and not having anyone, besides Helen, who understands the loss."

I don't need to know this, but more to the point, I don't want to know it.

Besides her old man, she's the only person in my sad existence to make me feel something other than hatred and self-loathing. If I buy into what Kevin's trying to sell me, it threatens everything I spent the last twenty years building.

I'll allow myself to feel again, and just like he seems to think, I'll go back with my tail between my legs. Home to the mistakes and the mess I left behind.

Home to her.

"You're being a little overdramatic, don't you think?"

Kevin doesn't even have to answer and I already know he's not.

Alyssa, at least the girl I remember, was never fond of large groups of people. What comes with popularity, was the last thing on her agenda. She was more content digging in the dirt with a couple of moronic boys than she was dressing up, going out and partying.

It's half the reason we called her AJ. She was one of the guys.

At least she was until I went and screwed it up.

I'm also having a hard time believing in the twenty years since I bailed, she hasn't moved on with her life. Sure, she was all about her family; especially her father, but there wasn't a person we came in contact with who didn't love the girl.

Not the same way I came to feel about her, but they damn sure felt something. Which makes me wonder if Kevin is just using her as a way to get me back in town.

It wouldn't be the first time.

"You really think I enjoy picking up the phone and having to tell you this? I get better than anyone why you left. I also know all about your goal to stay fucking gone. But sometimes we've got to do things for people, no matter how uncomfortable it makes us."

"Kev—"

"No, you know what, Josh? You can stow whatever excuse you're gonna give because they're all just the same regurgitated crap you've been saying for years. For once in your life, can you just bottle your shit and think about somebody else?"

"AJ isn't just somebody else."

"Yeah, I know. She's *the* somebody. Which, by my estimation, means you're going to do what I said and book the first flight out."

It pains me how easy he makes it sound.

Like it wouldn't take every ounce of strength I have to get off the sofa right now and pack a bag, calling the airline and booking a flight.

There's nothing easy about any of this.

"Let's say I do what you want and catch the next flight out. What happens when I get there and she slams the door in my face? What's the bright idea then, Einstein?"

"You keep knocking until the slammed door opens."

Well, shit. I can't exactly argue with that.

"Stop being so pigheaded, Josh. It's been twenty years. Get your ass back here and get your girl."

My girl.

That's what she used to be, and if I'm honest with myself, I'm pretty sure it's what she's always going to be.

The real question is, can I willingly go back and throw myself at the mercy of not only her but her mom again after the way I left things?

Of course. It's not like you've got anything substantial going on. Unless indulging in meaningless sex with strangers has somehow become more than it appears.

There's an easy enough myth to dispel.

Heading out a couple of times a year and giving in to the need to have a warm body beside me for a night, means absolutely nothing, giving me no reason, especially with not being needed here for work, to stay.

Alyssa Jeffries, though. She is sure as hell enough of a reason to leave.

I hate admitting it, but Kevin's right. It's been twenty damn years. Even if he's using AJ as a reason to get me home, it's time I stopped running.

Start admitting that the setup isn't working and something's still missing.

Someone's missing.

I miss my girl and I'm getting sick of denying it.

"You're gonna do it, aren't you?" he exclaims. "I'm finally getting through your thick skull!"

The level of smugness I hear annoys me to no end, but he's right, and there's no sense dragging it out any longer than I already have. Something tells me he knew this was how things were going to go before he even got on the phone.

"I'm gonna do it, but Kev, not a damn word."

It's a last-minute thought, but important.

If I'm gonna do what he said and head back to Toronto to win back AJ, I don't want her to see it coming.

"A word about what?" he laughs, and after a few minutes of back and forth, along with a promise to let him know the flight information when I've got it, I hit end on the call.

I can't believe I'm entertaining this, much less about to get up and pack in order to make it a reality. But with the way the thought of seeing her again is giving me life, I know I'm well past the point of backing out.

The first time I fell for the girl next door, I was seven.

The next time, an idiotic fifteen-year-old with a chip on his shoulder.

Twenty years of change, growth, and time have passed now.

I'm older, wiser, and the chip on my shoulder has been almost whittled down to nothing. The only running I want to do these days is in a completely different direction.

Toward her.

AJ.

And this time when I catch her, I'm never running again.

Chapter One
The Hardest Goodbye

Alyssa

Open the door, accept condolences, smile, making sure to show teeth so it appears more authentic. Close the door, repeating the cycle over again in fifteen minutes when the doorbell's shrill blast goes off like clockwork.

My heart—if there's anything left of it—is breaking, and I know these people mean well, but if I have to hear the words, *I'm sorry for your loss,* one more time, I'm not going to be responsible for what I do. It's not the worst of it, though. No, it's the ones who tell me they understand what I'm going through that make me want to grab the baseball bat out of the closet and wail on something.

Anything.

Maybe even their faces.

How can they understand what I'm going through when they didn't know Wayne Jeffries the way I did?

They weren't the ones being lulled to sleep as a child to the sound of his voice as he sang off-key lullabies. The tough guy who when I broke my leg falling off a bike at seven, cried even more than I did. The man so proud the day I graduated high school, he jumped up out of his seat halfway through the ceremony, making sure the world knew how amazing Alyssa Jeffries was.

More than all of those things, he's the person who spent the last thirty-five years showing me who and what a real man is. Who, even on his deathbed, made sure I knew I was the best damn thing he ever did with his life.

These people don't know that side of Wayne Jeffries.

That's something only for me, which makes what I'm having to do now even harder. Everywhere I turn in this house, the memories haunt me and make my heart shatter all over again.

Why'd you leave us, huh? How are we supposed to stand here and be strong when the very man whose strength we depended on is gone?

"Daddy," I whisper to the empty space. "I can't do this without you."

Another memory.

My speaking to the air this way, and his belief it was useful because it's how the people who are lost communicate with the ones left behind.

"It's long distance phone calls for the people who have crossed over, dove. Whenever you're feeling alone and nothing seems to ease it, just speak the words aloud and they'll carry through the breeze like invisible phone lines. And if you listen closely, you'll hear their answer."

He said it so often growing up that for a long time I believed it.

When my grandma died just after my fifth birthday, I would talk to her just the way my daddy taught me. Of course, I never heard anything back, but I figured at the time it didn't work so well when you're little. The older I became, the more I saw it for what it really was.

His way of handling the losses.

Shortly after, I gave up believing.

Until now.

"Daddy, please tell me how to live without you..." I whisper into the air just as the doorbell goes off.

Okay Aly, time to put your game face on.

No matter how much it aches or how gaping the hole is in my heart, I've got to grin and bear it, remembering the other part of what he told me as a young child.

It won't last forever.

Joshua

After landing and becoming reacquainted with my hatred for Pearson airport, I secure my bag and head out to meet Kevin.

His eyes once I've made my way over honing in on the shoebox in my hand, but thankfully, his mouth staying shut as he grabs my suitcase and heads around to the trunk.

A silence not nearly long enough when a few seconds later, he stops holding back.

"Not for nothing, Josh, but you always bring a girl shoes when she loses a parent?"

If shoes were in the box, they would have gotten tossed in the trunk the same way everything else did. This isn't a pair of shoes, though.

It's a lifetime.

My lifetime with AJ, one I'm not letting out of my sight.

"Oh yeah. What says *I'm sorry for your loss* better than a pair of eight-inch heels? Isn't that what everyone does?"

"No need to be a smartass." Waving toward the door before jogging around to the driver's side, he grunts. "Now get in. You know how I feel about airports."

I definitely do.

If there's one person in the world who prefers driving everywhere, it's Kevin Williams.

Pulling on the handle and leaning in, I place the box gingerly down between our seats and slip my body in after it, pulling it back into my lap the second I've got the belt secured.

"You wanna tell me what the deal is with you and that box, or you gonna leave me to guess?"

Looking at the box of memories, knowing what's inside and what every single item means to me *and* my past with Alyssa, I just shake my head and grin. Let him stew in his curiosity for a while.

The box and its contents are only for me.

"If I told you, I'd have to kill you, and you know if that happens your mom would never forgive me."

"Some days I think if you did, she'd be the first in line thanking you."

It's good to see some things never change. In this instance, Kevin's flair for the dramatic.

For fifteen years there were two certainties when it came to adults in my life. There were two parents on our street who gave a shit. Wayne Jeffries and Rosalie Williams, Kevin's mom. I have a hard time believing even after all this time she'd be the first in line to see anyone die, much less her own flesh and blood.

"Glad to see you're still melodramatic. Though, it appears to have gotten worse since we saw each other last."

"No one's the same person they were twenty years ago, man. Can you honestly sit here and tell me you are?"

Considering time seemed to stop for me at sixteen and even with the move and the life I built for myself after the fact, it still hasn't seemed to start back up, my answer to this wouldn't like everyone else's.

Sure, I've changed, but not in the obvious ways everyone else has.

I've just been going through the motions.

"So, you sure Sammie's cool with me staying with you guys while I'm here?" I attempt to change the subject.

"If I let you go to a hotel, not only would Sammie whip my ass, but so would my mom. I'm already in the doghouse enough with the both of them, I'm not looking to add more to it."

Kevin's wife Samantha was a cheerleader the last time I saw her. I hadn't come back for their wedding, which neither of them have let me live down, but even if I had, I would still find it hard to believe those two ended up together.

Any time I imagined Sammie in the future, it was always her running off and marrying the captain of the football team. Not the IT geek Kevin eventually became.

Just goes to show how appearances can be deceiving, and you're powerless against who your heart calls to and falls in love with.

The same way I did with Alyssa.

Damn. Not even in the car fifteen minutes and she's already flooding my brain.

"How is Sammie doing?"

Another change in the subject attempt, one I'm in desperate need of with the bottomless pit of emotion just thinking her name evokes in me.

"She's five months pregnant. How do you think she is?"

"Hormones getting to her?"

"More like getting to me, but if she asks, I never said that."

"You used to spend days hacking into some of the largest government databases in the world. You're telling me you can't handle a pregnant woman?"

"Oh man." He chuckles. "I cannot *wait* for you to stay with us now. Hacking is a walk in the park compared to Sammie and her moods."

"But you love her anyway."

"That I do." He agrees and the way his face goes from pensive to soft, his small grin growing larger by the second, there's no room for doubt. He's definitely got it bad for his wife.

Getting to see this after spending years just hearing it over the phone, is hard to stomach. It serves as a reminder of everything I don't have and spent the last twenty years running from. Content with my lack of personal connections and living my life alone.

Witnessing now the way your life can be enriched by having the right person in it, I'm definitely jealous.

I want what my best friend has.

"Little known fact, Joshua. If you can somehow get back into Aly's good graces, you might want to look into putting a bun in her oven."

Oh, for fuck sakes, here we go.

We've gone from adoration to perversion. Another of Kevin's strong suits.

"Do I even want to know why?"

Turning just slightly and angling his eyes at me, he grins.

"You think sex is hot when you're doing it with some random and there's no attachments or feelings involved?" I swallow the lump in my throat hearing him throw my own words at me. "Try doing it with a pregnant chick. It's off the damn charts. The best part being, they're damn near insatiable."

"Remind me to ask Sammie about that when we get there."

This shuts him up and gives me the break I need from the twist in my gut.

I may not have the first clue about marriage, but love, sex, and pregnancy, they all hit a little too close to home.

"She's a wreck, man."

I wondered how long it was gonna take him to talk about Aly.

"So, your bright idea is to have me come in with my mess and what? Create a bigger one?"

"You're disconnected, brother. You're not a mess. Even if you were though, some of the best things in life are messy."

"Tell me that in six months when you're cleaning baby puke from your suit jacket."

He laughs and after a few seconds, I join him.

"Thanks for making my point for me. You know how useless I am without coffee this early."

He may not be the same friend I left behind twenty years ago, but there's no doubt his addiction to all things caffeinated is still as strong as ever.

"I could have easily gotten a cab from the airport if you wanted to stay home and feed your need."

"And I'm straight up telling you again. If I'd done that, I'd be picking you up without balls. And just in case it's not obvious, I kind of like having my boys intact."

Sharing another laugh together, the car goes quiet as he pulls out onto the highway and merges into the express lanes, leaving me to use the quiet to my advantage. Closing my eyes, I allow myself to nod off, but not before the darkness that comes as my eyes shut goes Technicolor as a brown-haired angel walks toward me, a smile on her face, her lips parted and repeating the only five words I've never tired of hearing.

Words I hope I can pull from my daydream and make her repeat again, more than once, every single day until we've made up for the twenty years without them.

I love you, Joshua Brantley.

Chapter Two
The Day the Earth Stood Still

Alyssa

I don't think I can do this.

It was hard enough when I had to sit beside my mom in the church, listening to the pastor speak of my dad. Sharing memories of a time forever ago, when my dad would reach out to help kids in the neighborhood, working in tandem with the pastor, attempting to shape their lives in a more positive way.

My mother is unable to keep it together despite what must have been her best attempt and finally releasing the hold on her emotions, letting them boil over as he spoke, collapsing into my body, needing me to be the strong one.

The sound and feel from the vibration of her emotions smothering me as they filtered through the church.

Making my way from the town car that brought us here, my hand still being held tightly in hers as we slowly start moving across the lightly dewed grass toward my daddy's final resting place, it becomes even harder to ignore.

I'm *positive* I can't do this.

My rigid body and broken heart aware with each step we take, just how close I am to having to do what everyone just expects will be easy for me to do.

Deliver a eulogy.

Say goodbye to the only man who has ever loved me as fiercely as I did him. And the man I will never be able to wrap my arms around again.

Saying goodbye, moving on, in time this day becoming a memory in a long line of them, I've already done it too much and those people weren't him.

They weren't my dad.

How can anyone, my mother included, expect me to do this?

I'm tired of goodbyes.

Just once I would like to be able to deliver one heck of a hello.

Am I doomed to always be the goodbye girl?

As we're making our way over the hill, I take in the rows of chairs, some still empty but a lot filled by a group of young men and women, along with an older set. All of their lives forever altered by what I always hope will be his legacy.

I may not be able to say goodbye to him, but I can admit that my daddy changed the world.

Pausing once we've reached our seats, front and center for what is about to take place next, I lower myself down until my mother is seated, before following suit, all the while my eyes remaining locked and loaded on the scene unfolding.

"Why couldn't he be cremated?"

Insensitive question, sure. The worst possible time to ask it, definitely, but despite knowing it, I can't help thinking that if he had agreed to cremation when they went about having their wills written, this ache and all of this pomp and circumstance could have been avoided.

We could have taken the urn, one made of stained glass— just like the windows at church—down to the water and said our own private goodbye to the man we loved so deeply, instead of having to stand here and draw the pain out longer.

"Your father always did his best work building things from the ashes, Aly. He was never a fan of being turned into it." My mother responds as if it's not the first time the question has been asked of her, and despite my deep seeded need to argue in favor of cremation, her words stop me cold.

She's right. This is how it had to be for him. No other way would do.

With a squeeze to my hand, calling my attention away from the large wooden box in front of me, I meet her eyes and that's when I see what she had been desperately trying to summon during the church service, but had failed her.

Strength.

And not just any strength.

My fathers'.

For the first time since people started dropping by the house after hearing of his passing, I'm starting to see what I couldn't through my own grief.

His physical form may be gone, but it's the heart, soul, strength, and love he bestowed on every single person he came into contact with that won't ever be.

"He's here," I whisper and what should be the strangest sight with what we're all about to face, my mother's lips begin to rise and she merely nods, as if she's known it all this time.

"Did you really think he would miss this?" She pauses, her eyes lifting from mine as she takes in the people around us. "Generations of people, baby girl. He wouldn't have missed this for anything."

Nodding and letting my eyes wander slowly, running over all of the men, women and children alike—generations—just like she said, all here to say goodbye and honor the man I was lucky enough to call dad.

All but one.

Try as I might not to be let down by his absence, my heart seems to break just a little more with the knowledge that not even the death of the man he once called "Dad" himself was enough to bring him home.

With all the years that have passed since the fateful day he shot like a lightning bolt out of my life, he has to realize his being here would have been accepted. Okay.

It's where he should be.

Just another reminder of how well I perfected saying goodbye. I'm so well versed in it that the one boy I'd never gotten the chance to say it to, but who had shaped every day after his leaving, still couldn't find his way back home in order to give it to the one person who deserved it.

Damn you, Joshua Brantley. You don't have the right to own any more of my heart, especially not today. Today isn't about you and I hate that even for a second, I've managed to make it that way.

In letting my thoughts wander, my mind easily treading back into territory I've spent the last twenty years trying to forget, erase and write over, I've become completely unaware of the pastor now standing beside me until my mom squeezes my arm lightly and brings me back.

It's time.

Only this time, with the renewed strength and earlier words from my mother, I'm determined this won't be a goodbye. It's an *I'll see you soon,* or better yet, the most tender, heartfelt and beautiful hello because when it comes to Wayne—my best friend, my daddy, and my champion—nothing but all I've got will do.

Joshua

It should be hard to see from this vantage point, most of my body being blocked by the tree I'm hidden behind, but it's not. It seems not even pieces of nature, twenty years of being away, or my ever-dwindling eyesight can stop me from honing in on her the second I arrive.

I'm especially sensitive to the vacant look I can make out in her eyes as she rises from her seat and takes crisp, yet even steps toward the podium, smiling weakly at the pastor before he steps down, allowing her to take her rightful place.

The only place I would expect her to be today.

A place that if I hadn't walked away, I would be standing with her as she delivered.

Instead, I'm regulated to being hidden from the masses, watching from a distance, as my heart calls to hers, the same way it's always done since I met her. It's a call I have to squash down and ignore. I have every intention of making my presence known, but respect for everything Wayne Jeffries gave me in life stops it from being now.

Has she noticed my absence?

Who am I kidding? I've spent the last twenty years making sure I never had to come back. Of course, she didn't search for me. Hiding here and watching her from a distance only proves I'm letting her down again now.

What was I thinking coming back here? Determined to insert myself back into a life I'd given up the right to be a part of when I left without so much as a goodbye the day after she dropped the news.

The minute she informed me that life as I knew it was about to change.

No matter how much I loved Wayne, I lost the right to be here the minute I left his daughter behind because I couldn't deal.

"I have to admit, I questioned whether you would make an appearance today."

Stripping my gaze from the shaking form of the only girl I've ever loved, I focus on the voice now standing in front of me, the smallest touch of a wistful smile on her lips.

Caroline Wayland. Another kid from the old neighborhood Wayne had helped. Also, the girl who would wind up being my girl's best friend.

"Nowhere else I need to be."

"Funny you say it like that. I'm thinking those six words would have been better received if you'd said them before you hightailed it out of town."

Hatred, anger, distrust and raw and unbridled pain. I expect all of those things from Alyssa when I finally come face to face with her again, but standing here of all places and hearing it from someone who has no clue what was going on for either of us back then, I don't need to hear it.

Attempting to hide my grimace, I move around her, determined with my hiding spot compromised to find another one.

"There's nowhere else to hide, Joshua. You either come out of hiding and destroy Aly for the fourth time or you stay here and entertain an old friend."

"We were never friends." I scoff, offended at the implication. She was my girl's best friend. That's all there was to her and me. No matter how similar our backgrounds may have been, it was a good day when I could mildly tolerate Cara.

With all the time and distance between us, I don't have to do that anymore. Especially with the knowledge I have of the current state of their friendship. If there's anyone here more unwelcome than me, it's her.

"You're right. We weren't, because I knew what she couldn't see until years after you split. She was too good for you. Then and now."

"That's rich, coming from the girl who tried more than once to get me in a position to where she could take advantage of me, despite knowing how I felt about her best friend. Spare me the good friend act, Cara. We both know as far as friends go, you're the worst kind."

Damn. Coming back here wasn't supposed to be about this.

I really don't want to be taking this walk down memory lane, especially not with Caroline.

Waiting for her to mount some kind of a comeback and coming up empty, I let myself be carried away again as I hear the microphone being positioned, Alyssa getting ready to memorialize the man she loved even more than she had me.

The man we both loved.

Catching the soft tremor in her voice as she finally begins to speak, I move around Caroline, bringing myself out of hiding, ready and willing to face whatever the consequences will be.

It's only when I'm completely out of the shadows, making my way over the grooves in the grass and more into her line of sight as she looks out over the crowd of people gathered that it happens.

Her head pauses in its inspection. Her eyes, I can feel them before I look up to meet them, her sharp intake of breath clear as day through the mic and resonating all the way down through the rows of people.

The sound enough to make more than a few turn their heads toward what has caused her to gasp, but a move I'm only vaguely aware of as my eyes, my body, my god damned soul, all center on her.

And in the few silent beats it takes before she begins speaking again, shaking off her surprise, I can feel the first wall begin to fall.

I'm home.

Chapter Three
You Can Let Go

Alyssa

No. It can't be. He can't be here.

This is because I was thinking about him earlier. He's been on my mind despite my every attempt not to think about him, and now my mind has teamed up with my heart and conjured up the ghost of him to haunt me.

Except for a ghost, he's surprisingly agile. His body now stilled, was moving only a few seconds ago. And where his gaze had lingered to the ground in front of him before, now he's staring straight at me.

Straight *through* me.

My initial surprise at seeing him has given him away, and with the way he seems to move his weight from one foot to the next, yet make no move to look away now that we've connected, tells me he's uncomfortable with even the small amount of attention he's now getting from the rest of the people present.

Joshua Brantley is really here.

I'm torn.

On the one hand, I know I need to deliver this eulogy, but there's also the very strong urge from somewhere inside the heart I've kept under strict lock and key, that wants to back down from this podium, run to him and never let him go.

Such a natural and simplistic move but one even with how my heart still responds to his, I have to ignore.

It may have taken me a long time to move on from the disaster of our love story, but move on I did, and now, no matter what seeing him again makes me feel, I need to do what I came here to do.

Honor my father.

With a final deep exhale, I focus my attention on the people now turning their attention on me, doing just that.

"The first memory I have of my daddy, was shortly after I turned two. A couple of days before, he'd come home with a Walkman for my brother Scott. Unbeknownst to him, Scott wouldn't have it for an hour before I went out of my way to get it. It didn't work and I'd been pretty upset about it, but Daddy didn't let me stay that way for long. He bought me one of my very own, and the second he placed it in my tiny little hands, I climbed up on their bed with it, put the earphones on the way I saw Scott do, and the rest is history."

Pausing, taking a breath as I let the memory wash over me, I smile. That simple memory bringing to light thousands of others. Events where my father went out of his way to make sure our faces were always lifted instead of falling.

"About a year later, he did something similar again. This time a few days before Christmas in 1983."

"He'd snagged a Santa outfit from work and brought it home. Keeping it a secret from all of us, he held onto it until Christmas Eve and while we were all sitting around the tree, he came out from behind the safety of our kitchen, loud as ever. Holding his belly, shaking it as he hollered out a hearty 'Ho, Ho, Ho', and dropping a sack onto the floor in front of us. It's so clear in my mind because it was at that moment, I knew just how special we were to him. He was willing to break tradition, dress up in a stained, well-worn and used costume, in order to create a lasting memory of our happiness."

"It was always like that with my dad, you know? He would always go out of his way to create these memories that at the time they happen, don't really mean much, but now, standing here as I'm flooded with them, mean everything. Moments of pure joy and amazement because no matter where he found himself, at the end of each day, all he seemed to really care about was the wellbeing and happiness of others. Whether they were his biological family or the one he created in the neighborhood from the time he was old enough to vote."

"Wayne Jeffries touched a lot of people's lives. All of you wouldn't be here now if he didn't, but he touched no life more than mine. And for a short while before he passed on, my brother Scott. A boy who just like with a lot of the kids in the neighborhood, he met one day when he was two and took on as his own, no questions asked."

This is where things are about to get hard and where I need his strength more than ever to make it through. The point in time where I'm throwing the script out the window and instead of saying goodbye, I say hello.

"For a few days before he took his final breath, I could tell something wasn't right. He was tired, worn, and needing to rest. But it was his lack of humor bothering me most. I think deep down, I knew it was only a matter of time, but if there's one thing I know when it comes to my daddy, it's that he was still fighting, even when he couldn't anymore. Even in the amount of pain he was in, he didn't want to let go, and honestly, until about ten minutes ago, I didn't want to let him."

Taking another deep breath, closing my eyes and for the first time in weeks, truly breathing in the air around me, I feel the first of what I'm sure will be many tears slowly begin making its way down my cheek, but instead of stopping, lifting my hand and wiping it away, I let it stay.

Opening my eyes and focusing on the people all sitting reverently with their heads bowed in respect as I speak, I say the only thing left to say.

"It's okay, Daddy. I can do this on my own. You can let go."

Chapter Four
Stuck in a Moment You Can't Get Out Of

Joshua

The service has been over for a few minutes, the sea of people there to honor Wayne finally dwindling down until the only three people remaining are my best friend, Alyssa, and her mother.

As far as services go, it was everything the elder Jeffries would have wanted. After Alyssa spoke, Pastor Michael said a few words before the brass band from the church began to play and set the tone perfectly for what this day is really all about.

The celebration of a man's life.

With all the other mourners having cleared out, it would seem like the best moment to step forward and allow myself the chance to say a final goodbye to the best man I've ever known, but I hang back. As eager as I am to lessen the mountain of space between Alyssa and me, I'm not an idiot. Seeing me earlier was a surprise and I'm not looking to compound it.

When her mother turns and squeezes her daughters' hand before slipping her arm through Kevin's as he begins to lead her away, I prepare myself for the second hardest part of being back.

Coming face to face with the other woman I let down.

Helen Jeffries was the perfect counter to her husband. Where he was often times tough and rigid, she was the softy. The one we could go to when we felt we let him down. She would hold us, rub our backs, reassuring us we were still loved, even if at the moment it didn't much feel like it.

The non-judgmental woman who raised her daughter to be the same, though with Alyssa, that particular part of her—the softness—being magnified. She was the walking/talking combination of the best parts of her parents, and despite all the years I spent denying it and treating her like a friend, she was impossible not to fall in love with.

"As I live and breathe! Joshua Brantley."

"Hey, Mrs. J," I respond with a minuscule upturn of my lips before catching eyes from Kevin and nodding in our own brand of acknowledgment.

"I'm so glad you could make it. Wayne wouldn't have much cared about who else showed up, but I do know he wanted you here."

Shoving down the familiar pang of guilt that's been plaguing me since I got on the plane, I summon up the most sympathetic smile I can manage and step forward the minute her arms open.

As I bend my body to accommodate her small stature, I hear her chuckle and I suffer a moment of pause. Of all of the things I expected to happen when I came face to face with Helen again, the softest brush of laughter wasn't one of them.

"You always were the considerate one."

"I learned from the best," I answer honestly, which as I finally pull back and take her in, I see has earned me another soft laugh, which when finished, lingers in the smile lining her features.

A smile I've missed.

Looking from Helen to Kevin, I catch movement behind my best friend and looking out, see Alyssa moving closer to the casket until she's leaning over it, pressing her body into the plethora of red and white roses covering the top.

"Well, Kevin, I do believe it's time I head back to the house. It won't be long now before my doorstep is filled with dishes, and I think we should give Joshua and Alyssa some privacy."

Not entirely sure why, but wanting to make sure she doesn't get the wrong idea about my reason for being here, I reach out before she can walk away and attempt to explain.

"You don't have to do that, Mrs. Jeffries. That's not—"

With a lift of her hand, she cuts me off. "Are you going to tell me she's not the reason you're back?"

Do I lie or agree? It's the moment of truth.

"If I said it wasn't, would you believe me?"

"Not even a little bit, and if Wayne were here, he'd tell you the same thing. Look," she says, bridging the gap between us and resting her hand on my arm, squeezing softly. "It may have taken longer than any of us liked, but you being here means something, even if it's not clear to you."

"W—what does it mean?" I stammer, biting back the annoyance I feel at having let this strong woman see me break, even if it was a slip and only momentarily.

"It means, whatever you were running from then, it caught up with you and it's brought you back where you belong. To the only person in the world you belong with."

I can't argue with her. She's right. I'd been running long enough, and it hadn't gotten me anywhere, except lonely and missing the one piece of the puzzle that could and would complete me.

"What if this person doesn't agree with you?"

"Then don't stop trying until they do. No matter how against hearing it they are."

Leaning in and placing her lips to my cheek, she embraces me one final time before turning and looping her arm through Kevin's again, this time beginning the trek that will bring them down the hill to where the car awaits.

Leaving me not only with a hell of a lot to think about but also the sad eyes of the only person in the world I belong with.

The most beautiful girl I ever laid eyes on, living inside of the stunning woman now turning in my direction, facing me down, completely unaware as, much like when I was seven, she takes my breath away.

Alyssa

I can't believe he's here.
Really here.
And him being here, standing about four feet away, is making my heart flutter and soar the way it used to, almost as if there's been no time or distance between us at all.

I'm fifteen again, a sophomore, blissfully happy and in love.
Damnit. This can't happen now. I've been handed too much.
Joshua Brantley is a complication I don't need.

But despite the pep talk and knowing this is the last thing I need, I can't help taking him in. Not the boy who ran and left me behind, but the man standing here now.

Time has treated him well. He looks good. Healthy. Even if his face is lined with the scruff of one too many days without a razor, and his eyes look tired.

I mean he fills out the suit nicely, but the first two buttons of his white shirt are unbuttoned and a tie loosely hangs down, as if he'd somehow forgotten how to tie one and just gave up. His hands are buried deep in his pockets, and the way he moves his weight from one leg to the other as he stands speaking to my mother, it's obvious he's uncertain.

Something we have in common.

Except in the time it takes to compose myself, my mother is gone, having been walked away by Kevin and it's just the two of us. Standing in place, staring at one another, neither one of us ready to take the first step and change the distance between us.

I really wish I had the strength to take the first step, but I don't. All of the fight, the will to get through this day I had when I arrived here has depleted, leaving me completely barren. It was supposed to see me through the worst of it. I didn't plan on needing more.

Sensing movement, I inhale sharply as he does what I'm unable to, bridging the gap of space between us, one solid foot in front of the other until there is less than a foot between us. To make matters worse, he does another thing I can't drum up the strength to do.

He speaks.

"Hey, AJ."

AJ. The shortened version of my full name the guys I hung out within the neighborhood deemed me because it was easier than calling me, Aly or Alyssa.

The name no one has called me since the day the man standing before me walked away without so much as a goodbye.

"JJ..." I mumble, though the heaviness weighing on my chest as I use the term of endearment almost too much to bear.

I'm jealous, you see. Jealous of the way he can so easily say my name as if he's spoken it repeatedly over the last twenty years and how hollow, yet painfully heartfelt mine comes out because I've been determined not to.

"I'm sorry," he pauses, and I wonder what his apology is for.

For leaving? For being away so long? For breaking my heart or ruining me for moving on and being happy?

"You know...about Wayne. Your loss."

My loss? Really?

The beat of my heart, which until this moment had been rapid and unsteady, the nerves over what we would say to each other, how this would go, completely taking over, is now slowed to a complete crawl. I wonder if it's even beating at all or if him being back has completely broken it.

"Thank you."

God, end this now. Put me out of my misery.

"I didn't even know he was sick." He muses. "How long?"

"Awhile. The stroke last year," I respond robotically, having answered this question more than my fair share of times since he passed on. "He never really recovered from it, despite what he wanted everyone else to believe. It wasn't exactly expected, him having another one, especially with the work they had done on his heart, but also not surprising."

He nods his understanding before moving again, taking another couple of steps closer, only stopping when his closeness to me is too much and I take an uneven step back, catching myself before I completely make a fool out of myself and fall.

"I'm sorry."

"You already said that."

"I know I did, but I..." his voice tapers off and I scream, but it's only in the confines of my own head.

"You what?"

"It was a different sorry."

"Oh."

"Yeah."

I need to end this torture. Tell him I'm expected back at the house and walk away, letting him get a good view of my backside as it walks away from him, the way it should have gone down twenty years ago when he did the same.

This conversation doesn't need to happen. It's been too long. A few years ago, maybe him being here and saying sorry would have worked and something could have been saved, but now, I'm not sure it's worth it.

"I should really get going. Give you a chance to say your goodbyes to Daddy."

Not meeting his eyes, I begin to make my way around him, making it a couple of steps, almost believing he's going to let me leave when he reaches out and stops me cold.

"Don't go."

"Give me one good reason I should stay."

Pulling his hand away from mine quickly, as if the small touch has burned him, I make no move to leave as I catch his hand linger at the breast pocket of his suit jacket, moving around inside of it until he's pulled something and taken the steps that find him lingering ever so closely behind me.

"Because I need to give you this."

Letting his hands rest on my side, he turns my body ever so slightly as he reaches out and takes my hand, opening it and placing the item from his pocket in the middle. Closing it before I can catch a glimpse and stepping back.

Wanting to shift my eyes from him, see what he's placed there, but seemingly locked in position on the sad and look of utter loss and despair in his now damp eyes, my breath hitches as he leans into me, his breath falling easily across my cheeks as he speaks again.

"Can the girl who gave me this spare a few minutes for a jackass undeserving of even holding onto something as precious as it is?"

I was right earlier. Joshua being back is a dangerous thing. It really is as though we've gone back in time. I'm no longer the thirty-five-year-old woman who stood before a crowd of people and spoke so beautifully of a father gone, but not forgotten. I'm the sixteen-year-old, head over feet in love girl who thought her life was perfect all because of the boy standing in front of her now.

Heart beats faster, breath becomes hitched, caught and hard to release, as his words sink in and I lower my gaze back to what I'm holding in my hand.

A memento of our time together.

He's given me the guardian angel pendant.

Joshua is standing here in the middle of a cemetery giving something back I never thought I'd have again.

A piece of me.

"You kept it..."

"I kept a lot of things, AJ."

"Why now, Joshua?" I ask, purposely ignoring the butterflies fluttering away in my chest. "Why come back and give this to me now?"

"Because when you gave it to me, you said it was so even when we weren't together, I wasn't alone. I had you with me. And even though it took a horrible loss and twenty damn years, I'm tired of carrying it around with me. I want the real thing, AJ. I want you."

Chapter Five
The Kids Aren't Alright
Fall 1986

Joshua

"I know this all seems scary right now, Joshua, but give it a chance. I think you'll end up liking it here."

Yeah, because I haven't heard that before. It's not the same line the last three social workers have given when they've dumped me off at a new home, proclaiming it my fresh start.

When you've been through what I have since I was stripped away from my parents six years ago, you grow up quick. I didn't have time to be a happy little kid.

Nah, I had to fight and claw for everything I'd been given, which considering how small the backpack is on my back, is not a whole lot when you think about it in terms of stuff.

Sure, the house I'm standing in front of looks really nice, but so did the last one I was placed. This one's white, just like the last one. Two floors with bright green grass coating the lawn and a light green fence running all the way around it.

It looks like it was built to house a family, but not the kind who takes in a stray off the street. A ready-made one with two parents, two kids—a boy and a girl— complete with bright and happy smiles.

I don't care what the social worker thinks. This is not going to be the place for me.

Digging my heels into the grass, determined not to move another step unless it's back towards the car we just exited from. I don't even realize our privacy has been usurped until the intruder speaks.

"Hi!"

Turning toward the voice, my body moving in tandem with my workers and coming face to face with the intruder, I'm surprised to see who it actually is.

In every neighborhood I've lived in, there have always been a few nosy kids who make their way over, wanting to know who the stranger to their perfect existence is, but it's never been someone like this.

A girl.

Not just any girl, but one with dirt and grass stains marring the knees of her pants, and a smudge of dark brown something coating her forehead and running down across her cheek, wearing the biggest smile.

The strangest girl I've ever seen.

Even the girls I knew in the system managed to make themselves look at least remotely presentable in any situation, especially if they wanted to have a full-time adoption in their future. None of them ever looked like this.

I notice her eyes next. Bright blue orbs that seem to glisten and glow even more as the sun finds them, giving me the opposite of morbid curiosity.

Denny, a guy from the old neighborhood I used to hang with would call her a walking contradiction.

Words I didn't understand at the time, but after I learned, describe this girl perfectly.

"Hello." My worker responds, ruining the moment by clearing her throat and turning to me, pressuring me without speaking to say something.

"You're the Watkin's nephew, right?" The girl asks, and after clearing her throat, my worker confirms for me.

That's another difference between the other homes and this one. None of the others had been family before. They'd all been strangers who were in it for the checks every month. This time, they'd finally tracked down my mom's sister.

What no one seems to get is, I'd rather be with the drug abuser and the space cadet woman he married, then with this rendition of the Cleavers. But here I am, and for the time being, at least until they find a reason to boot me out for something I didn't do, I'm stuck with it.

"Joshua, don't you wanna say hello to the young lady?"

"Nope."

There, I've spoken. It's not what she wants as she releases an annoyed sigh, but it's gonna have to do. I might have to do this, but it doesn't mean I have to like it and I definitely don't and won't be making any friends.

Connections are overrated.

"My daddy saw your car pull up and wanted me to come over and introduce myself."

That's not scripted at all. I think as she speaks, attempting to ignore the fascination I have with the lilt in her voice. How it rises and falls with every word she says. She sounds like a bird, but not the annoying ones who squawk incessantly. She's sing-songy.

Another way she's not like anyone else.

Sure, she sounds like a girl, but not like any girl I've heard. Most people when they talk, do it in the same singular tone, but with this girl, it's like all the rules have been thrown out the window. She's all over the place.

"Well, that was nice of him. It's nice to meet you—"

"Alyssa Marie Jeffries, ma'am."

God. Even her name is music.

"The boy who seems to have lost his voice, is Joshua Brantley, Jr and I'm sure once we've gotten him settled in, you two will become fast friends."

Not on your life.

Like this girl would want to hang out with me.

Even if she is dirtier than half the boys in the group home.

"Oh yeah! My daddy also told me to tell you to come over for the barbeque once you're all settled in."

Even though she's saying it to me, my earlier response must have awoken a beast inside my worker because before I've even had the chance to come up with a response, she's answering for me.

"That sounds lovely. Please extend my thanks to your father for the invitation."

"Okie Dokie!" Alyssa responds excitedly, sounding more like the kid she's supposed to be, before turning her attention back to me. "See you later, JJ."

JJ?

Turning her back and looking down both sides of the street, she runs across the road, not stopping until she's taking her front steps two at a time and reaching the top. It's then she spins around and even with the distance between us, responds in a way that should be normal to me now, but is anything but.

She waves.

Alyssa

He's here.

The boy I've heard my parents talking about for the last couple of weeks.

The nephew of Frank and Genie Watkins is finally here!

Daddy made sure I went over to say hello when he caught sight of the car pulling in. He does that a lot. Whenever he hears there's someone new coming in, he wants them to know they're welcome. He says it's because moving to a new place is super hard and he wants to be the one to make a little easier, but I know better.

It's because of what happened to Scott last year.

Losing my brother was hard, and even though he hasn't really changed all that much, in this way he has. All the boys who live around us, they're close to him now, and before they always kept their distance. So, instead of having the one boy and losing him, he's gained a whole neighborhood full.

I also like to think he does it because he's an angel.

Mommy claims it's just silly talk, but that's because she's old and doesn't get it like I do.

"Did you do what I asked, Aly?"

"Sure did, Daddy. I said hello just the way you said and invited them to the barbeque later."

"Then what's with the sad eyes?"

Whoops.

I was supposed to stop doing it before he caught on, but despite smiling and waving at the boy before coming inside, I can't seem to shake the feeling the reason Joshua Brantley is here isn't a good one.

"He doesn't seem happy."

"Well, dove, it's like we talked about. Moving is hard, especially when you're a kid. I'm sure he's going to need some time to adjust. Happiness, when it comes, is well worth the wait, but sometimes, you've got to give it extra time to happen."

This is why I think my daddy is an angel. He always knows the right thing to say to turn the sadness I feel around. Helping me make sense of the things I don't understand.

"Go on and wash up. Your mom's almost done with lunch."

Doing what he asks and heading up the stairs, I stop at the bathroom door. Joshua's face comes to mind, his unwillingness to speak even when spoken to, confusing me. The empty look in his eyes and the slouch to his body the entire time I stood outside. It all comes at me in a rush until I'm turning my back on the bathroom and racing into my room—the one room in the house facing his new home—and stopping just to the side of the window.

Watching as the woman I talked to earlier heads to the trunk of her car, opens it and pulls out a tiny blue suitcase. Slamming the top down, she makes her way back over to where he's still standing frozen like a stone, and the knot in my chest from earlier hits again.

How can he be moving here for good and not have more stuff? Are the holey backpack and the little blue suitcase really all he has?

As the questions pile up, I do my best to shut them down, remembering what Daddy said about prying into business that's none of yours and how wrong it is.

It's just too bad it doesn't work.

I'm filled with curious questions and I know it's not gonna stop bugging me until I get the answers.

What's Joshua's story? Why is he really here, and why does he seem like this is the very last place he wants to be?

But more important than all of those questions is the one I haven't had since Scotty died and I had to try and navigate this whole life thingy on my own.

How do I get him to be my friend?

Chapter Six
Home Sweet Home

Joshua

"I'm sorry. I need to go."

In the short time it had taken for me to spill my guts at her feet, falling back into familiar patterns and remembering the first day I met her, she'd pulled her hand back out of mine, murmured the words and turn and run.

I knew it was going to go down this way. Not this exact way, but I knew going in I would say or do something—in this case, show my hand too early—and it would spook her and make her run.

Doing it to her today of all days twists me up, because I didn't just make her run from me, but from her father too.

This is such a mistake.

I fell in love with a girl when I was a kid, let her go when I got older, and by some dumb luck been given a second chance with her, only to do what I've always done, and bail on her at the worst possible moment. Leaving her, my best friend, and every other person who gave a damn about me to rot in the wind.

That's not exactly something you can sweep under the rug. Alyssa had every right to run from me because if I was in her shoes, I would have done the same thing.

Turned my back, run, and never looked back.

Wait, I'm an idiot. I already did it.

What I wouldn't give to go back and do it all over again. Starting when I showed up on her street that sweltering hot day in late September. Seven-year-old me, he would say something this time. Reach out to the girl with the sing-songy voice and tell her everything.

How, despite knowing deep down being stripped from my addict parents was the right move, I still loved and missed them every single day, and sometimes, when the whiskey doesn't do its job, I still do. Tell her that when she showed up with dirt all over her face, sweat pouring down and only making the mess even worse, she was the prettiest damn thing I'd ever seen and I wanted to grab her and never let go.

I wouldn't have held onto those things so long.

I would have told her all of it even though it wouldn't have made a bit of sense.

Things would have been so damn different. I would have made sure of it, so when she came to me when she was fifteen and dropped the bomb, it would have brought us closer instead of tearing us apart.

But that's the shitty thing about life.

You don't get to live it all over again. Sure, you get chance after chance to rectify situations, do things the way you should have now that you're older, but you never get the shot to go back and completely write a new story.

You just have to make do with the one you've got and make every second count.

A Wayne Jeffries lesson if there ever was one, and like usual with me back when he tried to teach it to me, one I emphatically ignored in favor of carving my own path.

"Why'd you have to go and die on me, huh?" I yell at the casket, my words echoing out over the empty space, the silence deafening. "You were still needed! How am I supposed to come back and make everything right when I don't have the first clue what the hell I'm even doing?"

Kevin's earlier words flood me, followed quickly by Helen's, but they aren't him.

"I love her, Dad," I admit, the name, a term of endearment for the man who shaped a good portion of my life falling effortless. "I don't know how to make her believe it. How to make her see. Damnit, Wayne. I still need you. Why'd you have to up and leave?"

Attempting to push back the emotion threatening to break me, I slam my fist down hard on the casket, shaking loose a few of the single roses and knocking them to the ground. One, a faded shade of red, falling directly at my feet.

Bending down and slipping it through my fingers, the softness of the petals doing nothing to ease the hardness I've spent the last twenty years bathed in, I just let my gaze linger on it and that's when it hits me.

Helen's words from earlier about my being here meaning something. Wayne's belief that even after you've lost someone, you can still find a way to communicate with them and get the answers you need in order to move on, it's all here in this rose.

I've gotten an answer.

This flower is the answer to everything because just like the guardian angel pendant, it's another reminder of the life I had before. The life I can have again. If only I do what Wayne, his daughter, and even at times my best friend have been trying to get me to do from the start.

Believe.

Chapter Seven
Fire and Ice
1988

Alyssa

"Don't you dare!" Squealing as he completely ignores me and turns the hose in my direction, the cold spray hitting like a tidal wave and stealing the breath from my lungs as he breaks into a fit of giggles, I cry out again. "JJ, you jerk! Stop!"

"Are you gonna put makeup on my face when I'm sleeping again?"

One time.

I put a tiny bit of makeup and nail polish on his nails during a sleepover and he's been finding ways to make me pay ever since. It was six months ago. You'd think he would have gotten over it by now.

It's not like I painted his nails every time he was over.

Feeling my cheeks overheat, I lift my hands and just like every other time I swear not to do something to him, I cross my heart and hope to die.

"You promise not to give me a cold shower again?" I ask and for a second it looks like he's about to turn the hose on me again, but instead, he nods before following the same motion with his hands over his heart.

"It's officially a truce."

"And we're officially gonna be dead when my dad sees this mess." I laugh as I take a look around my lawn. Water is everywhere, sponges tossed in the driveway and all over the grass, along with two buckets of warm water turned on their sides, no longer full. Soap coating everything from the car to us and everything in between.

"He won't kill us. He's just gonna turn the hose on us."

"No, that's just you." I laugh, sticking my tongue out, which the second he catches makes him jump in my direction and for me to take off running as fast as my gangly legs can go.

"Oh, come on, AJ! Why you gotta be like that?" he calls out, chasing after me now, but instead of stopping, turning around like I've done so many times over the last two years I just keep going, straight across the road, veering off to the side and heading into the brush of trees we've used as the perfect hide and seek spot.

"Because you're gonna tickle me when you catch me, that's why!"

"I swear I won't."

Finding shelter against a tree once I'm sure I'm hidden far enough from view, I attempt to catch my breath as I wait him out. It's only a matter of time before just like all the other times we've done this, he finds me, and tickles me until I'm close to wetting myself.

It's our thing.

What had been a hard shell to crack when he moved here two years ago, has become so much easier now. Where Josh had been a closed book, not willing to be opened before, now it's hard to get it closed most times.

I'd like to take all the credit, especially with the way I'm starting to feel about him, but it's not all me. A lot of it might surround me, but only because my daddy managed to break through his shell the day of the barbeque and has taken a sledgehammer to his walls every day since.

"Caught you."

Looking up and realizing with the way he's got me pinned against the tree, I really am caught, I laugh softly before preparing my body for the kicking I'm about to do in order to get away again.

But what I expect him to do, he doesn't. Instead of resting until his breath returns to normal, he leans in and before I can adapt, his lips are on mine and my heart completely stills.

One beat. Two beats. Three beats.

That's all it takes for me to realize what's happening.

My lips were frozen in position against his, while the beat of my heart matches with the pounding in my head.

This is my first kiss.

Joshua is my first kiss.

Moving ever so slightly, lifting my body back off the tree and putting more force behind my lips as I press back against his, the spell of the moment is broken as he breaks the connection and backs away. But not before I see his fingers lift and touch the spot where my lips rested and the contented sigh escaping through them.

He wanted to kiss me. He *liked* kissing me.

I wonder if he wants to do it again.

"Josh—"

"AJ, no." he hushes me, his eyes finally finding their way back to mine as his hand comes out in front of him, the same fingers that had just traced his own lips, standing up straight against mine. "Don't say a word."

He's joking. He has to be. There's no way he can kiss me out of nowhere and expect me not to say something.

Pulling his hand back and bringing it to his side, his face, which had been so relaxed and peaceful, finally turns to stone, and before I can react, he's the one running.

Following close, I run and don't stop until I reach my house.

Where I found him the last time he took off.

Taking the steps two at a time, I barrel past my mom as she makes her way out through the door and take the steps again all the way to my room, expecting when I get there to find him on my bed.

When I finally reach the room, though, shoving my way through the door with no regard to how much noise I'm making or how crazy I might look, the bed is empty. As crisply and cleanly made as it was when my mom came in and did it earlier.

He's not here and after running back down the stairs, out the door, and across the street, banging on the Watkin's door and begging to be let in once his aunt opens it, I find out he's not home either.

Josh has done something he swore to me a year and a half ago, he would never do.

He's run away.

Joshua

I'm a dead man.

When Wayne finds out I kissed his daughter, that I got carried away seeing the minuscule rise of her lips, the flushed color of her face and the bead of sweat slipping down once she looked up and realized I caught her, I'm going to pay.

And I don't mean pay in the physical sense, because despite being a big burly dude, Wayne's not like that. I'm going to pay by losing something way more important.

I'll lose him and the bond I have with the family. The closeness. Most of all, I'll lose her.

The girl with the chocolate brown hair who not once in the last two years has given up on trying to get through to me. The girl who despite learning about the huge level of crap in the first six years of my life, still makes it her mission to hang out with me.

Smile at me. Enjoy being around me.

I can't believe I did something so selfish.

She's cute. I've been trying to deny noticing it for a while now. Swallowing down the urge to awkwardly press my lips to hers, just to see what they feel like. I've had a lot of urges lately, to do some pretty stupid stuff, but this one takes the cake.

This is definitely the stupidest thing I've ever done and what's worse is, I didn't even stick around once it was over and try to explain it to her. I'd taken off and hidden away.

I'm still hiding away.

All because a couple of weeks ago in the backyard while Wayne was barbequing, he had to go and ask me to refer to him as dad.

"I know we don't share any blood between us, Joshua, but for a long time after losing Scott, I didn't think I'd experience what it felt like to be a boy's father again. You've given it back to me in spades over the last two years. So, if you're comfortable with it, I'd really like if you'd call me dad."

What Wayne doesn't know because I didn't have the guts to tell him is, the last person I called Dad was only called it because of the biological tie I had to him. He wasn't a father to me, so the word is almost foreign sounding. Calling him dad, he's earned it. Between him and his daughter, along with the way they both are with Helen, they've shown me what real parents are supposed to be. So, the name, at least when it's Wayne it's being used on, feels right. Almost like it's the way it should have been all along.

I reach a moment like that in my life and what do I go and do?

The one thing sure to strip it all away when he gets wind of it.

"Now it's my turn to find you." She whispers softly as she steps closer, the sound of the dry leaves crunching under her feet, following her until she plops her body down onto the grass beside me.

"I didn't want to be found."

"Then you shouldn't have shown me this place."

Ignoring the truth of her statement, I just hang my head lower and shake it. "You should go."

"I will, but only when you tell me why you ran before."

"Not exactly fond of sticking around to get in trouble."

Flinching and backing away as she moves in closer and makes a weak attempt with her hands to get me to raise my head to look at her, she tenses and I sigh.

This girl is my best friend, and right now I'm treating her like she's my worst enemy. Not what I want to do, but with what happened, I've got to do.

"Trouble for what?" she pushes on and I shrug. If she can't figure out why I would assume I'd be in trouble than I don't know what to tell her.

"JJ, come on! Tell me what you're gonna get in trouble for. Is this about the mess back at the house? Don't worry if it is, I already talked to my dad and he thinks it's funny."

"I don't care about some stupid mess, AJ."

"Then what?" she pleads, this time getting her way and putting all of her strength into twisting my face so it's looking directly at hers.

"I kissed you."

"I know, I was there. I think I might have kissed back, you know. Just a little."

The way she says it, unable to keep a straight face, her eyes lighting up, it alleviates some of the torture I've been putting myself through.

If she can look at it playfully, even though she has to know it was a total mistake, then maybe she won't tell Wayne and things can just go back to being the way they always have.

Maybe I don't need to lose anything after all.

"It was more than just a little." I chuckle softly and am rewarded when I notice her cheeks flush and a soft laugh of her own escapes.

"Why did you do it?"

"Why does anyone kiss someone, AJ?"

"Lots of different reasons, really. I wanna know yours."

Do I tell her I've been wanting to kiss her for a while? Admit I wanted to see what her lips felt like? If they'd be as soft as I'd imagined them or as rough around the edges as she can be sometimes? Or do I just say nothing, shrug, and hope she doesn't push?

"Did you want to kiss me?" She asks.

"I wanted to know what they felt like."

"Okay," she pauses, as her teeth slip out over her lips and she begins to bite down. A move so simple, but one that despite wanting to look away, I can't do, completely fascinated by the way she looks when she's nervous.

"AJ, I wanted to kiss you for a while, but I shouldn't have. We're like fire and ice, you and me. It can't happen again or it's gonna turn into a total disaster."

As if she hasn't heard a word I've said, she smiles and continues, her next questions getting right to the heart of the matter.

"Do you like me?"

"You know I do."

"No, JJ. I don't mean do you like being my friend or whatever. I mean, do you really like me?"

I can't answer this. The disaster I was talking about earlier, the result that comes from answering this question, it's wrong, and I can't make things any worse than they already are.

"Because, JJ, I like you a whole lot. I wanted you to kiss me."

Huh?

"You're just saying what you think I want to hear. You don't know what you want."

Shaking her head, she leans over and presses her forehead to mine and despite the right move being to back away and put as much distance between us as possible, I'm powerless. Her skin against mine feels right.

"Do you remember the day you moved here?"

"Yeah, what...about it?" I question, my voice cracking, fearful of what comes next.

"I watched you from my window. I saw you come out of the house after your social worker left, making your way around the entire house before stopping on your doorstep and looking across to mine. At first, I thought you caught me staring, but after a few minutes of you standing there, I knew you didn't."

"So, what you're saying is, you've always been a peeping tom?"

"Ha-ha. Very funny." She rolls her eyes. "There was only one thing I wanted that day."

"Which was?"

"To figure out a way to make you my friend."

"Oh."

"I got what I wanted, but the more time we hung out and the more I watched you, I wanted more."

"Me to push you against a tree and kiss you?"

"Eww, no. My first kiss wasn't supposed to be against a tree, but you're partly right because I did want you to kiss me. I wanted to know if it would feel as good as I imagined it would."

"You imagined kissing...me?" I don't want to be happy about this, but I can't get the words to form because I've been doing the same thing with her.

"Yeah, I did. A lot actually. What I'm trying to say is, you say I don't know what I want, but I do. I've always known. What you see as a disaster from fire and ice colliding, I see differently."

"How do you see it?"

"Fire and ice together create water, but not just any water. The purest kind."

Holy crap.

Despite being fearful of the answer, I can't do anything to stop the next question or the way my heart seems to settle once it hears the answer.

"You said you know what you want, so what is it? What does Alyssa Jeffries want?"

"She wants you, JJ. Just you."

Chapter Eight
I Remember You

Alyssa

When you're young, everything seems so big.

The places, the people, the things, even the situations you end up finding yourself in.

Everything is just monumentally bigger.

At the time, you don't believe some of the small stuff you're sweating is actually not that big of a deal. All you know is it's there, you're confronting it, and it's got the power to ruin you.

Joshua Brantley was a lot like that for me.

I mean, sure, he was my size, give or take a couple of inches, and very comfortable to be around, but still larger than life.

Growing up is tough. Experiencing feelings that you've never had to concern yourself with before, even harder, and it's tricky navigating through the minefield all of it piled on together becomes.

But if it was hard on me, it was exponentially harder on Joshua.

Within two weeks of him moving to our street, he'd made a name for himself in our house. My dad enjoyed having him over, and it seemed to be reflected back on Josh. An hour visit turning into a few hours, which morphed into a day, sometimes even an entire weekend.

The annoyed and angry boy he'd been that day in front of his house, he wasn't any longer.

It was right around then he told us how he ended up here, or rather, he told my dad, and attempting to be a super sleuth at the time, I listened in on the whole thing.

To hear him tell it, both of his parents were addicts. Cocaine first, then, shortly before getting pregnant with him, making the switch to heroin. One of his workers told him years later it was so bad he had been born addicted.

If that wasn't bad enough on its own, it only seemed to follow him as the years went on.

The first time he was taken, he was just a little over a year old. There had been a party at the house they were staying in and a fight broke out between his father and some guy who his dad owed money to. Police were called and when they got to the scene, upon seeing the state of the house and the shape of the supposed caregivers in it, he'd been taken out.

Over the span of the next three years, he had been placed back with them three times and even to this day, I question why.

According to what Joshua told my dad, his parents did the bare minimum and because of it he was thrown back into the same situation until again, authorities were called and the sickening cycle repeated.

At just over the age of four, his first memory of the system stuck.

He was placed in his first group home.

When we were like eight, we were goofing around and he apologized to me.

He was apologizing for being angry around me. After I tried telling him I didn't mind, he'd shaken it off and told me I was cute but wrong.

I never understood then why he was so adamant I was wrong.

I do now.

After a year in the group home, a new couple came and took him home and according to him, they hated him on sight. Nothing he ever did was good enough and any chance they had, they beat him in an effort to make him compliant.

It was in one of these incidents he found himself in the hospital.

One of his neighbors at the time had an older female cat that had given birth to kittens and one day, maybe a couple of months later, one of them had gone missing. When no one could find this cat, instead of searching the area or putting up flyers, hell, even asking around to see if anyone had seen it, his foster parents chose to do the unthinkable.

They blamed him for the loss of the kitten and then proceeded to take every bit of anger and frustration they had out on him. Injuring him so bad that he spent a week in the intensive care unit, during which time, red flags had again gone up and he was stripped away becoming a ward of the province.

Remembering all of this, the pain etched on his face as he told my dad everything he'd been through, I hate it. It kept me up when we were kids, and now, so many years later, my stomach is twisted in knots and I'm wanting desperately to run and hide in my room again.

This is a bad idea.

Thinking about this; about him.

Making my way into the kitchen, opening the fridge and eyeing the bottle of wine in the door, it takes only a couple of seconds to talk myself into why having a glass is a good idea, slipping it out and placing it on the counter.

Crossing to the other cupboard, the one that's been off limits for the last several years, I grab the closest glass, pausing for only a second, as a voice of warning rises.

Never again.

I swore to myself after the loss of Mark, I was done. No more drinking, alone or socially. Not when the reason for it, especially towards the end was more about dulling the pain than actually enjoying the drink.

Leave it to seeing Joshua again to throw the plan out the window in favor of diving head first into numbing myself.

Shaking off the voice continuing to warn me off, I make quick work of popping the cork, pouring and downing the first glass, quickly following it up with another.

I don't care what the voice in my head says. If I'm going to keep remembering a time better left forgotten, I'm gonna get pleasantly numb at the same time.

Making my way into the living room and placing the glass on the coffee table, I flop back onto the sofa and just like earlier when I'd come through the door and the past slammed me in the face, it does so again. This time picking up right where it left off.

What brought Joshua to my doorstep.

After healing enough to officially be released, he'd been sent back to a home with fifteen other boys. There had been three to a room, he'd told my dad, but instead of grouping them together by age the way one would expect, there had been no rhyme or reason to it at all.

He admitted nothing was ever the same after he was placed there.

Least of all him.

His time there had hardened him, his own admittance of having an edge to him evident in the times early on when he did have flashes of anger. He didn't trust anyone or anything. He admitted easily that in every situation he found himself in, he was always waiting for the inevitable fallout to occur.

Between being tossed aside and having to fight for everything he had in the group home, most of the time because he was smaller than the other boys, getting beat up and treated like garbage, he had grown up a lot faster than he should have.

So, a boy who started out in Sarnia, been shipped to Toronto, only to end up in Richmond Hill, finally made his way here.

To the little white house across the street, with family, and a life that despite how much he opened up and shed the ways of the past, still haunted him every single day.

Joshua has always operated on one setting and one setting only.

Running.

He ran when he was six, because he wanted to rebel against the family he had been stuck with, and then again four years later when he was ten. There were a couple more before those, but the coup de grace came in the dead of night at sixteen.

Bringing the wine glass to my lips, allowing the cold red liquid to run down quickly, I don't stop until its drained, not only wanting to drink away the memories of the boy who ran, but block them completely.

I can't let him do this.

Unlike all of the times in the past he's done it, if I allow him back now, especially with the way I'm already reacting, when he inevitably takes off again and goes back wherever the hell he came from, he won't be the only thing that ends up missing.

I will be too.

Joshua

"Josh, my man! Where the hell have you been?" Kevin calls out before I've even made it through the door. Coming around the kitchen, his face lights up, his eyebrows twitching. "You weren't with Aly this whole time! Man, you move quick!"

"Not funny, bro."

Maybe it's the scowl on my face or the rigid way I'm carrying myself, but the amused look he was wearing fades quick.

Now he gets it.

"Well if you weren't with Aly, where've you been?"

"Driving around. Stopped in at Pop's and had a couple of beers. Now I'm here, tired, and need my bed."

Moving around him, more than a little ready to take the stairs three or four at a time in order to get myself locked away in the upstairs room faster, he blocks my path.

"It went that well, huh?"

"Oh yeah, because scaring the girl I haven't been able to spend one night in twenty years not thinking about is just fantastic. I don't even know what the hell I was thinking coming back here."

"Whoa. Slow your roll, pal. You're back because you belong here, and if you didn't come, I would have gotten on the first plane out and dragged you back here myself."

"Bullshit, Kev."

"How do you figure?"

"You're the only one who knew where I was all this time. Well, other than the time Wayne found me. If you were gonna drag me back here kicking and screaming, you would have done it years ago."

"Maybe, but back then you weren't ready. Maybe you're still not, but you're as together as you can be without her, so better now than never."

"After the way things went down at the cemetery, I'm thinking never would have been the way to go."

Pushing past him before he has another chance to react and stop me, I climb the steps, picking up the pace until I'm in what's to be my room for the duration of my stay.

What I said to Kevin was right, even if he doesn't want to believe it.

Coming back here, especially right now, wasn't the right move. It would have been better if I'd just sent a sympathy card to the family without a return address and kept doing what I've spent years perfecting.

Staying gone. Going through the motions. Not making connections and hating anyone on sight who even dares to try.

The way things were when I moved in with my family thirty years ago, it's how it should have stayed and one has to look no further than the reaction to my being home now to see it.

If it wasn't for you moving here and meeting Alyssa, you never would have known the way things could be. You wouldn't have gotten the chance to live the life you deserve. It's not a mistake you changed how you were, and it's not a mistake you're here now.

It's no surprise my inner voice sounds a lot like my best friend. Though we were both good at causing shit when we were younger, at the end of the day he was always my conscience. The one to tell me when to head forward and when to pull back.

It's in acknowledging the voice, I'm able to get the nerve to climb off the bed and make my way over to the bedroom door again, hoping my friend is willing to give me one more push.

Moving forward the last thing I expect is to run head-on into him.

"For a second there, I actually thought you were gonna spend the night moping. Glad I was wrong."

"Me too," I admit. "You think you can do me a favor?"

"Won't know 'til you ask, brother."

"Alyssa's number. You got it?"

"Yeah." He grins.

"You feel like giving it to me?"

"Well, now that you mention it, I was thinking about letting you stew in your own shit for a little while, you know, really make you work for it, but with as pathetic as you look right now, it almost seems like too much punishment."

Rolling my eyes, I shove him in the shoulder and laugh. "That a yes?"

"It's a yes, but Josh, you ever talk about bailing again, I promise you, you won't even get the chance to."

"Sammie would get to me first, huh?"

"You know it, and if there's one thing I've learned since she dropped the damn stick in my lap...you don't wanna piss off a pregnant lady."

Slamming a piece of paper against my chest, what I realize once I turn it over is the very number I was after, I look at him, this time all traces of my earlier disappointment gone and grinning like a Cheshire cat.

"Thanks, bro."

Motioning to the bedroom, knowing full well what has to happen now and the privacy I'm going to want and need in order to do it, he smiles knowingly before turning and beginning the trek down the stairs.

It's only when he's gotten about halfway down and I'm about to shut the bedroom door, I hear him again.

"This time, you might wanna lead with the box!"

Just the small passing reference to the box, a blue one, with the company name written across the front, my heart is warmed and I can't shake the smile building.

A company name that to so many people wouldn't mean a damn thing, but to me, with what is contained within it, means damn near everything.

Impressions Shoe Co. Est. 1978

Over the course of almost thirty years, I managed to find, be given, and collect ten different items which left their mark on me. Or as the box states, their impression. And all of them were left by the girl with the brown hair, blue eyes, and constant dirt caked to her face who penetrated what was once an impenetrable heart.

A box that when I hand it over, I hope will leave one hell of an impression on her too.

Chapter Nine
The Great Valley
1989

Alyssa

"Alyssa, honey, can you come here for a minute?"

Hearing my mom call out as I come through the door and start making my way up the stairs, I pause, my eyes shooting down over the banister to the kitchen and a sharp pang of guilt causes my heart to pause momentarily.

Being out at the ravine, skipping rocks with Jacob, Michael, and JJ, I'd lost track of time, missing dinner completely.

Which means I'm in big trouble.

"Aly? That's you, right?" she calls again.

"Yeah, mom, it's me. Be right there."

Moving as slow as possible, I come back down the stairs and practically drag my feet until I'm standing in the doorway, her body turning from its position at the sink, her face lit up as she smiles.

"I'm sorry I wasn't here earlier. I was at the ravine. I lost track of time and I really didn't mean to miss dinner, but I was having such a good time that I didn't want to stop—"

"Take a breath, honey." She laughs. "I figured that's where you were when I looked out and didn't see Joshua anywhere. I wanted to speak to you for another reason."

"What's up?"

Moving from the sink, she points to the table before motioning with her hands for me to come closer.

"Do you remember asking me for something a few weeks ago?"

Truth is, I ask her for a lot of things, all the time. So, if she wants me to remember she's going to need to be more specific.

"Not really."

"Well, take a look at what's on the table and maybe it'll spark your memory."

Moving in and looking at the envelope, I slide my hands in and pull out the contents. Taking in the big block lettering, everything finally making sense.

Last week, when we had family movie night and Josh was over like usual, I saw a commercial for a new movie releasing, and I went a bit over the top in my eagerness to see it. At the time, though, they said no because it was something I wanted to see on my own.

But now, there are two tickets inside the envelope and a huge smile on my mom's face as she watches me inspect them, which can only mean one thing.

They're letting me go to the movie.

"Does this mean what I think it does?"

"Your dad and I have spent the last few days discussing it, and despite our initial fears, we trust you and think this one time, we can see how it goes."

"For real? You mean I can go see the movie on my own?"

She shakes her head and my heart drops. I knew there had to be a catch. They were so against me going when I brought it up. With there being two tickets in the envelope I should have guessed it wasn't going to be the way I wanted.

I probably have to take one of them with me.

"There are two tickets, so you going on your own isn't happening."

"Which one of you am I taking?" I quietly ask, my eyes never once leaving the tickets as if by some stroke of luck, I'm hoping I can will one of them away.

"Neither. We got you two tickets because we figured you might want to ask one of your friends to go with you."

Wait. What?

"I don't have to bring you or Daddy?"

She shakes her head again only this time, it's in a way I was hoping to see.

Oh my god! I can't wait to tell JJ!

Squealing as I run around the table and leap into her unsuspecting arms, she laughs when I squeeze tighter before pulling away and shooting me the serious mom look again.

"Now you know if you're going to do this, there's gonna be rules. For instance, you have to call me from the pay phone outside the theatre when you get off the bus, and then again before you come home. We need to be able to know where you are at all times. We want to be sure you're safe."

"Yes! Yes! Yes! Anything you want. Holy moly, I can't believe this is happening!"

"Well, be sure and thank your father. I wasn't entirely on board with this, but he seems to think this is something you can handle."

Of course, he does.

"I will! Is he home? I'll thank him right now! Ahh! Mom! This is the best day ever!"

Hugging my body to hers again and listening to the sound of her laughter, I slip the tickets out of the envelope and into my pants and run out, making a beeline straight for the stairs and what will eventually be my parents' bedroom.

Last week my dad was chosen to lead the service at church on Sunday, so for the last few days, he's been locked away in his room working on everything. If I want to thank him for trusting me and letting me do this, I know just where I'm going to find him.

Knocking excitedly with no immediate response, I put my fist back on the door, ready to knock again when it opens and I'm met by the smiling face of the best man in the entire universe.

"Thank you, thank you, thank you!" I repeat over and over until through his laughter, I hear *you're welcome*. Letting him go, I attempt to calm myself as I question him.

"What made you change your mind?"

"Well, that would be you. With your birthday coming up, and your excitement over this movie, I thought there was no better time to do this. I mean it's not every day a girl turns nine."

My birthday is in a couple of weeks. It's also the first year where I haven't wanted to make a big deal of it, so for the most part, it hasn't even been brought up. Him wanting to do this now, it being less about the present and more about the trust and responsibility he's giving me, is huge.

"Have you given any thought to who you're going to give the other ticket to?"

Like he doesn't already know.

"You're doing it again, Daddy."

"What would that be?"

"Asking me questions you already know the answer to, silly!"

"Then what are you doing standing here talking to your old man? Isn't there someplace else you need to be right now?"

Right! Of course!

And just like that, my excitement builds and overflows again, and with one more quick hug, I stand up on my toes, place the softest kiss to his cheek and I'm running again.

Down the stairs, until I'm swinging the front door open, jumping from my porch to the ground and looking both ways before speeding across the street. Stopping once I've reached his doorbell and press down on it, not even bothering to let go and ease up on the sound going off on the inside.

Rolling back and forth on my feet as I wait for someone to answer, I hit pay dirt when it opens a few seconds later and I'm face to face with the person I'm dying to see.

"Where's the fire, AJ?"

"Huh? Fire? What?" I ask, confused and that's when he laughs and makes his way outside until the door is shutting behind him and we're alone.

"I watched you burn rubber to get here and you went manic on my doorbell. So, where's the fire?"

"No fire, just super amazing news!" I scream, releasing the overload of energy by jumping up and down, JJ's handheld in mine and his body moving with me the harder I jump.

"Okay. Stop." He says, slipping his hand out of mine and putting both of them on my shoulders to steady me, keeping them planted until my body is still. "Start from the beginning. I gotta know why you've got all that steam coming out of your ears."

Looking from side to side and then taking one of my hands and bringing it up to my ear, really expecting there to be steam billowing out, I'm disappointed when I realize he's joking again.

"Ha-ha. Very funny, JJ."

"I know. So, you gonna tell me what's got you so crazy?"

"We did it! I mean, I did it, or maybe it was us. I don't know. But it doesn't really matter who did it because it's happening. It's really, really happening!"

"What is?"

"We're going to see *The Land Before Time!*"

Motioning to the steps and sitting once I've sat down, I pass the tickets over to him and where his face hadn't registered much of anything when I told him the news, it does now.

His eyes widen before settling back to normal as the sweetest smile I think I've ever seen lifts on his face. Staring at the tickets, his fingers running over them the same way mine had done earlier, making sure they're real, he swears in surprise before turning and pulling me into a hug.

Ever since he kissed me a few weeks ago, he's made sure to keep his distance, this hug being the first bit of contact we've had. And even though I know he's only hugging me because he's excited, there's a part of me that feels funny when he pulls away because I want it to last longer.

I miss the way it used to be before the stupid kiss had to come along and ruin it.

"So, they're really letting you go?"

"Yep! And the best part is, I don't have to go alone."

"I thought that's what you wanted."

"It was, but I don't mean it like that. I mean, I get to take someone else with me. Anyone I want! Isn't it the coolest?"

"Yeah..." he agrees, though his voice lowers and seems less excited than he'd been a few seconds ago. "I guess you're taking Cara, right?"

Caroline and her mom moved into our neighborhood about a year after Joshua and when I'm not hanging with the guys, I'm usually with her. It's natural he would think I'd invite her since she wants to see this movie almost as badly as I do, but I'm definitely not taking Cara.

"Nope. I don't wanna do this with her."

"So, if you're not taking Cara, who are you taking?"

"Well, I was thinking about taking the guy who lives across the street who hates admitting his best friend is a girl, and who likes to spray me with water and pull my hair a lot. You think he'd go with me if I asked?"

His face, which had been angled toward the ground, lifts, and the dejected feeling I got from him is gone as he hollers super loud before pulling me in for another hug.

"Hell yes, he would!"

Laughing once he's released his hold, I lean my hand on his shoulder.

"You really thought I'd choose Cara over you?"

"Wouldn't have blamed you if you did. I mean, she is your friend and a girl and all."

"Yeah, you're right. She is my friend *and* she is a girl, but there's something she's not."

"What's that?"

"She's not you, JJ."

Joshua

"Alright guys, move in. This is a big moment for you both."

When I agreed to see the movie with AJ, the last thing I was expecting to do when I got here was take pictures.

I mean it's only a movie. It's not like we're going off to college or moving away, but with as great as Helen and Wayne have been to me, I'm finding it hard to put up much of a fuss.

If they want a picture of us, I'm not stopping them.

Stepping to the left at the same time as AJ moves to the right, our arms bump together and we laugh and just as we turn, smiles still lighting our faces, the flash of the camera hits us.

"Mom, really? You couldn't give us a second to get ready?"

"Not when both of you were smiling so naturally. Gotta seize the moment."

Catching the roll of her eyes, I laugh and slip my hand into hers, same as I've done so many times before. Only this time, when my hand makes contact, my perspiration is met with a slick coat of her own.

Yeah, this is definitely more than just a movie.

"Re—ready?" I stammer, and before her parents can stop us or ask to take more pictures she nods and we're walking out the door and making our way down the steps.

Alyssa only pausing when she hears the sound of the door open and her dad call out.

"Remember, Aly. Call us the second you get to the theatre and no stops there or back."

"I know! Bus, theatre, movie, and then straight home. No stops or breaks in between." She calls back before turning her attention to me. "Hurry up, JJ, before they decide they want to come with us after all."

Heeding her words, I keep pace as she jogs her way to the bus stop, slipping her body into the metal seat, crossing her legs and preparing to wait, my own body following suit.

"Sorry about the pictures."

Twisting my head and taking her in, I shake my head. She might not like that they wanted to document the day, but considering I have virtually no pictures to speak of before my life here, I'm not bothered by it.

"It's okay."

"No, it's not." She sighs and again I just shake my head and shrug. "It's embarrassing."

Wanting to prove to her that I don't feel the same, I do the very last thing she'll expect.

"Do you think they'd mind giving me a copy once it's developed?"

"You really want one?"

"Course I do. This is my first time getting sprung from the house to do something too, you know."

She smiles but turns her head away, her eyes looking down the street and towards the bus moving toward us. Standing up and wiping at her jeans, she turns to face me and the smile that had been there only a couple of seconds before, the one for whatever reason she felt she needed to hide, along with the flush I saw creeping across her cheeks, is gone and replaced with a look of determination.

"You ready?" she asks as she moves around me as the bus pulls up.

Exhaling deeply, I nod. "As I'll ever be."

*****

"See? I can take care of myself - all by myself. I'm not afraid to be alone."

When Alyssa chose this movie, I figured it was safe. A movie that wouldn't remind me of my life. Just some silly flick about dinosaurs.

Except the more we sit here watching, every line the characters say just seems to jump out at me. No one line more than the one the girl triceratops, Cera says and it's got my stomach tied in knots. Though it's not just the characters doing it, but Alyssa too. She just doesn't know it.

She's wiped her eyes about fifteen times since the movie started, and it's gotten so bad I left the theatre and headed to the concession stands at the front about ten minutes ago to grab her some tissues because I was afraid if I didn't there would end up being a puddle on the floor.

What she doesn't realize is she's not the only one affected. Sure, a lot of the way I am is from watching her react. Seeing AJ cry isn't something I'm used to, so when it happens, it makes me feel weird, but it's also because I'm a lot like Littlefoot.

Sure, my folks didn't die fighting a Sharptooth, but in a way, they're on the same path because of drugs, and in the end, they left me on my own, just like him. The only part I can't identify with that I really wish I could, is his mother left him with the idea of having something special—the tree star—and when I got taken, all my mom left me with was the image of her lying across the sofa with a needle in her arm.

God, I need to watch it or I'm gonna be the one needing tissues.

"Then Littlefoot knew for certain he was alone, and although the Great Valley was far away, the journey there was perilous. He would have to find his way, or the chain of life would be broken."

My Great Valley is Toronto, I'm sure of it. All it takes is one look at the tear-stained face of the girl next to me, completely oblivious to the way I see her, for me to know it's true.

I might only be nine, and not know shit about the world, but I do know the road to get me here, where I'm most happy was just like the voice in the movie said. It was perilous and rough, but since I've been here, it's been the opposite.

Wayne Jeffries and his wife, along with their daughter, well, it's as close to happy and at peace as I've ever been and I want to hold onto it for as long as I can.

Lost in the movie, taking in the scenes with a swirl of the words spoken circling around my head the way stars sometimes do in the cartoons, I'm completely unaware that the movie is over until I feel a tight squeeze on my arm and look up to find AJ ready to repeat her actions and pinch me again.

Lights turn on, flooding the half-full theatre and as I watch her dab her eyes with the tissue one more time, I lean in and pinch her cheek, causing her to shriek and me to laugh.

"You're such a jerk, JJ!"

"Maybe, but you love this jerk."

"In your dreams."

"Every single night," I announce confidently before standing, pulling her to her feet and sticking my tongue out.

"Real mature."

"Would you rather I tickle you?"

"Don't you dare!" she calls out as her eyes go wide at my threat, only causing me to laugh again at the fear etched on her face.

"Then take it back."

"No. You can't take back the truth. Once it's out there, there's no takesies backsies."

"Now who's the one being immature?"

Tapping her chin, she grins. "Still you."

Taking off before I've got the chance to reach out and grab her, she swerves through the throngs of people, stopping when she gets to the hall, where I finally catch up, pulling her to the wall and falling in a cascade of her giggles and my breathless laughter, the earlier discomfort at how close to home the movie really was forgotten, and the only thing I can see being her.

This is what I'd been hoping for tonight. A chance to goof off and act silly without anyone's watchful eyes on us.

Maybe even finding the right time to kiss her again.

When we've finally calmed our racing hearts and steadied our breathing, from her position beside me, she leans her head down onto my shoulder, and for a brief moment, I just enjoy the smell wafting from her hair and across my nose.

Flowers with a hint of vanilla. The same smell she's had since I met her two years ago and the one that even with all the dirt she seems to accumulate hanging out with boys, never seems to go away.

The scent of familiarity.

Of home.

Alyssa Jeffries is home.

"Did you know it was going to be like that?" I ask, leaning back against the wall once her body shifts and her head lifts. "Is that why you picked it?"

Eyebrows furrowed and lips pursed, the confusion arising from my question clear. She has no clue what I'm even talking about.

Great.

"Never mind. Stupid question."

"There aren't stupid questions, JJ. Just stupid answers, remember?"

"Well this one is stupid, so forget I said anything."

"No can do. Spill it, buddy."

Do I admit the movie got to me? How close I was to crying and how near the end, I did?

"If you don't tell me I'll just find a way to get it out of you, so you might as well save yourself the torture and just spill the beans."

"Did you choose the movie because I'm like Littlefoot to you?" I blurt out, and when her eyes widen, it's as clear as her confusion was a minute ago. She didn't have a clue and I've just embarrassed myself admitting it.

"No. I chose it because I heard Duckie's voice on the commercial and thought it was awesome! You were there, remember?" She pauses, tapping her finger on her chin before raising her eyes back to mine again, this time, concern lining them.

The look I saw countless times in the group home.

"You really think you're like Littlefoot?"

"Well, you saw the movie same as me. Can you say I'm not?"

"Last I checked, you weren't a dinosaur, JJ." She giggles. "Unless there's something you wanna tell me."

"Like what?"

"Are you a shapeshifter?"

"You read too many books."

"Maybe, but answer the question." She admits before poking me in the side. "Is there something you need to tell me?"

Choking back a laugh, the sound coming out garbled like I'm clearing my throat, I go for broke. I tell her the truth in the only way I know will make the most sense.

"You, your family, and where we are...AJ, you're it."

"I'm what?"

"My Great Valley."

Chapter Ten
Setting Fire to Yesterday

Alyssa

When my cell rang, I expected it to be my mom. I was due back at the house after all. But pressing talk and hearing heavy breathing, it was evident almost immediately that the last person on the line was my mother.

It only became more apparent when he talked and my mind instantly went back in time for the third time today. And not to just any point in time either, but the ones where everything just felt right with the world.

My dad was still alive, we were all healthy and happy, and I had the best boy in the world as my best friend. The very boy on the other end of the line now, except, now a grown man.

"AJ, did you hear me?" His voice soothing my ears as my entire body seems to warm with the familiarity of it. It's almost as though with him being back, we haven't missed a beat.

Yet, history shows we've missed a lot of them.

"Are you there? Hello?"

"I'm here, Joshua." I finally speak, attempting to keep my voice even and still, despite the nervous shake beginning to develop.

I hate this. When I ran from him at the cemetery, it was supposed to be me leaving to go home, but instead, I'd downed a bunch of wine and ended up here. Going off the beaten path to a place only a few people know about in order to visit another dearly departed friend. A place that was supposed to be safety from him.

So much for being able to hide.

"What do you want?" I ask, my voice clipped, but worn. "I thought we said everything at the cemetery."

"Not everything, AJ. You ran off before that could happen."

"I heard everything I needed to. Goodbye, Joshua."

"No! Wait!" he shouts, and before I can hit the end call button, he speaks. "Please don't hang up."

"I can't do this," I admit and he sighs.

"I know, and I understand why you can't. I know this is a lot, me being back, but..." His voice fades out, but before I can fill the awkward and painful silence with noise, he beats me to it. "I want to see you. Please. Just ten minutes."

"Why, Joshua?" Disappointed with myself, hearing the submission in my tone.

"I want...no, I need to see you. I can't explain why. It's too complicated. I just have to do it."

Familiar words. Ones he hasn't said since the day he came back into my life at fourteen, but ones with the same end result.

"Sometimes it's not right to do what you want."

"And sometimes it is. Please, AJ. Just tell me where you are and I'll come to you. Are you at the house with your mom? Your place? Would you rather meet someplace more public? Whatever you want. Just tell me."

Decision time.

Do I tell him and let him invade this spot the same way he invaded my daddy's resting place earlier, or do I lie, put him off and hope he goes away?

"Come on, princess. You know you wanna tell me."

"In your dreams."

And with just those words, we've gone back to every single time we were out together in the past. The familiar back and forth banter as easy as it ever was.

"Joshua, this isn't good. We can't do this. We can't be this way. It's been too long."

"I don't think you've got much of a choice here, Alyssa. The reason we're like this and it's so damn easy is because it's what's meant to be."

"Says the guy who ran away from it."

He sighs and I can imagine his hands raking through his hair with a slight tug on the ends, his annoyance at having what happened between us thrown in his face again. An annoyance he might as well get used to because despite how easy this feels talking to him again, it doesn't change facts.

"You're right, and I deserve that, but I'm not running away. This time I have something to run toward. Now tell me where you are."

Despite wanting to argue, I cave, giving him exactly what he wants and praying the second it comes out, I don't live to regret it.

"Cody. I'm with Cody."

Joshua

I'm with Cody.

I guess it shouldn't surprise me that on the day she loses Wayne she ends up there.

What they say about a dog being man's best friend is true, but no more so than in the case of Alyssa and Cody.

A treat from her father when she was nine, lasting until he passed away five years later, aside from the times when she referred to me as her best friend, Cody was it for her. They did everything together and the fact that they had birthdays one day shy of each other only made the bond she had with him stronger.

He was fully grown when they got him, having been passed back and forth between one family to the next, moving from house to apartment until finally landing at the Jeffries. Sometimes with the way she was with him, it was as if she had gotten her brother Scott back through him.

Pushing my way through the trees and heading down deep into the brush, I see the tree first, and the closer I get and the memories that rise with each step I take, I make her out next.

Cody was laid to rest in the one place at the time it happened, had meant the most to her. Buried directly in front of the tree that at eight years old I had pushed her against and kissed her. A spot when we reconnected again in high school, had become the most sacred.

Coming to a stop on the left side of the tree and leaning my body against it, I use the short period of time before she acknowledges I'm here to really take her in. So much loss in such a short period of time, yet just like when we were kids, showing no signs of the debilitating ache that comes with it.

Knowing how much Cody meant to her, what laying him to rest here had meant back then, and what she is going through now, I feel like an intruder. The guilt I have at taking a place so sacred and inserting myself, rising fast. I needed and wanted to see her, but maybe the right thing to do would have been to wait until she was on neutral ground.

Not in the one place wrought with memories.

Lifting herself off her knees, she pushes her body up into a standing position and turns her head in my direction, for the second time today causing my breath to seize at the same moment my heart does when her eyes connect to mine.

The time for quiet reflection is officially over.

"Sometimes when I come out here, it still feels like yesterday we lost him. I wonder if when I visit Daddy if it'll feel the same way. Like will it still hurt twenty years after he's gone?"

I don't have much to go on, my only losses being those I ran from, but if the way it still feels twenty years after running is any indication of how long the wounds of pain can last, it's one I can answer and speak truthfully about.

"When you lose someone or something you love, no matter how much time passes, I think it always feels like it just happened, even when you don't want it to."

If she picks up on the way I worded things, she doesn't let on. She just dusts off her knees and makes her way over to the tree, situating herself on the side opposite mine, still keeping herself distant.

I haven't earned the right to be close to her the way we would have been had this happened in the past. But being here now is my first step towards making sure I can be in the future.

"I see him everywhere. At the house when I went home, even though he'd only visited and never stayed. It's full of memories of him. I thought coming here, it would alleviate it somehow, but it doesn't. He's everywhere."

For a moment I think she's talking about Cody, but once she mentions her home, it becomes clear we're talking about Wayne.

"Better he's everywhere than nowhere," I say, quoting yet another one of her father's famous lines.

"That's true, I guess."

"You guess?"

Turning toward me, her position almost hugging the tree, she winces as if she's been hit and I immediately question what I could have said to cause it.

"This might sound bad, but all day I've had these moments where I wish he was nowhere because then it wouldn't hurt so badly. I wished he had died and just died, you know? It beats leaving behind this slideshow of memories I can't seem to break free from." Pausing, her eyes trained on me as if gauging my reaction, she sighs. "That makes me a horrible person, doesn't it?"

"No," I admit easily. "It makes you human."

"When he started deteriorating, the doctors warned us to prepare ourselves. I distinctly remember one of them telling my mom we had to because no one could live forever. At the time I was so mad. Like how dare he say it like that? He was supposed to be the one giving us hope, but now all I feel is sick because I didn't listen. If I'd just taken his blunt words at face value instead of getting offended, maybe I could have somehow been ready for this. Been better prepared."

"I don't know much about dying, but I know loads about losing people, and there's no way even if you had believed the doctor, you would have been ready for this."

"You sound so sure."

"These days there's not a whole lot I'm positive about, but I am with this."

"How?"

"Because I know you and I know Wayne."

"Don't you mean, you knew us?"

The dig at the years of distance between us hurts, but there's no denying she's got a point. I'm basing what I believe to be true on the way she and her father used to be, and not what they may have turned into.

"No. I said it right the first time."

"That's crap, Joshua, and you know it."

"He came to see me a few years ago," I admit, and as my words register, I can see whatever light remaining in her eyes beginning to dim as she turns and looks away from my truth.

"I'd been careful after I left. No one but Kevin knew where I was and even with him for a long time it was State dependent and not an actual location. After a while, I let him know, but it was all quiet. No one knew, or at least I didn't think anyone did. Wayne proved me wrong."

"He came to see you a few years ago…" she repeats, making no mention of anything else I've said and when she looks back toward me, seemingly for confirmation of what she's trying to wrap her head around, I just nod meekly.

"Yeah. I had no idea he was coming until I went to leave in the morning and found him on my doorstep. So, you see," I say, switching gears. "I know you wouldn't have been ready or accepting of your daddy dying."

Where I expect her to question me more about how he found me or what we talked about, she does the opposite.

"Is that why you're back now, Josh? Did you come back to twist my memory of him? Make me realize he was keeping secrets?"

"Wait, what? No. That's not what this is."

"Then what is it?"

"I already told you what I'm doing here, and while part of it has to do with Wayne and paying my respects, it's got nothing to do with tarnishing your memory of him."

"This doesn't make any sense." She whispers, pulling her body off the tree and stepping away, putting more distance between us, before stopping and turning back to face me. "Why didn't he tell me he saw you? He knew how I felt."

I want to push further, question why her voice raised an octave or two higher when she mentioned him knowing how she felt, pushing her to admit to me what it means, but I don't. For whatever reason, she hasn't walked or even run away from me, and no matter how badly I want to do this, I can't give her a reason to do what I do best.

Leave.

"No matter how bad things were, how hurt I might be, he always told me the truth about everything. He told me he didn't want to have a relationship based around half-truths and sugar coating. He wanted me to grow up always knowing the reality of the world and people in it so I'd have a better chance of surviving it after he was gone."

Having begun to pace as she spoke, I'm not at all prepared for her to stop directly in front of me, lift her eyes to mine and look through me the way she does.

"When did he come to visit you?"

"A little less than five years ago."

Her eyes go wide, the time obviously meaning something, but just as quickly as she reacts, she takes in how close we are and immediately looks away, stepping back.

Time speeding up, as her foot hooks into a stray branch, her body tripping in her effort to get away, and my body on instinct alone, reaching out and catching her. My arms coming around her back effortlessly and pulling her upright, but more into me than I intended.

The familiar scent of her wafting its way up and straight into my nose, weakening me at the same time as it threatens to pull me back in time. A time where we were happier and didn't have all of this pain, loss, and animosity between us.

When we loved each other.

"Joshua, let—"

"Not yet."

"Please." She pleads, breaking up the impact of her intoxication of my senses and slamming me back into reality. A reality that once reached, has me letting her go once I know she's again on solid footing.

"I'm sorry."

"No, it's my fault. I should have been paying attention. This area's always been a mess."

Ignoring her opinion of the area, I change the subject. I need answers. I need to know why she reacted the way she did.

"What happened five years ago?"

"Huh?"

"You heard me, AJ. You've never been good at pretending."

"Nothing." She admits, and I sense the lie. Proving that not even twenty years can change the most significant of things. She still can't lie. Not to me.

"Is that your final answer?"

I can see her resolve start to crack. She wants to tell me what is so significant about five years ago despite her distrust, which means maybe I've got a shot at cracking her. Getting not only the girl I love back but my best friend too.

"This isn't an essay question, AJ. Something happened five years ago, and it's something Wayne obviously thought was important enough to track me down for and keep from you. So, spill it. You'll feel better when you do."

"Somehow I doubt there's much of anything that can make me feel better."

"Well, since I know you want answers and I think getting them lies somewhere in what happened back then, I have to figure it's worth a shot, even if in the end it only makes you feel worse. Unless you've totally changed, you know your mind won't settle until you do."

It's faint and disappears almost as quickly as it comes, but me calling attention to her insane need to have all the answers, it's made her lips lift and do the one thing I didn't think I'd get to see for a very long time.

She's smiling.

The sight of it, hitting me the way it did when I was seven, again when were eight, ten, twelve and fourteen. Liquefying me like quicksand to my spot by our tree, completely engulfing me. At least it does until she speaks again and shatters my barely held together heart.

"My life was going through a pretty drastic change then, Joshua. When Daddy came to see you, I was engaged. I was going to get married."

Chapter Eleven
Atrophy
1990

Joshua

I am so over this crap.

It's the third time this week we've gotten into it and nothing changes.

Uncle Frank gets into it with me, tells me I'm not pulling my weight, I call his bluff and he comes at me, with Aunt Genie in the background screaming at the two of us to knock it off.

The only difference this time is instead of just attempting to scare me the way he has for the last three years, when he moves forward to grab me, he actually lands his hit, leaving me with the marks to prove it.

I can't believe I thought things would be different coming here. With the way things have been falling apart lately, I would have been better off staying in the group home.

Coming here was a mistake.

Well, living here was.

"Oh, Joshua. He didn't mean to do that." Aunt Genie starts in, immediately making excuses. "You just push his buttons and he lost control."

Losing control. I know a whole lot about that. I do it a lot. With jerks at school, idiot guys in the neighborhood, and sometimes, when I've got no other outlet and in need of a release, with my best friend and her dad.

This was more than losing control, and to be honest, I'm not in the mood to hear any different.

"He's full of shit. That's the first and last time he'll ever put hands on me."

Frank and me, we've been butting heads since I got here. He loathed me on sight. I was the bastard kid of his wife's sister. Nothing more. The amount of time I spent over at the Jeffries house, though, I'd managed to build a pretty thick wall between it and me. Never letting it get to me the obvious way it is now.

The time for playing parts was over the second Frank's fist made contact with my face. I'm done swallowing it. It's time for action, and not even Aunt Genie's sad eyes are going to change it.

I'm getting the hell out of here.

"You know he's not normally like this, Josh. You just had to keep pushing."

"Is that really what you think?"

"If you had just agreed with him, things wouldn't have escalated to this point."

Unbelievable.

I know I'm not exactly a saint, and I do things to annoy them or piss them off, but for her to stand here and put all of the blame on me, is sick. She's delusional.

"You just keep telling yourself that. Maybe one day it will make it true. Until then, I'm out of here."

Slamming my way past her and stomping up the stairs, she calls my name and I just continue climbing, ignoring her altogether until she calls out again, this time with a question I don't have the answer to.

"Joshua, where are you gonna go? If you leave here, they're gonna throw you back into the system. A kid with your issues, you'll probably stay there until you age out."

"Who cares where I go?" I call down. "All I know is anywhere is better than here."

Heading for my room and slamming the door behind me, I head to the closet and yank out my duffel, pulling clothes off the hangers before turning my attention to the dresser drawers. Yanking out the contents before dumping it in my bag. Moving as quickly as I can so when Genie does come through the door, there's nothing to stop me.

Pausing at the mirror above the dresser, I take in the slight discoloration beginning around my left eye, before looking away and letting my gaze linger on what's left of the dresser to take.

Picture frames, six of them, all pictures of me with the Jeffries. Two of us all together, and the other four of me and Alyssa over almost four years together. My smile tight, but real, alongside the one she wore. The smile transforming her entire face, making her eyes glow, her cheeks lift, and her lips part perfectly.

Sliding my hand around the first picture, bending the back down, I continue the same motion until all of the pictures are wrapped up with my clothes in the bag, before zipping it shut and slinging it around my back.

Time to get the hell out of here.

"What do you think you're doing, boy?" the stern voice calls out as I turn to make my way out.

Great. It wasn't enough that he punched me, he's gonna add insult to injury and get into it with me again.

"Getting the hell away from you."

"Right. Where are you planning on going?"

"Anywhere that's not here. You deaf or something?"

"You got a smart mouth for such a little bastard."

"I'd rather be a smart-mouthed bastard than a complete idiot, so thanks."

Frank's body leans forward, and I immediately step back, calculating exactly what my smart mouth is about to cause and instead of giving him the chance to get another shot off, I maneuver around him until I'm on the other side of the door.

"You leave this house, you can bet your bottom dollar you're not coming back."

Smirking at his threat, along with his stupid belief I even want to come back, I laugh, before taking the stairs two at a time until I'm standing by Aunt Genie at the bottom.

"Go on then!" Frank yells from the top of the stairs. "Show us what a big man you are. Leave and try finding another place as good as you had it here."

"A cardboard box in the middle of Yonge Street is better than here." I snap before turning toward Genie and silently saying goodbye.

No matter how I feel about Frank, she wasn't all bad. I just wish I could somehow get through her brainwashing to make her come with me.

"I'm sorry, Joshua. It wasn't supposed to be like this."

"I know Auntie, but I can't be here anymore." I respond, my voice steady, the truth light and airy on my tongue. "I deserve better than him and so do you."

With those words as my goodbye, I make my way around and through the door, destination unclear, but a significant weight lifted the moment I've jumped down off the porch and made my way away from them.

Looking both ways, deciding on what course I've gotta take now that I'm out, a voice calls out, and it's only when I turn toward it, I realize my answer has been here all along.

Alyssa Jeffries is my answer.

Alyssa

Taking the steps quickly, I make my way through the gate as Joshua crosses the street, his blue bag chock-full of stuff and hanging in front of him.

"You going somewhere?" I ask when he finally comes to a stop.

"Yeah. As far away from there as I can get." He thumbs back toward his house.

"What happened?"

This isn't the first time he's been over here like this, saying the same words and then explaining them. Telling me what happens in the house, how often he fights with Frank and how he needs to get away. This time though, I can see it's not like the others.

"Same shit, different day. Frank accused me of not doing the chore list. Said I was spending all of my time over here screwing around with you and shirking my duties."

It's all things I've heard before. When JJ lifts his head though, shoving locks of his wavy hair out of his eyes, and I'm able to see the slight difference in the left side of his face from the right, it all makes sense.

Frank hurt him.

"You wanna come in and talk about it?"

"Talking is the last thing I want."

"Alright, so making out on my bed it is then." I laugh, and despite the seriousness of the situation and the vacant look in his eye, I'm rewarded when he laughs.

"Come on," I start, motioning to the door, this time my tone serious. "Mom's baking again and I happen to know it's your favorite."

"Is your dad home?"

"Yeah. He's upstairs working on something. Why?"

"I mean it, AJ. I'm not going back there, but if I want to make sure I've got somewhere to go when I leave here, I have to talk to your dad."

"Okay, well, come on. Cookies are waiting."

"Are you bribing me with cookies so I'll talk?"

"No. I'm bribing you with cookies since you laughed at my idea of making out."

Listening to the sound of his laughter as it escapes again, I start walking back up the steps, hearing the sound of his own slowly following. It's only when I get to the screen door and pull it back to step through that he speaks and I come to a full stop.

"How do you do that?"

"Do what?"

"Just know how to calm me down. Make me forget I just had the world's biggest fight with my uncle?"

"What can I say? It's a gift." I answer with a grin. "Now are you coming or not?"

Standing on the inside of the door and waiting as he makes his way through and tosses his bag on the ground, immediately gravitating toward the kitchen, I follow behind, wrapping my brain around what he admitted outside and what I can do to make sure it's the last thing that happens. If my dad can't find a way to make him stay, it's going to be up to me.

There's no way I'm letting JJ leave for good.

Over my dead body am I going to lose my best friend.

Chapter Twelve
Your Guardian Angel
1990

Joshua

"Sophie, thank you for taking the time."

"With all the scraps you've thrown my way over the last few years, it's my pleasure, Wayne. I'm just not sure what it is you want me to do. You weren't clear over the phone."

Scraps.

She means kids like me.

After Wayne got off the phone with her a few hours ago and informed us he had called someone whose job it was to help, he'd explained just what he was putting in motion.

Sophie Abrams is a child advocate. She speaks up for kids like me who can't do it themselves or for whatever reason, aren't being heard. Putting our best interests before anyone else's and getting us the end result we crave.

For me it's simple. I want out of that house.

Even if it means going back to the group home until I age out.

When I showed up two days ago and Alyssa insisted I stay with them, they'd agreed and I'd spent the time soaking up what I've been craving since the first barbeque.

Spending time with a real family. One that didn't exist on fighting, pain, and addiction. Where I was free to be myself and I was accepted for it, maybe even loved. Working on the car with Wayne, hanging out at school, and again after it with AJ, finally getting to enjoy life again.

I wanted the Jeffries family forever.

Now it's in the hands of the lady who just stepped through the door to get me there.

"Joshua!" Wayne calls out and ceasing my eavesdropping, finally push my way through the door, met with not only

Wayne's knowing smile but the warmth of the one from the lady beside him too.

"Come on in, son." He motions as he notices my trepidation before crossing over the threshold of the bedroom turned office. "Ms. Abrams would like to ask you a few questions."

"Okay, but I already told Wayne everything, so not sure what else there is to say," I admit and Sophie nods as she steps forward and rests her hand on my shoulder.

"I've taken everything Wayne has told me into account, but I do need to hear it from you. Are you alright with that, Joshua?"

"Yeah, I guess."

Truth is, I'm not really, but since it seems like I'm not getting out of this room until I at least give them something to go on, I'm gonna have to suck it up.

"How long have you lived with the Watkins?"

"Since the fall of 1986."

"And the nature of your relationship with Frank and Genie?"

"My mom's sister and brother in law."

"How was your relationship before you came to live with them?"

"Didn't know they existed," I respond truthfully, knowing nothing of my actual family before social services dumped me in their lap.

"And your relationship once you came to stay with them?"

"Alright at first. As good as it was in the group home."

"In your estimation, when did it start to change?"

"I'm not sure what you mean by change. You mean harder or what happened a couple of days ago?"

"Well, for right now I mean, when did you notice things escalating into what happened a few days ago?"

"About six months in. Uncle Frank would find ways to add to the list of my chores every week until sometimes it was hard to keep up with them and school stuff."

"Were you against doing chores?"

"No. I've been doing them for years. I'm earning my place that way."

Something I've said seems to take her off guard because even though she tries to hide it, I catch her eyes widening and her lips parting into a small circle.

"Who said you had to earn your place?"

"No one. It's just what you do."

"Okay." She responds softly before moving on. "Did you ever express to your family that you were feeling overwhelmed?"

"They weren't my family." I snap, swallowing the dirty taste that comes from even using the word family and my Uncle and Aunt in the same sentence. "But yeah, I did. A couple of times I didn't get everything done and I'd try and tell them why. It didn't matter."

"What would happen when you tried to explain?"

"Genie would get annoyed, complain to Frank, and he'd go off. Yelling and cursing."

"It never escalated past that point?"

"Not when I was younger, but the older I got, the more he'd get in my face." Closing my eyes, I attempt to soothe away the twisting sensation that comes with talking about this. "No offense, but how is all of this supposed to help me?"

"Joshua, right now I'm trying to get a feel for the way your life has been since you came here. Create a timeline so when this goes to court, everything is on the table."

"Why does it have to go to court? Just call my worker and send me back to the home. I know the way this goes. I'll be alright there."

Before Sophie can respond, Wayne steps forward and moving in, leans down until his eyes are level with mine, giving me the answers I'm really after. The reason all of this is happening at all.

"She's asking you these questions, we're going to go to court instead of following through on what you want because I'm petitioning the court for temporary custody."

Wayne's doing what?

"You've come a long way since you arrived here Joshua, and for that reason, we feel it best we keep you here so it can continue."

"You want me to stay with you?"

"Yes. Temporarily. If it doesn't work out, you're free to leave and go back to the group home if you want, but Helen and I have talked about this and we'd really like to give it a go."

Wayne wants me to stay.

I can't believe this.

"Is this some kind of joke?"

"I assure you, son, it's not."

Sophie takes that moment to cut back in, bringing the questions around again and taking me away from what's been thrown in my lap.

"Up until a couple of days ago, did Frank or Genie put their hands on you in any way that would be considered inappropriate?"

"No, and they won't either. Once is enough."

I hope this is the end of her questions because I've got a few of my own now. Like, what Wayne is thinking wanting to do this for a kid he doesn't even know. It's not like he's obligated to help me. I'm just some kid who moved into the neighborhood.

Having crawled into my own thoughts and zoned out on what the two of them are doing, I've got no idea if the conversation has continued on without me until I see Wayne turn and shake hands with Sophie and her turn and head to the door.

When we're alone again, I turn my attention back, asking the only question I can.

"What happens now?"

"Now we wait and let Sophie do her job."

If only he knew how powerful his statement is.

Temporary custody, something after a period of time and being paraded through the courts again in the future could very well lead to a more permanent situation with the family I care about, is a dream come true for any foster kid.

Living with the Jeffries family could finally give me a place to call home, but what Wayne doesn't know and I don't know if I've got the heart to tell him is, I'm not sure it's the right thing for me.

As much as I appreciate what he's done, what AJ and her mom have done, I can't shake the fact I've burdened them enough and I can't put them through anymore.

It's time for me to move on.

Alyssa

Okay, I've put up with this long enough.

JJ can tell me he's fine all he wants, but I know it's not true. He hasn't been fine since the day I came in from outside and caught him talking to my dad and the lady.

He's been quieter than normal, sticking to the house more, not wanting to go out, even with the bribing I did with another movie.

It's also written all over his face. The way he's either zoned out a million miles away or frowning.

Two days of it is enough. Him being here was supposed to be a good thing, but with the way things have gone, it seems like it's gotten worse.

I'm done.

He doesn't want to give me answers, fine. I'm going to try something different.

I just hope it works the way it does in my head because I really need my best friend back. With him slipping away a little more every day, it won't be long before he's lost to me forever. I can't let that happen.

I care about him too much.

Call it a crush or puppy love all you want, but I like myself and my life a whole lot better since JJ came into it. I'm not letting it go without a fight. My first real friend, my first kiss. The first person to make my heart beat something other than steady. He's all of those things and more.

JJ is my everything and it's about time I showed him.

Knocking on the door and waiting, after a minute or two passes, he gives me what I'm after as he opens the door.

"What do you want, AJ?"

"Hello to you too."

"Hi." He responds sarcastically. "What do you want?"

"I was wondering if you wanted to take a walk with me."

"Not really in the mood."

"Please?" I beg.

"Why?"

"Because I want to show you something."

"Show me what?"

"It's a surprise. I came across it a couple of days ago when you bailed on hanging out with me at the ravine. Will you come so I can show you?"

He doesn't even attempt to hide the struggle he's having, his hands immediately coming up and rubbing his forehead, while his lips perk up for the first time in days and twitch as he smirks.

"I hate surprises."

"You won't hate this one. Pinkie Promise."

"Wow. You must be serious if you're breaking out the pinkie promise. You haven't used that since we were eight."

"Totally serious," I grin, as the warmth of him remembering the last time we used those words settles over me. "So, are you gonna make you kidnap you or come willingly?"

"If I go with you now, will you chill on the smothering you've been doing lately?"

"Can't promise anything. I care about you. I can space it out, though."

"Deal." Turning from the door and grabbing the flannel shirt hanging over the back of the chair pushed into the desk, he slips his body into it and makes his way through the doorway.

After taking the stairs and heading out of the house, taking the path designed to bring us to our spot, our tree and where before things got bad at home for him, we'd spend the majority of our time, he stops cold at the tree and leans his body against it, his gaze landing on me.

"Time to tell the truth, AJ. You didn't find anything out here, did you?"

"Actually, I did. It's just not here anymore."

"Then what the hell are we doing here?"

I wasn't sure just how deep the changes ran until now. The cold way he asks, along with the stony look and the hardness of his face, it's all the answer I need. Whatever happened with him and my dad, it's left scars.

This is the seven-year-old JJ, not the one he's become in the four years since.

"You needed to get out of the house. It's been days since you left."

"Not exactly up for company or the same old shit, AJ."

"This isn't the same old shit, JJ. And you're not the same either."

Scoffing and adding another eye roll to match the ones from earlier, my stomach twists.

"Wondered how long it was gonna take you to say that. I know you've been dying to lately. Gotta say though, I expected worse."

"Worse how?"

Moving from his position against the tree and stalking slowly and deliberately toward me, he stops when he's almost straight on top of me, running his hand down over my jawline and smirking, before leaning in, our lips a breath apart, my heart picking up and him ruining the moment by speaking.

"You want to swear at me, AJ. You know it and I know it. I've been a total asshole to you. I know you wanna call me on it."

"You're—wrong." I stammer and instead of smirking, he chuckles before taking a step back and crossing his arms across his chest, waiting me out.

"Fine, I'll bite. If you didn't bring me here to unload on me or to be a little do-gooder, why are we here?"

Slipping my hand into my jeans until they're gripping the surprise, I hand it over. Dropping it into his hand before closing his fingers around it. Releasing his hand, I wait with bated breath as he opens his hand and takes in the small trinket now in his possession.

When I was out here a few days ago, I caught the shimmer of it in the ground as the sun hit it. Digging my fingernails in the ground, I'd found what I was after and with everything that's been going on, it seemed like a sign.

One I needed to find so I could show him.

"Where did you get this?"

"Found it half buried out here a couple of days ago. So, see! I wasn't lying about finding something."

The way his fingers roam ever so softly, his eyes noticeably softer than before, it's obvious not only was this a sign I needed to find but one that has some meaning to him.

"I don't understand. Why would you want to show *me* this?"

"Because you're my best friend and I show you everything."

"No, I get that, but there's gotta be more to it."

"Sometimes there's not."

"And sometimes, when your best friend is Alyssa Jeffries, nothing is ever black and white."

"You might be right about that." I concede, finally giving up on skirting around the issue and instead of going with the truth instead. "I was out here thinking, wondering really. I had this friend, who shall remain nameless, who went from sharing everything with me to pushing me away."

"This friend sounds like a real jerk."

"Oh, he is, totally, but usually it's directed at everyone else. Lately, it's been directed at me, and I guess I was out here trying to come up with a reason why. The sun broke through the tree just right and that's when I saw it."

Motioning down to the guardian angel pendant in his hand, he speaks. "You saw this."

"Yeah. It seemed perfect because at around the same time, I think I figured out what's going on with you."

"I thought this *friend* was remaining nameless."

"No fun in that."

"What did you figure out?" He switches gears, asking as he turns back toward the tree, leans his body against it and slowly lowers himself to the ground.

"I know why you're acting this way, JJ. What I can't figure out is why you think you need to."

"I'll bite. Why am I acting extra jerky these days?"

"Because you want to leave."

If I had just met Josh, the slight widening of his eyes, along with the way he seems to bury his face even deeper into his knees wouldn't mean much to me. It wouldn't confirm or deny what I think, but I do know him.

"I'm right."

"Is there any use denying it?" he asks once he's lifted his head back up.

"Nope. Not really. But I gotta know, JJ. Why?"

"Four years is the longest I've stayed anywhere before, Aly." He admits. "I knew I had a shelf life here when I moved in. I just thought it would be a lot sooner. It's time."

"So that's it then? You just wanna give up and leave?"

"It's the best thing for everyone."

"Now I'm the one who doesn't get it. You have it good here. My dad loves you the same way he loved Scott, and for him, that's a really big thing. It's like Scott sent you to us when he died."

He can try and hide it, but I catch the way he flinches when I admit the truth. Sure, this is all stuff he wouldn't know because my dad wouldn't come right out and admit it, but after four years of watching them together, I know it's true and its time Josh did too.

"That's not true, Aly."

"It's the truest thing I've ever said. You didn't get to see him when you went home most nights. The way he would stand watch at the window, making sure you got home okay but was also sad you had to leave at all. He loves you, JJ. It's the reason why he talked with my mom about helping you stay with us."

He wants to argue this, but what he should know by now is when it's me he's doing it with, he won't ever win. Especially when it's something like this.

"It doesn't matter, Aly."

Now it's my turn to flinch. I thought if anything, knowing the truth about how my dad views him would mean pretty much everything. Not this.

"Then what matters, JJ? If my daddy accepting you and wanting you with us doesn't matter, what else is there?"

"This." He answers matter of fact before again motioning toward the trinket in his hand.

"I knew you wanted to leave. I could feel it. It's the only real reason you'd change the way you are. The guardian angel is about watching over people, right? Protecting them at all times, when everyone else fails you. I guess I figured if you were really serious about leaving and going back to the group home, you could take it with you."

"W—Why?"

"If I can't be with you, then at least you won't have to go through everything that happens next, alone. Where I can't be, this can."

Chapter Thirteen
Revelations

Joshua

Engaged.

The girl who no matter the time, has always just belonged to me, was engaged. I came so close to losing her for good and had my head up my ass so far, I didn't even know it.

"I'm sorry, I don't think I heard you right. Did you just say you were going to get married five years ago?"

"Yes."

It's not storytelling or fable to say I always pictured when the time came for marriage it would be Alyssa walking down the long and winding aisle toward me. Even after the way I left things, and the hermit I turned into, apart from work and the occasional dalliance, it always came back to her.

Hearing that even if it was for a short period of time in a twenty-year time span, she didn't feel the same, is enough to gut me. Making me thankful before she dropped her bomb, I'd leaned back against the tree for support.

I can't believe this.

Coming back here, if things had been the way they were when Wayne came to see me, could have ended completely different. I could be pining after another man's wife.

"I don't know what to say," I admit and where I expect her to nod, give me even a small flicker of understanding, the tables turn and she quickly flips into defense mode.

"What did you think would happen, Joshua? That after the way things ended for us, I would spend every single day at home pining away for what could have been if you had just talked to me instead of running?"

"Yeah! Is it so wrong? I mean it's what I did."

"The thing is, you could have easily got what you came for years before. It took a very long time for me to stop blaming myself for the way things turned out and move on with my life. I held onto you and what we had very tightly. I couldn't and wouldn't let you go."

"So, what changed?"

"I met Mark. Who after spending years watching his wife slowly succumb to cancer until she finally passed, understood at least a little bit what it was like. He took his time, becoming my friend first, helping me work through things until what was happening between us could be passed off as friends anymore."

"That's beautiful, AJ, it really is, but if he was such a great guy, why are you standing at our tree with me and not off enjoying a happily ever after with him?"

I know the edge in my voice isn't lost on her, but where I expect her to do things the way she would have in the past, she stands her ground, staring me down without so much as a blink, giving back as good as I'm giving.

"He died."

Of course. Open mouth, insert foot.

Doing a real bang-up job here, Brantley.

"I'm sorry."

"It's fine. You didn't know."

"No, it's not fine. I should never have acted like that."

The time for her accepting my craptastic attitude is over. She's right. She's been right the entire time. Just because I kept pieces of her with me all these years, doesn't mean she had to.

Besides, considering I'm the reason things are as strained as they are, I've really got no right to sit here and act self-righteous. Alyssa did what I made her do.

"How long?"

"How long what?"

"You and Mark. How long were you two together?"

"A year to the day he proposed. Friends for about three years."

Another truth I can barely stomach but need to hear. She was telling me the truth earlier when she said it hadn't been easy for Mark to break through her walls.

"Were you happy?"

"Yes...and no."

"I don't get it."

"Well, Joshua, that might be because you're not meant to get it."

"Then explain it to me. Why is it both?"

"As it turns out, no matter how much you talk yourself into something, how ready you think you are to move on, if your heart isn't in it, it won't work out. I just wish I'd known back then. Maybe things could have been different."

For the first time since I threw myself back into her life, she's opening up to me. Admitting that despite caring for the man she would have eventually married, she really had been like me and been unable to completely move on.

Alyssa is admitting she loved me. Maybe loves me still.

"Do you think he knew you felt that way?"

"Did my fiancé know he was marrying a master pretender? No, I don't think he did, but had things been different, he would have. I couldn't pretend forever."

This is something I know easily about her. She isn't a liar. At least not outright, and if she is anything now the way she was when we were younger, she didn't stick it out with this guy to hurt him, she stuck it out because she wanted to love him.

She wanted him to be something he could never be.

"What happened to him?" I cautiously ask, before realizing just how none of my business this is and try and retract. "You know what? Never mind. It's personal and clearly not my business."

"Car accident." She answers softly. "I'd been telling him for weeks to get his tires switched out, that at the worst possible moment we were gonna end up getting hit with a storm and they weren't going to be able to handle it. He kept putting me off, telling me I was paranoid." Pausing to laugh, she shakes her head. "I'm never just paranoid, but I dropped it. He was coming over after work one night, we were going to go over wedding plans and the storm hit. He lost control of the car and it slammed into a guardrail, the airbag malfunctioning and..."

"I got it, you don't have to tell me the rest."

"But I do. You know, when you left years ago, everyone urged me to talk about it. It will be therapeutic, they said. Help me get a handle on my emotions and move forward. I didn't say a word. I didn't talk about it with anyone, not even my parents. The same thing happened again after Mark's accident. I kept being told to talk, but couldn't. Now that I am, I think I need to see it through. Even if it is with you."

Nodding my understanding, I wait for her to start again, finish telling me what happened to this man she wanted to love so badly, but never got the chance to. After a few more seconds with no sound, she makes her way over to the tree and lowers herself down until we're sitting side by side with our backs firmly planted against it, clearing her throat and speaking again.

"His head slammed off the dash before swinging backward. He broke his neck, and that, coupled with the bleeding on his brain from hitting it off the steering column, was too much. He died before he made it to the hospital."

I've read about loss, experienced a bit of it in varying degrees over the years, but never anything like this. I don't have the first clue how to respond.

"Scott, Cody, you and our baby. Then Mark, and now my Dad. You'd think after losing so many people I'd be a pro at handling it when it happens. Even *the way* it happens. Car accidents, sick animals, cruel twists of fate, and heart attacks, I should be used to it, but I'm not. The only thing I am a pro at is how much I hate losing people."

"It's not worth a whole lot, but you can take me off the list. I might have run, but you never lost me."

"Didn't I?" she asks, lifting herself off of the tree and turning toward me. "Twenty years, Joshua. Twenty years of not knowing whether you were alive or dead. Yes, you're right. You did run and you're here now, proving you didn't die, but with the way it felt when it happened, it sure as hell felt like you were dead."

"But I didn't and I'm here now."

"For how long? How long do I get you this time, Joshua? A couple of days? A week? A few months? How long will it be before you choose running over staying again?"

The use of my name and the flood of emotion it unleashes aside, I've got much bigger issues to deal with. Making her understand what I've known from the second I got the call from

Kevin days ago. I didn't come back to say goodbye to the only father I ever had.

I came back to say hello to her.

I need to make her understand my being here now is for keeps. I'll never leave her again. The boy who was always running turned into a man who is finally ready to stop.

"For as long as forever is for us, AJ. That's how long."

"I wish I could believe you, I really do, but your track record says otherwise."

"I know it does, which is why I'm asking for the chance to prove it. What you said earlier about pretending, that's what the last twenty years have been like for me. Just one big show I starred in. I made people see the person they wanted to see because being the one I wanted to be was too difficult. I spent thirty-six years living in a fear of my own design, and I want to spend the next thirty-six living free from it. No more running. No more hiding. I want to be me with you."

"Josh—"

"No, don't try and come up with an argument against this or tell me the past proves I'm going to fail. I know already."

"I wasn't going to say that."

Well, color me confused.

"What were you going to say?"

"Welcome home."

Chapter Fourteen

Black Cloud Rain
September 1994

Alyssa

Here goes nothing.

It's officially the first day of high school.

Freshman, minor niner, the girl the seniors will mop the floor with once they catch sight of me. I'm all of these things, and this is officially the last place I want to be.

Is it too late to go back to junior high?

What are you thinking, Jeffries? It's not like those last two years were any better than what you're about to face once you get up the nerve to walk through the front door.

Gotta give it up to my inner voice. She's right. It wasn't any better. Nothing's been great for four years if I'm keeping track of time.

Ah, yes. The voice mocks. *The night Joshua Brantley couldn't get away from you fast enough.*

Shut up. I can remember all on my own, thanks.

With the voice in my head quiet, I step forward, taking in the lengthy set of windows laid out in front of me. Swallowing down the rising nerves being here, I take a few tentative steps toward the door, stopping only when I hear my name being called.

It's only when I work up the nerve to turn, I catch sight of who was calling out and I don't even attempt to hide the groan.

Another person mysteriously absent from my life since JJ up and left.

He never should have called out.

Kevin is the worst reminder of everything I'd much rather forget.

"What do you want, Kev?"

"It's been awhile, huh?"

Yeah, no shit Sherlock. Real brain surgeon, this guy.

"I repeat, what do you want?"

Shifting back on the soles of his feet, his eyes scanning over the crowd of people moving around us, he ignores my question and takes another route.

"How's your dad doing? It's been a while since he came down to the center."

The center he's talking about is the recreational center a few minutes from our house.

A place where after Scott died, my dad would frequent religiously. Hanging out with the young guys, playing basketball, hockey, and every other sport under the sun. Sometimes, even just popping in and doing nothing but imparting his years of wisdom on them.

Also, the place he hasn't been able to stomach going to since he found out what really happened to Joshua.

His leaving, what he'll probably never get, it didn't just affect me. It had gotten my daddy too. Maybe even more so.

"If you came by the house once in a while, you wouldn't have to ask me."

There he goes again. Shifting his feet. He's uncomfortable. Nervous.

Good. He's another jerk in a long line of them who deserve to feel that way. If it's sympathy or forgiveness he's after, he's not gonna get it here.

"You know how shit was back then, AJ."

"Don't call me that."

There's another change. A nickname everyone used to use for me but meant the most coming from Joshua, I haven't been able to stomach again.

Four years.

1460 days.

All of that time passing and I still hate the way it sounds coming from anyone else.

Four years gone and just standing here with Kevin is leaving me raw, like a scab freshly picked and bleeding.

Joshua Brantley can rot in hell.

"Look, I'm sorry, okay? I know when Josh left, I bailed on you and your old man. I'm sorry for it, I really am, but if I had kept coming around, do you really think it would have been okay? Would have been the same?"

"I guess since you didn't, we'll never know, huh?" I snap, repositioning my backpack over my shoulder and turning my back on him.

"He's back," Kevin calls out after I've made it no more than a foot away, and just like the puppet I became for everyone so long ago, two words act like strings and bring me to a complete stop.

He doesn't even need to elaborate. I know who *he* is. There is only one I would ever care about.

Joshua.

Kevin is standing here dropping the mother of all bombshells on me.

Joshua Brantley is back in town.

Spinning around, I bridge the distance between us, pausing only when I find myself directly in front of him. Staring him down, the shock of what he's dropped on me mixing with the rage I feel over the way he's doing it, has my hand rising until I'm full on slapping him in the face.

His stupid, stupid face.

"How dare you?!"

Touching the spot where my hand made the most impact, his eyes steel, the blue of them cold as his lips follow suit and straighten.

Good. Let him react. He deserves this.

I have no doubt he's known about Joshua being back for a while now and he held onto that knowledge, waiting to tell me until he could make the biggest impact.

Getting hit in the head with a hockey stick constantly must have made what was left of his brains seep out.

Who drops something this big on a girl right before she's about to start one of the hardest days of her life?

"What the hell was that for?"

"You know what the hell it was for!" I yell, my body hardening and refusing to back down.

"Like hell I do! I thought you'd be happy!"

"How long has he been back?" I demand, but before he can answer I shove my hand out to stop him. "On second thought, why don't you tell me how long you've known he was back first?"

This gets him. I can see by the way he averts his eyes that he wants to lie, but I'm not having it. I knew I was right. He's known a whole lot longer than the few minutes to get here and find me.

"How long, Kevin?"

"He's been back for a few weeks. He's been holed up at my house. My parents agreed to let him stay with us after his last foster family threw him out."

"You're an asshole."

"AJ—"

"What did I say about calling me that?"

"Shit. Fine. Al-ys-sa." He draws out my name, earning an eye roll and a back turn in response. The only way I can make him see just how done I am.

With him *and* this conversation.

Aware as the heavy sigh escapes, but not turning around in order to deal with it, I'm blocked when he comes around the left side, halting me in place. Continuing to move with every attempt I make that follows to get around him.

"Don't be like this. I know I should have said something sooner, but he didn't want you to know. You of all people know how it goes, Aly. He's like a brother to me."

Yeah, you're damn right I know. But before he took off, I could have sworn I was something more than that to Joshua. The same way he was more to me.

Naïve little Aly thought he hung the moon.

"And once upon a time, you were like my brother too. I deserved better than this but fine. JJ is back. That's great for him. I hope you guys live happily ever after."

Ignoring the curse when I finally fake him out long enough to skirt my way around, I take off at a run for the door, desperate for the sanctuary, the school will provide.

This can't matter now.

Joshua Brantley can't matter.

There's only one problem, though.

Even after four years apart, he's still the only person who does.

Joshua

"She knows."

"Yeah, she knows. She also went postal on my ass when I told her too, thanks."

I've got to admit; her reaction surprises me.

With all the time that's passed since I bailed, I assumed she would have gotten over it. I mean, just because I can still smell the soft scent of her vanilla shampoo every night when I close my eyes, doesn't mean she's going through the same thing.

Leaving was supposed to put an end to what I knew was starting with her.

With the respect I had for Wayne and everything he did for me during the four years I lived across the street, the thoughts I was having about his daughter weren't right. I owed him better.

I owed all of them better.

Too bad it didn't do that.

Four years went by and I still missed her every single day. It never alleviated or went away. It was always just there, haunting me. All me leaving really did was make my mind grasp on tighter to the memories we'd already made.

Memories I wish I could find her now and expand on, but I've got to be content keeping to myself. Her reaction to Kevin's announcement proof enough.

We're better off apart.

"She's still pissed."

"Pissed is an understatement. When it comes to you, bro, she's a fire breathing dragon. You might wanna keep your distance."

Not bad advice. Too bad it's the same line I gave myself when Kevin's parents took me in, and I've been breaking every second since. Going by her house when I know no one would be home was the first step, and it carried over to me keeping tabs on her from a distance since we got here a few hours ago.

I might be keeping physical distance between us, but that's as far as it goes. Because where it matters, we're still the same way we were then.

Best friends. Crushes. Two kids on a precipice, where if we fell, would have thrown us into what could have been a pretty epic love story.

Yeah, I know, it's sappy shit, but I've been around. I've seen a lot. What I felt for her, it went a lot deeper than friendship.

It still does and I'm starting to think it always will.

"I don't get you, man. It's pretty obvious you two have unfinished business. You clearly care about her, especially if you're dragging me into it. So why not talk to her? Why all this cloak and dagger crap?"

"It's the way it has to be. You know the way my life is. I can't drag her into it."

"What happened wasn't your fault."

Kevin might be right, but not everyone is gonna see it that way.

Some would even say I asked for it. What ended up happening, I put the wheels in motion by leaving in the first place.

"Doesn't matter. I'm a fucking mess, she's better off without it, and this conversation is over."

"Whatever you say, bro, but I remember hanging with Aly. She was cool back then, and I'm pretty sure if you could get past the massive wall of hate she built up when you left, she'd be just as cool now."

"Doesn't matter. It's not happening."

I don't even know who the fuck I'm trying to kid here. He's right about all of it. It would be so easy to fall back into old routines with this girl. Find her in the hall and tell her how much I missed her. How much I wish I could go back in time and never leave.

Be what we always were to each other.

It would be so damn easy.

Problem is, she knows nothing of what's gone down since I left and it's all of that, my inability to fuck up her life more by telling her about it, that makes something so easy, incredibly hard.

Totally off limits.

It's the way things have to be.

Chapter Fifteen
Let the Games Begin
September 1994

Alyssa

Avoiding someone is surprisingly easy when you don't share any of the same classes, and anything you might be doing extracurricular wise doesn't add up either.

What I thought would be hard, considering the gravitational pull I feel whenever I'm within a few feet of JJ, turned out to be surprisingly easy after the first day. Before I know it, I've made it two weeks without so much as one run in with the boy who still managed to hold a very big piece of my heart.

But any celebration I might have thought of having melted fast when I realized the same couldn't be said for Kevin Williams.

He was everywhere.

At first, I thought the reason he seemed to be in all my classes was dumb luck, but when he started showing up at the library during the off times, I knew there was nothing random about it.

Kevin has never cracked open a book he wasn't forced to in the entire time I've known him, and something told me he wasn't itching to start now.

What I'm starting to see, on the fourth day of him showing up and throwing his body down in the seat across me at the round table is, he's also not doing it for Joshua.

This is all him. I just wish I could understand why.

Grinning when he catches me studying him, and full on laughing when I attempt to blow it off by burying my face back in the textbook deliberately standing up in front of us, I give up any attempt at trying to figure him out and ask him point blank.

"Not for nothing, Kev, but it's pretty obvious this is the last place you wanna be, so why don't you just spit out the reason you're here so we can move on with our lives?"

"I don't know what you mean, Alyssa."

"Sure, you don't." I roll my eyes before looking back down to the text I'm supposed to be reading for history class.

"Can't I want to spend time with an old friend?"

"Normally, I'd say sure, but you and I haven't been friends for a long time. So, no. I think there's more to it."

"If I said I thought you were cute and was working up the courage to ask you out?"

I can't help it. Something about the struggle he's experiencing trying to keep a straight face and what he's said causes me to burst out laughing.

"You can't seriously expect me to believe that." I finally admit when in an attempt to hide away in the text, he pulls it out of my hands and slides it to the other end of the table.

"What's harder to believe? The fact I find you cute or me wanting to ask you out?"

"Both?"

This gets him. The grin is gone, but the look it's replaced with isn't much better. What I've said is obviously enough to make him switch gears.

"Do you remember when we were eight and your dad took all of us to the field for a game? And despite his repeated warnings to stay behind, you ended up sneaking over there anyway?"

I don't even know why he bothers asking things like this. I remember everything from when we were kids. They were some of the best times of my life.

"What about it?"

"You weren't like the other girls, AJ." Cringing at the sound of the nickname, he clears his throat and does his best attempt to rectify. "Shit, sorry. Aly."

"I still don't understand what that has to do with you stalking me for the last four days."

"You might have been off limits to us because we had mad respect for your old man, but it didn't mean we didn't notice you. I'm bringing this ancient shit up because you wanted to know what I'm doing here. Now you know."

"Actually, Kevin, I don't know. All you've done is confuse me more."

It's a lie of course. I can read quite easily into what he's getting at. I just don't know how much of it I believe. We were eight years old for crying out loud.

"Look, I really need to study if I want to pass this test tomorrow, so if you could just speed this whole thing along..."

Gone is the confidence I've come to expect. With the lowering of his head and the aversion of his eyes down to his hands, along with the way they seem to be shaking, it's like Kevin isn't even here anymore.

I'm sitting with someone else entirely.

"I'm probably gonna get killed for admitting this, but I miss hanging out with you. I miss the way things used to be. I'd really like it if we could at least try and get it back."

"You...miss me?"

"Hanging with you." He clarifies, but not before clearing his throat and starting up again. "Shit. Screw it. Yes, okay? I miss you."

This is so incredibly weird, and I have no idea what to say or do with what I'm hearing.

I've got to come up with something to say, though. The silence is more awkward than his admission to missing me is.

"That wasn't so hard, was it?" I joke, but when I meet his eyes, I see I'm the only one who finds it humorous. "Why would you get killed for admitting this?"

"No reason. I was just rambling." He responds almost too quickly. His movements betraying him as he starts looking around the room instead of focusing on me the way I expect.

"That's bullshit, Kev, but fine. Keep your secrets."

Breathing a sigh of relief, he meets my eyes again, this time with the signature grin of his right back where it belongs.

"With all of that out of the way, I was thinking. A few of the old crew are getting together after school, and I thought if you didn't have anything else going on, maybe you'd wanna come?"

Well, if his admission of missing me was out of left field, this is even more so.

There is no way Kevin Williams just asked me out.

"Come on, Jeffries. I know you wanna say yes. It'll be like old times."

Old times I've spent the last four years trying to move past, but times Kevin doesn't have the same issue with.

"If I say yes, will you leave me alone?"

"It depends," he says, wiggling his brow. "Is that your way of saying yes?"

"No. It's my way of trying to figure out exactly what the game is here."

"No game, Aly. Just miss my friend and wanna hang with her. So, you in or not?"

Despite my head screaming at me to say no; to not trust a damn thing he's saying, it's not at all what comes out when I do finally speak.

"I'm in."

"Yes!" he yells, throwing his body up and out of the chair, causing all eyes in the place to fall on us. "You won't regret this, Aly."

"I better not." I hiss at the exact moment he chooses to push my book back across the table.

"I'll get out of your hair and let you study." He smiles. "But I'm looking forward to seeing you later."

With those words as his parting shot, he salutes the people still staring before turning and quickly making a beeline for the door. Only stopping once he's made his way through to look back at me with a grin.

As he turns and goes out of sight, all I'm left with is the bad feeling in my stomach telling me this is a mistake. In fact, I'm pretty sure I'm going to live to regret saying yes in the first place. It looks like my avoidance of all things Joshua is about to come to an end.

Great.

Joshua

"You did what?!"

Bailing on me to spend time with AJ was one thing, but I've obviously got shit clogging my ability to hear right because there's no way my best friend just said what I think he did.

"You heard me, Josh."

"No, I'm positive I didn't, because I could have sworn you said you asked AJ out."

"You heard right the first time, bro. I asked her to come to hang out while we play."

No fucking way.

"Why?"

"Man, you really haven't paid attention to anything I said, have you?"

I heard every damn thing he said. I'm just not about to admit it because everything he's said up until now is only making me want to unload on his face.

Has he forgotten the part where she's off-fucking-limits?

I've spent the last two weeks doing everything in my power to stay out of her way. Been succeeding at it too given the fact that I haven't so much as seen a hair on her head in the halls. It's made what I said to Kevin before, the plan of mine to keep my distance, easy.

Until now.

What part of me not wanting to bring Alyssa back into my shit is he not getting?

"Tell me you don't miss hanging out with her," Kevin smirks, and it takes everything I've got to swallow down the urge to punch him.

"Not going there."

"That's the problem, isn't it? You never wanna go there. You tell me you miss her and want to reach out to her and her pops in one breath, and then in the next, go all woe is me and say she's better off without you. But, when you catch wind of someone showing any interest, you act like a rabid dog."

"What's your point?"

"You need to make up your mind, bro. Either you reconnect with her or get the fuck out of the way and let someone else do it."

"Someone else, being you?"

The anger coursing through me should cause Kevin to step back, but it's not happening. Gone is the Kevin of old, and in his place, someone more stubborn than me.

"Yeah, man." He grunts. "You know how things used to be with all of us. I miss it, even if you don't. Not to mention the girl is fucking gorgeous. I'd be stupid not to at least try."

I can't argue with him. She's not the same girl I left behind when I walked away. She has most definitely grown up. You'd have to be blind not to see it, and with all of the watching before coming back to school I've been doing, I definitely noticed.

Doesn't mean I've got to be cool with anyone else doing it.

I don't care if I don't have any claim anymore.

Alyssa is mine.

She'll always be mine.

"If she's coming, I'm not." I threaten, and Kevin just stands there laughing and shaking his head.

"Then don't come, because I'm not going back and telling her we're calling it off. I meant what I said. I want to get to know her again."

The idea of Kevin getting within a foot of her, especially with the ease at which he admits to missing her, guts me. I know he's right and I have to put up or shut up here, but any mention of him and her in the same sentence makes me forget all logic.

All I can see is red.

"Fine. Let her come. Do whatever you want with her, I don't care. As you said, she's fair game."

I want to puke the second the words are out.

"So, you won't mind if I ask her to be my date for the Halloween dance?"

Jesus, Kev. Twist the knife in a little deeper, why don't you?

There's no turning back now. I've already slung the bullshit even though something tells me even Kevin knows not a word is true. Might as well keep it going. It's not like staking a claim right now would do much good anyway.

"Nah, man. Go ahead. I was thinking of asking Ronnie anyway."

Ronnie Watson. As in the principal's daughter, Ronnie.

The one girl in the entire school even more off limits than AJ is.

"Man, you really do have a death wish." Kevin whistles, and I laugh.

If it wasn't total bullshit, I'd agree.

"Gotta find out if the rumors are true, don't I?"

Acid fills my lungs as my chest seizes under the weight of yet another lie.

I've been doing this for weeks. Blowing off what might have been and still could be with AJ, focusing instead on the shallower end and shoving myself straight into the line of the high school fire.

"Better you than me, I guess. Look, I gotta go. I wanted to catch up with Alyssa and see if we could walk home together. Before I do, though, I gotta ask again. You sure you're cool with this?"

"Yeah, man. You're right. I gave up my shot with her, which means I can't be pissed when someone else wants to ask her out. Besides, better you than some of the dicks on the field hockey team with us."

Even knowing I'm still slinging bullshit, there's some truth to this. If I've gotta put up with anyone near AJ when I can't be, I would rather it be someone I trust.

The lesser of two evils it is.

Doesn't do a damn thing for the need to pummel him I'm still dealing with, though.

That's still alive and well.

It's also something I need to get a handle on in the next couple of hours, or my plan to stay away from her is going to go up in flames. Alyssa can never know how I really feel.

That's got to be for me only.

Kevin

I can't believe how easy they're making this.

Months of listening to Josh go back and forth over the girl, along with the anger from Alyssa stemming from her unresolved feelings for the guy, it's like taking candy from a baby.

They're eating right out of my hand.

Though, I gotta admit things were sketchy there for a bit with Aly.

Even when we were little she could always see past the expressions on my face. So, when she eyed me in the library, I thought for sure she figured out my game.

As it turns out though, actually missing her worked in my favor because it made her believe me.

There's a small part of me that feels like a horse's ass for doing things this way. Risking the two most important friendships I have in order to get them to see they're perfect for each other.

It's just not enough to make me stop.

I've always prided myself on being upfront and honest in everything I do. Cuts out the unnecessary bullshit, but with as stubborn as they both seem to have gotten since Josh left, playing them is the only way to make this work.

Matchmaker Kevin at your service.

The Halloween dance didn't factor into my plans when I started but is a happy little accident I'm going to use to my advantage now that it's on the board.

I mean, that's what works on chicks, right?

Grand gestures. The bigger and more elaborate, the better?

Given what I've got to work with, what better place and time can there be for these two idiots to finally admit how they feel about each other?

It's absolute genius.

Game on.

Chapter Sixteen
Slow Dance
October 1994

Alyssa

I can't believe I let myself be talked into this.

Coming here alone was one thing, but agreeing to wear this red monstrosity is something else entirely. I never should have done it, especially since the reason I'm wearing it at all isn't here to appreciate the effort.

Trust me, I've looked.

No Kevin to be found.

I'm on my own.

I guess I shouldn't be surprised. When Kevin threw out the idea of us going to the dance together, and even worse, suggested dressing up as characters from when we were kids, I should have seen it for the joke it obviously was.

If we'd come dressed as characters from Sailor Moon, Power Rangers, hell, even the Ninja Turtles, it would have made more sense, especially with the sheer amount of cartoon anime girls I'm seeing all over the gym.

Lydia Deetz and Beetlejuice, though?

What the hell was I thinking?

Of course, he's not going to show his face.

Being dressed as a character from one of my favorite movies shouldn't be the big deal I'm making it out to be, because to everyone else in the room, it's all they're seeing.

Alyssa Jeffries being a freak.

They don't know the real reason I was so eager to wear this costume. They don't get why it's my favorite movie or even why standing here alone without the match to it is causing my heart to shatter and break.

Kevin doesn't even know.

My first date with JJ.

Well, my first one if you can believe a nine-year-old knows what a date even is.

Hand holding and slipping with how greasy from popcorn and sweat our hands were. The random little bird peck kisses he'd turn and give me when I seemed too hyper-focused on what was happening in the movie. The way he made me giggle and blush when he told me I looked cute.

I could go on, but just thinking about the history of this movie and what it means, let alone standing here and wearing a costume for someone who isn't JJ, has me slamming the breaks on.

Lydia wasn't the same without Beetlejuice in the movie, the same way Alyssa isn't and won't ever be the same without her Joshua.

"Holy shit!" The surprised voice calls bringing me forcefully back to reality. "You actually did it."

Kevin.

Looking up and meeting his eyes, I return the grin on his face with one of my own until I see his costume.

It playing effortlessly into the whole movie theme we were going for, but where I expected him to be the counterpart to my red monstrosity, he's dressed in what Beetlejuice hated most of all.

The sandworm.

"You jerk!"

Driven by the sheer disappointment that comes with him standing here wearing what he is, I shove my hands hard into his chest, knocking him back.

"Jesus," he curses before attempting to right himself. "Aly…"

"I should have known the second you asked me to wear this stupid costume you would pull something like this."

It's clear by the utter confusion on his face as he rights himself and attempts to silence me by grabbing my arm and turning me around, my reaction isn't what he was expecting. It's also painfully apparent, even in the midst of it, I'm blowing things out of proportion.

He's still dressed like something from the movie.

If anything, I should be happy he isn't standing here dressed like Beetlejuice.

"About the costume..." he attempts to explain, but before he can finish whatever excuse he's about to give, I'm paused by a shift behind us. My breath catching when making their way around, the person stops just to my left.

I don't want to look at him, much less meet his eyes, but it seems the gravitational pull that's always been there between us has other plans, and I take him in.

Joshua.

My Beetlejuice.

Clearing his throat and bringing my attention back to the other person in the triangle formation we've made, Kevin grins.

"Ladies and gentleman, my work here is done."

Before I can make sense of what he means, all I make out is his back as he slips through a crowd of students and he's gone.

"Asshole." Joshua curses and despite my confusion, I laugh.

"Wow."

Angling my body and getting a better view of not only the costume but the fuller body filling it out, I focus on what I just heard him say.

"Wow, what?"

"It's been so long since I heard you laugh, I was starting to think I'd never hear it again."

"Well, you did. And for what it's worth, I agree with your original sentiment."

Kevin is most definitely an asshole.

But a loveable one. Especially now that I see what he was trying to do. He played me.

Played us.

"Figured you might."

Rolling back and forth on my heel, hating that standing here with someone I used to consider my best friend is this awkward, I pull a move from Kevin's book and clear my throat, waiting patiently until he finally meets my eyes.

"He played me."

Clearly, with the frown he's sporting and the way he comes to the same realization I already have, it's clear he doesn't want to be here.

Worse yet, wants nothing to do with this.

With me.

"You don't need to stay, Josh. I get what Kevin was trying to do. It's sweet and all, but if you have somewhere else to be, you can go. We don't have to talk or anything."

"Don't we?" He asks, head dipping to the side with those damn eyes of his staring straight through me.

"I d-don't know." I stammer, surprised both by his words and the change in tone. "Do we?"

"Alyssa..." he says with a pause. "I hate the fact I didn't see this coming. I mean, it's Kevin for Christ sakes. I should have known all the attention he's been showering you with for weeks was for my benefit, to drive me crazy. But now that it's done and I'm here, especially seeing you dressed the way you are, there's nowhere else I need to be."

Not wanting to fall into the weight of what he's said, I let my eyes fall over everyone milling about around us.

"AJ..."

The second he says my name, I want to call out. Turn and do what I did to Kevin the first day of school. Slap him. Tell him to stop using the nickname, but I can't because as my body takes control and forces me to respond, my heart aches with the need for him to say it again.

"JJ..." I respond in kind and he laughs awkwardly, his own feet now doing the same dance mine have been since Kevin left us alone. Proving him to be just as nervous at the moment as I am.

"I missed you." He sighs and my heart stills. "I tried really hard not to, but after the first couple of nights, I knew it was a lost cause. It got so bad sometimes that I started to think the only thing I was capable of doing *was* missing you."

"What a-are you d-doing?" I manage to stammer out through the overpowering beat of my heart now filling my ears.

"I'm doing what I should have done years ago. I'm being honest."

Well, two can play that game, buddy.

"When you took off, you broke my heart." I blurt, freezing when I see his body flinch from the impact, but I don't stop. If being honest is what he wants, then it's what he's going to get. "I couldn't eat or sleep, much less breathe, for what felt like the entire four years, but was really only about six months. When I finally did break free of the loss, I conditioned myself to hate you. Made myself believe I didn't care if you were alive or dead. Then, just when I think I've gotten through the worst of it, Kevin tells me you're back."

Laughing at how pathetic I sound, how truly broken I was and now am again remembering how it felt, I shake my head.

"Why did you stop?" he asks softly, bridging the space between us until we're as close as two people can get when he pulls me to him, his arms finding their way around my back.

"Because it hurts too much to keep going."

"Why?"

Something about the way he asks the question, the plea I can barely make out in the clipped response gives me the strength I need to finally look him in the eye. A burst of strength I haven't felt in years rising and feeding off the building annoyance I have over him not already knowing the answer.

"Because you weren't the only one missing someone, alright?!"

This is too much. The two of us, how we're standing, who we are dressed up as, and the way that even after four years apart, we still connect like puzzle pieces, it's too damned much. I can physically feel parts of me splintering, and it won't be long if we keep doing this stupid little dance before those splinters make me bleed.

"Come on," He says, pulling his arms away but keeping me planted to him by slipping his hand easily over mine. "We're obviously going to do this, which is fine, but we're not doing it here."

Swept up in the pleasant warmth the second our fingers touch and the way it climbs so swiftly up my arm as he begins making his way slowly with me at his side through the room, I don't realize exactly how far we've come until we've made our way out through the gymnasium doors.

An awakening that has me yanking my hand out of his harshly and making him pull to a complete stop.

A fight that even though I'm trying, he still manages to beat me at as he takes hold of my hand again, not nearly as politely as before heading down the hallway, not stopping this time until he's shoved his way into the front doors of the school and brought us outside.

Softening his grip, he rubs his thumb over the spot where he'd held so tightly, sighing before finally releasing the hold and stalking a few feet away. The cold look in his eyes when he finally turns to face me more than enough motivation to make me back up the second his feet begin to move again, but my placement leaving me nowhere to go.

"Weeks, AJ!" he yells before sucking in a breath and repeating himself again, this time softer. "I had to sit there for weeks thinking about Kevin touching you. He asked you to this stupid dance, suggested those costumes, torturing me every day because I couldn't stop thinking about the two of you, *my best friends*, being together."

"He played me too, you idiot!"

Shaking his head and ignoring what I've said, drives me crazy. Somehow, Kevin deciding to play this game with us for Josh has become my fault.

Like hell it is.

"This has nothing to do with Kevin! You wanna have this out, hear the truth, fine. What about what you did four years ago, huh? Mister, *I'm so freaking tortured.* You left! You promised me you would stay, and you lied! You said goodnight, kissed my forehead and you left!"

"I had to!"

"Bullshit, Joshua."

Despite the crackling, I can feel in the air as we're yelling back and forth, he does the strangest thing once I call him on his crap. He smiles. And not just the tiny smirk from earlier, but a full on, brighter than the damn sun, smile.

"You're cute when you curse, AJ."

"Stop changing the subject."

"As you wish." He jokes. "What I said wasn't bullshit, though."

"Yes, it was." I immediately argue. "The only thing you *had* to do was stay with me. Everything would have been fine if you'd done that."

Again he flinches, but this time it's harder for me to ignore. As upset as I am with him, causing him pain was never something I wanted. At least not intentionally.

It really is true what they say.

The truth *does* hurt.

"I wanted to stay. God, AJ. The idea of getting to live with your family was a dream come true!"

"Then why'd you leave?"

"There was a chance staying with your family wouldn't be permanent. I didn't want to stay and get even more attached, only to get pulled out a few weeks later when the courts decided I was better off with the pieces of shit I'm supposed to call family."

There's truth in what he's saying. It's there plain as day in the rigidness of his face, and for a split second, it makes me doubt everything my father told me a couple of weeks after Joshua came back, but only for a second because once I feel his eyes, I can see there's more he's not saying.

"Is that the only reason?"

"What other reason could there be?"

"I don't know, you tell me."

"Do you want me to tell you I left because I felt myself falling in love with you and didn't want to do it? Didn't want to risk losing the father figure I'd found in your old man because I'd been stupid enough to fall for his little girl? Is that what you wanna hear, AJ?"

"Yes!" I yell. "If it's the truth, then yes. It's exactly what I want to hear!"

One breath. Two. He stalks toward me, further boxing me in, stopping just shy of making contact with my body. Just enough space between us for me to see the cold air from my breath fall over him.

"I promised myself the night I left I'd come back for you, AJ. *To you*. I wasn't going to leave you forever. It just took a lot longer than I thought it would."

His words are like music to my ears, but not sweet enough to ignore the facts. If he'd just taken a chance on me—on my parents—he never would have had to worry about coming back because he never would have left.

"JJ..." I sigh. "He knew. My dad knew how we felt about each other. You didn't have to leave."

"I know that now. He told me when he came to see me at Kevin's."

"Everything you wanted...you could have had."

"And now?" he whispers, completely bridging the gap between us and pulling me into him. "Can I have what I want now or am I too late?"

"W-what do you want?"

His answer is in the softness of his lips as they brush against my forehead. It's in the way his arms tighten around me, my own response evident in the way my body melts so easily into his, and the tear slipping out of my eyes.

It's in the way we're surrendering all control.

"I want my best friend. I want you and me, AJ. I tried doing the right thing by staying away. I even tried being happy for you and Kev when I thought he wanted to be with you, but all it did was make me realize even more what I lost. What I didn't deserve to have back even though I wanted it more than anything."

"What about my dad?" I ask. "I know what you told him."

"Well, since I plan on taking back what I said, I suppose I'm going to have to talk to him. I mean, if there's anything *to* talk about."

It's now or never. With Joshua back and my feelings for him seemingly getting stronger instead of lessening the way I'd hoped, there's only one way this can go. I have to take the chance and take what I've known from the age of six was meant to be mine.

Him.

"You're not too late."

Joshua

"What happened to you after you left?" AJ cautiously questions once we're settled on the bleachers and away from the prying eyes of the school.

Completely alone apart from the moon glowing effervescent above us. It's shape and positioning in the sky proving to be as full as the heart beating steadily in my chest.

Being here with her, even though her line of questioning isn't one I'm eager to get into, is the first time in years I've felt completely at peace. For the first time since I made my way back here, everything is right.

"How much did Wayne tell you?"

"Not a lot, but you know Daddy. He wouldn't tell someone else's story."

I do know that about him. Even when a lot of what I lived through affects his daughter because of my feelings for her, he wouldn't break the confidence.

"When I bailed, I had no clue where I was going or what I was going to do. All I knew was I had to get as far away from my aunt and uncle as possible. And well, you."

"But you didn't—"

"I know, AJ." I interrupt. "But I didn't see anything the way it was back then."

"Okay, I'm sorry. Continue."

"I headed to the mall first, using one of the payphones to call my worker. Didn't stick around after. Still didn't have a plan, but my goal for the night was to find a bench somewhere, and head down to the office in the morning to fill my worker in."

"That never happened though, did it?"

She catches on quick which I'm thankful for. I'm not sure if it's because of the little Wayne did tell her or if she just knows me, but the less I have to repeat myself or relive the way the last four years have gone, the better.

"No. After a cop caught me at the park and told me to beat it, I used the little change I had and jumped on the subway. I honestly don't know what the hell I expected was gonna happen when I got downtown, but none of the people down there took kindly to a brat hoarding in on their space. I got into the first of many fights the first night."

"JJ…"

"It's fine. It's been a long time, and as you can see, I'm okay."

"My definition of okay and yours are drastically different." She mumbles and I laugh despite myself.

"Well, since I'm not laid out in a pine box somewhere, I'd classify that as okay."

"What happened next?"

"I moved around a lot."

Lifting her head from my chest and meeting my eyes, the slight dip to it giving away her confusion, she studies me silently while waiting for me to continue.

"What I mean is, I'd keep on the move. I'd stay a few days in one place here or there, but for the most part, I'd just walk until I couldn't feel my feet anymore."

"My dad said you were on the street for a year. Is he right?"

"I don't know," I admit honestly. "After the first few weeks, the days blended together. Seems about right, though."

"There's something I don't get."

"What's that?"

"Why didn't you go see your worker the next day like you planned?"

"Well, at first it was because I didn't have the money for bus fare, and where I'd ended up, the way I looked after getting into it with the old guy who thought I was going to roll him, no one would so much as meet my eyes to give it to me."

"You were just a kid!" she exclaims. "I don't care how you looked. Someone should have helped you."

The way this girl feels about me, I don't think I'll ever get used to it. The way she has my back unequivocally, I'm not deserving of.

"I guess people figured if I was on the street there was a reason and they didn't want any part of it. But AJ, I'm okay. I swear."

"Yeah, you're okay *now*."

"Are you sure you want to hear this? I just got you back. I don't want to get into this if it's going to risk losing you."

"Not possible," She says, surprising me when she places her lips to the side of my face. A natural move for two people who are as into each other as we are, but unfamiliar with as long as I've gone without it.

It's definitely a touch I could get used to.

After four years of experiencing what I'm sure is the worst the world has to offer in terms of people I encountered, and the foster families I ended up placed with once I stopped running, she has no idea how heavenly the feel of her lips pressed against any part of me is.

"Keep going, please. I'll stop interrupting."

The warmth of her breath against my face along with the soft way the words are spoken gives me the courage I need to cup her chin with my hand and pull her to me. My lips on hers for the first time since I'd brushed softly against them four years ago.

A fire erupting from deep inside as we collide. The warmth flooding through me, but the reality of the moment—our conversation—a bucket of icy water keeping me from taking things any further.

"I spent four years dreaming about kissing you again," I admit and revel in the tiny smile I'm rewarded with. "It was better than I imagined."

"I'm sorry, JJ." She says against my lips and on instinct, I shake my head.

She has nothing to be sorry for. She wasn't the one who made the choices and put us in the position we'd found ourselves in.

"You sure you wanna hear the rest?"

"If you're sure you want to tell me."

"I'm sure."

Smiling tightly before letting her eyes fall to our connected hands, she uses her free hand to trace over our fingers before finally resting it on top and squeezing.

"So, you said you didn't go to your worker because you couldn't afford it, but the change couldn't have been hard to come by, so why didn't you go later?"

"I started thinking about what would happen when I went to her. The cycle we'd go through again, and after a few nights on the street where I had nothing but time to think, I decided I'd rather take my chances moving around then end up in another place where I wasn't wanted."

It's got to hurt, or at the very least bother her, hearing me talk about how unwanted I feel. What had been shown to me for years before I met her and then in the four years after I walked away. It's expected because, for her, all she can see is me walking away from a sure thing for no reason.

"I still don't get it. I don't get how the system works, but I mean, I have to believe your worker didn't just forget you existed. She had to be looking for you, right? Why did it take over a year to find you?"

This is where things are about to get tricky. She's going to look at me differently when she learns the truth. As tough as AJ claims to be, how tough I've seen with my own eyes she can be, she's still the picture of purity when it comes to the way the rest of the world works. She's been sheltered. Kept away from the darker parts of life.

What I have to tell her now is going to twist that purity.

"I never stayed in one area long enough to get detected. I purposely took off whenever I got a whiff of someone possibly finding me. AJ, I wasn't just on the street. I was in some other places too. Bad places."

"Define bad places."

"You know what the best thing about being placed with an overworked social worker is? When you end up in their office and they turn their back, sometimes its seconds, other times minutes. Forgetting altogether about the mountain of information they've left open on their desk for anyone's eyes to see. For the kids to see. Turns out, my worker was incredibly detailed with her notes. Names, places, and their relationship to me and my family, it was all there for the taking. So, I took it."

"I don't get it. If you hadn't gotten in contact with your worker, how were you able to get the information?"

"When I came to live across the road, the meetings were monthly, AJ. I took the info back then. I just held onto it, not planning to do anything, just wanting to have it. When I was on the street, I decided to put it to use."

"How?"

"There were a few places downtown my parents used to use to score drugs from, so when I was finally able to get there, that's where I stayed. Turns out, a lot of the people there, in the beginning, remembered my folks and were more than happy to let me crash."

She's silent after my admission, the only evidence she's even still there, the rise and fall of her chest and the warmth of her hands under and around mine. I want her to say something. Sympathize the way I know she wants to, or hell, curse me out and tell me what an idiot I am for doing the things I did after leaving. Anything to end the silence. It doesn't happen though, which means it's up to me to put an end to it.

"I know it was stupid, but at the time, with the way I was thinking, it was the right move. I couldn't let my worker find me and place me somewhere I'd just end up getting kicked out of later."

"You wouldn't have gotten kicked out with my family..."

"In my head, with your parents and you, it wasn't about getting kicked out. It was about you all being better off."

"My dad said something pretty bad happened before you were found and brought back to the foster home. What was it?"

Running through everything I told Wayne when I first got to Kevin's, nothing jumps out other than the fighting. Something tells me with the expectant look in her eyes now, it's not those she's getting at.

"I only told your dad about the fights, so I'm not really sure what you mean."

"Oh, okay. He must have meant those."

Except he didn't. Which means Wayne found the information another way. He must have gone over me.

He spoke to my worker.

"He's wasn't talking about the fights, AJ. He just didn't get it from me."

"Get what?"

"Alyssa...something happened in one of the places I was holed up in." I pause, giving it a chance to sink in before laying the rest out. "I saw my mom."

"You what?"

"Yeah. About six months in at the first place, one of the guys who took me under his wing brought me to a place to make a drop. She was there."

"What happened?" she asks and I can feel my face fall the second it happens.

This is it.

The moment I've been dreading most. What I never wanted anyone to know.

"I was stupid. I got sucked up into her shit."

"I don't understand."

"I was young when I was taken away from them, but she remembered me like it all happened yesterday. She was so happy to see me, and in the moment, I was hooked by her happiness. Someone actually wanted me."

Even though years have passed since it happened, the rush I experienced when I saw how happy she was is still fresh in my mind.

"The first little bit was great, considering where we were. After a few months though, things shifted. She started talking about my old man. Putting the blame for what happened to him. Her issues were all his fault. She was an addict because of him. They lost custody of me because of him. I kept believing in it, even though I knew deep down it was crap. I just kept seeing how happy she was having me there, so nothing else mattered. It didn't take long after me buying into it that things escalated."

"Escalated how?" she pushes, and despite my need to ease her into this, when I open my mouth to speak again, it all comes pouring out.

"The drugs came first. I was already familiar with selling it. It's one of the ways things became easier the longer I was on my own, but with her, it went from selling and delivering, to using. I was so enamored when she first brought up smoking a little weed, I didn't even take a second to see how wrong it was. I just did it. We did it together."

The sharp intake of breath gives me pause, but only for a second. I'm too close to the end of the line now, there can't be any going back.

"Over time it went from weed to acid, but for her, even harder stuff. I was the one holding the needles. Helping her shoot up. God, looking back, it seems so stupid that I didn't see how wrong all of it was, but I was blind. A month after I started giving her the heroin, it happened."

"What?"

"It started out with just her touching me, you know. A rub of the arm here and there, and then sometimes she would rub my back, massaging me. Always saying it's what I deserved for all the hard work I was doing for everyone. It felt harmless, the back rubs and stuff. I figured that's just what moms did. Only, it's not, and it wasn't the end of it."

Freeing herself, she wretches first, before separating herself from our closeness entirely, making a mad dash across the bleachers to the end, bending over and spilling her guts out onto the ground below.

"I'm sorry." She whispers when she finally makes her way back and slips her again over mine. "I just…"

"I get it, baby, I do. I've done the same thing a lot since I've been back."

"How could she…I mean, why would she?"

"The therapist Kevin's mom hooked me up with told me my mom could see the damage done to me. She could see the target I wore showing I was vulnerable. So, she started with the drugs first. She used those as a way to keep me complacent for what came next. She was so strung out the doctor thinks she didn't even realize it was her son she was doing these things with."

"I don't believe that."

I'm glad. It makes this next bombshell easier to admit to.

"She knew what she was doing, Aly. When she started touching me—kissing me— she'd lean into me, moaning and whispering my name. There was no way in hell she didn't know who she was doing it with."

Another sharp intake of breath. "Oh my god."

"God was nowhere to be found."

"Did she—did you two..." her voice fades off before the question can fall and lifting her chin with my hand, making sure her eyes are on me and completely focused, I shake my head. I need her to see things never went too far.

"I swear to you, it never got to that point. She used her hands and eventually her mouth, wanting me to do the same with her, but nothing else."

"You say it like it's a good thing."

"When it was happening, I didn't see it the way I do now. I thought I was doing what a good son does. What a *good boy* does. With as happy as it seemed to make her, I liked doing it. It felt like I was doing something right for a change."

"And now?"

"There was nothing good about it. The therapist I'm seeing is helping me see everything for what it actually was."

"She never tried anything more?"

"Once. She tried once, and I don't even know why I did what I did. I shoved her. Pushed her off me. If the rest of the stuff we were doing together was okay, I'm not sure why I thought this wasn't, but I did. I couldn't let her do what she wanted."

Take my virginity.

Have sex. Fuck me.

It doesn't matter what you call it, even in my haze I knew I wasn't going to let it happen. My mom could take everything else, but she wasn't getting that.

"I want to be glad it didn't go further, but none of this seems like something to be happy about. But, JJ...you should know. Even if she had gotten what she wanted and things had gone even farther than they did, it wouldn't have changed anything."

What does that mean? Is she giving up? Was this too much? Is this where she gets up and walks away for good?

Pulling me from the wave of thoughts now bombarding my mind, she brushes her fingers across my face, under my eyes and when I open them again, really take her in, her lip curves up just slightly and she smiles.

"What I mean is, it wouldn't change anything between us. I would still feel the same way about you I always have. Well, no, that's not true. I would feel more. I would still be right by your side because it's where I always want to be. It's where I belong."

Chapter Seventeen
Far from Home

Joshua

I have an arsenal of knowledge when it comes to the girl she was, but next to no information on the woman she inevitably became in my absence.

What I do know is, as much as my heart would enjoy nothing more than to soar at those two words, it can't. I can't let it. There is far too much water under our bridge to believe I've been forgiven so easily.

"I expected you to be surprised, especially with what happened at the cemetery, but Joshua, I didn't think it was enough to make you speechless."

Her voice falters as the dry uncomfortable laugh she lets escape falls.

A clear sign I've still got my work cut out for me.

I knew it wasn't going to be easy, especially with as many times as I've made her relive this same scene, but I hoped after what I said before and how secure she was when she welcomed me home, I'd at least gained a few steps. As awkward as she seems with my silence, it's as though I've taken a few steps back and I'm standing in the same place.

Something I can't let happen.

"Not all silence is bad, AJ." I quietly explain, waiting with halted breath until my words spark movement as she turns to me.

"What kind of silence was it if not bad?"

Holding my hand out and motioning to the block of wood a couple of feet away, my chest warms the instant her hand slips into mine and we walk in silence to sit.

"A contemplative one. A surprised one, like you said earlier. A silence where like all the times before, I reflect on what you've said and realize how undeserving of it I am."

The slight shake of her head, the need to again argue, causes my lips to lift and a laugh to escape.

"What's so funny?"

"You know the saying; the more things change the more they stay the same?"

"Of course."

"Well, the way you want to argue against what I said, along with the little twitch and raise of your eyebrow just now, is the perfect example. As much as you've grown and ultimately changed, you're still the same AJ underneath."

She doesn't even waste a beat.

"The same could be said for you too, Joshua."

The distance present since I showed up and we began speaking, it's gotten significantly smaller over the span of a few minutes, but with the way I feel hearing her call me Joshua, it's threatening to separate us again.

Something as small and insignificant as a childhood nickname shouldn't be enough to push us apart, but with the many ways in which I've heard her say it over the years, it's threatening to do just that.

"You might be right," I attempt to deflect, not wanting her to catch wind of my discomfort. "But since I'm sitting here with you instead of almost a thousand miles away, I'd say not everything is the same."

"You make a good point."

Aware of every move, I take her in as she lays her gloved hands down on either side of her, leaning back and breathing in deeply before releasing it in a familiar sigh.

She's always loved being out here, hidden away from the rest of the world. Same as me. This was our escape from the heavier parts of what this city provides.

"When was the last time you were here?"

"After Daddy had his first stroke."

"Why then?"

Lifting her gaze from the ground and turning just enough to meet my eyes again, she grimaces before her head begins to lower.

A move I can't allow when it feels so good having her eyes on me.

Reaching out and resting a hand on her shoulder, while taking the other and brushing the tips of my fingers across her cheek in an effort to give her pause, I halt when she goes rigid, but almost want to shout out in victory when she doesn't look away.

"Tell me, AJ."

"What does any of it matter, Jos—"

"Stop, please. I wasn't going to say anything, but if you call me Joshua one more time, I'm going to lose it. We don't do this, AJ. We don't act so damn formally with each other."

I'm well aware I have no right asking for this, but I'm not lying when I say I'm dangerously close to losing it with the almost robotic way she keeps saying my name. Even the way she draws it out each time, almost like it's foreign to her own tongue, makes me sick.

"How is it so easy for you?" she asks and I'm at a loss.

"What exactly do you think is easy for me, AJ? Coming back here after twenty years? Standing by a casket I never thought I'd be standing in front of? Admitting what a screw up I am and have been? Fighting with everything I have to make the woman I've spent my entire life loving, forgive me? Or maybe I'm not done and you'd rather I do something like this to get back in your good graces."

Slipping from the block of wood until my knees hit the hard and unforgiving ground below, I turn until I'm close enough to her to reach out and touch her.

"I have always been, and may always be a screw-up, AJ. I made so many god damned mistakes with you, your family, and my own life that it would take me as many years as I've been messing it all up, to make amends for it. Maybe I can't even make amends. But if sitting here in front of you begging on my hands and knees is what will do it for you, I'll do it. I'll do anything I can to make up for the pain I caused."

Her silence continues for so long, I begin losing hope of her ever speaking again.

I've gone too far.

"I meant, how is it so easy for you to call me AJ?" Eyes never tearing away from mine, even though I can immediately tell she wants to, she takes an unstable breath and continues. "Because every single time I try, like when you appeared at the funeral, and again later at the casket, it's like my tongue twists and no sound can come out. Even now, when I see you as the boy you were, and want to slap you just as hard as I used to back then, I still can't say it. Those two small letters are the hardest thing I've ever had to say. They've always been."

There's a heaviness in my chest from everything I misinterpreted, but what she says last is what pushes me forward.

"What do you mean they've always been? When was it hard before?"

Rolling her eyes but making no attempt to turn away, she shifts her hands from the wooden block back into her lap and releasing an exasperated sigh, explains.

"When you came back in ninth grade. Though comparing then to the twenty years since seems silly. It was my own personal hell."

If I focus on what happened in ninth grade, I'm going to fall back into old habits and remember what took place two years later. A subject that if we're ever going to get back what we had, we have to discuss, but I don't think it's the right time for.

What we made together.

She lost alone.

Our baby.

"I'm sorry."

"I didn't tell you this for you to apologize, Joshua. This is clearly my issue. I was just curious as to why it was so easy for you."

"It's not easy for me. None of this is. I figure with the way I blew things out of proportion, you see it now. When it comes to what I call you, you've only ever been my AJ. I guess it's easier because I never let go of it. I never let go of you. Even when it would have been smarter if I had."

"Where have you been all this time?" she asks, just loud enough for me to hear, and as I'm about to tell her, her voice, stronger this time, falls over me again.

One word, two letters and that's all it takes for the speechlessness she accused me of earlier to rear its head.

"JJ."

"Say it again, AJ. Please."

It's selfish, especially after how she's explained it makes her feel every time she tries, but I don't care. I'll be a selfish bastard a million times over if it means I can have her with the same lilt in her voice, say my name the only way I've ever wanted it spoken.

It doesn't happen right away, but when it does, every single emotion I've spent years burying in an effort to just get through each day unscathed forces its way to the surface and I'm fourteen again.

She calls me JJ, repeating it over and over, each one stronger and more pronounced than the last, and for the first time in years, I feel wetness on my face.

Tears falling the way they should have been all this time, but I wouldn't allow for fear of being looked at as anything other than the cold unfeeling bastard I'd built myself up to be.

The laughter hits next, with what I recognize as sobs wrenching their way out through it. Ugly and harsh sounding to a casual observer, but in this second one of the most beautiful sounds I've ever heard.

Focusing on what's happened since the final time she said my name, I notice her knees on the ground beside mine, dug in deep, her breath falling over mine as her body is closer than it's been in two decades.

"It doesn't matter where I was, AJ. I wasn't where I should have been. Why...why did it take me so damn long to get it?"

The last bit isn't even remotely directed at her. It's all for me. I'm questioning where the hell my ability to rationalize went, and why it took me so damn long to admit what everyone else around me already knew.

What started out as running when I was sixteen, turned into something else the longer time went on. My self-imposed exile wasn't because of some noble act on my part, no matter how many times I tried saying it was.

I wasn't doing anyone, including myself, any favors with it. I was in actuality doing more damage the longer I was away from where they all needed me to be.

I was doing it because now, like then, I truly believed I was undeserving of anything remotely good, but most of all, anything resembling happiness and joy.

Child of addicts. A lifetime filled with various different abuses. A habit of being passed over, unwanted and uncared for.

How could anyone like that deserve anything?

Better yet, how could *I* deserve it?

Bending and curling into myself as emotion floods through me, my senses are aware of her scent first, followed by the tentative touch as her arms come to find their way around me. Making no attempt to break me free of my actions, only holding tighter as each second ticks by.

My girl, as always, knowing exactly what I need.

Hyper aware of everything about her in that moment, the familiarity no longer smothering as it was in younger years but desperately desired, my breath catches when I hear her voice, muffled but stronger than it's been in years, repeating words I haven't heard since they were spoken at sixteen.

"It's okay, JJ. I'm here and it's okay." Her voice pauses for a brief second before continuing. "I'm going to fall in love with you, you know? And you don't have to love me back, but I'm going to give you my heart."

Chapter Eighteen
Untamed Hearts
February 1996

Alyssa

"Okay, look. I wasn't going to say anything, but Aly, you haven't stopped moving since we came upstairs. If you're not pacing around the room or staring at that calendar of yours, you're fidgeting with your stuff. What's going on?"

From the time I rolled out of bed this morning, realizing what today is, I've gone out of my way not to focus on it too much. Pretending it was just another day and not *the* day.

Looks like with the way Cara is looking at me, her eyebrows furrowed and her eyes questioning, yet concerned, my plan is a fail.

"Nothing's going on."

Even to my own ears, it's easy to spot I'm lying, but I'm hoping she won't. As much as I want to talk to someone, I'm not sure Cara's the right person.

She's my friend, one of my best, but when it comes to all things Joshua, things get murky. She never wants to talk about him, and in the few times she has given me advice, it's almost always her saying I'm wasting my time with him.

"He's screwed up, Aly. Trust me on this. I should know. We've been through a lot of the same things. You're too good for him, and he's just going to end up leaving you again. He always leaves."

"You're lying."

Guess it wasn't passable.

Never being able to tell a lie in my life probably has something to do with it, but with the concern in her eyes, I start to believe I'm being too hard on her.

It's been a few months since we talked about JJ. Maybe she won't react the same way. It's not like any of what she said before was true anyway. He hasn't left. He's been right by my side every day for the last year and a half.

Surely that's enough time for her to see she was wrong. Besides, I really need to tell someone about this before I burst.

"I'm nervous."

There, I said it.

Shifting her position on the bed, Cara sits up and drags herself to the end, motioning with the pat of her hand for me to sit. And when I do as she wants, sitting cross-legged directly across from her, she doesn't waste any time.

"Nervous about what?"

Okay, Aly. Here goes nothing.

"I think this is it, Cara. Tonight after the movie, I think it's finally going to happen."

Narrowing her eyes, she frowns.

"What's going to happen?"

"Me..." *God, why is this so hard to spit out?* "JJ and I...I think we're going to take things to the next level."

Two things happen once I've gotten the words out. First, she releases a hard snort and then she rolls her eyes.

"Oh, Alyssa! You had me going there. For a second I thought you were serious."

I don't understand where this is coming from. Her reaction, I mean. How can she think I'd joke about something like this?

She knows me.

"I'm not kidding, Cara. I think it's a perfect time, especially with the movie we're seeing."

What I don't admit to is how quickly I put the plan in motion after my dad told me their plans to run the prayer group this week. Also omitting how things further fell into place when the old theatre down the road listed Untamed Heart as the movie pick of the week.

My favorite movie and the house all to myself?

It was like a sign from the gods or something.

With the way she's laughing now as if she really believes this is some kind of prank I'm pulling, it's painfully obvious her opinion on Joshua hasn't changed.

"I'm sorry, Aly." She chokes out through continued laughter. "I don't mean to laugh, especially since I can see you're serious, but I can't help it."

"Then just stop laughing. While you're at it, tell me why you think it's so funny."

I love Cara, but right now I'm seriously starting to question my choice in friends.

"I know you hate when I say things like this, but honestly, Aly." She sighs. "Of all the guys in our grade, Joshua Brantley is the last one you should be giving your virginity to. He's not the guy you have your first time with."

"How can you say that? He's your friend too!"

"It's because he's my friend I'm saying it. I know him, okay? I know you two have been friends since like forever or whatever, but you don't really get him the way I do. The shit we've both been through. Josh is the kind of guy you play around with but never get serious about. He's not a forever kind."

No. She's wrong.

Sure, he's run away before and he's always telling me how undeserving he is to be with me, but it doesn't mean he's not worth anything.

Not when he's worth everything.

I hate the way she insinuates I don't know him because our histories don't match. I do know him. I know him best and as much as I care about Cara, I'm not gonna sit here and take her berating him and me in some misguided attempt to tell me the truth.

Her truth isn't the same as mine.

"I love him, Cara."

"Oh, Alyssa." She sighs, her voice dripping in pity. "Don't be so stupid."

Where is all of this coming from?

"I thought...I thought you'd be happy for me, Cara. You know how I feel about him. Why are you acting like this? I've been dying to tell someone all day and this is what you're doing with it?"

I feel like such an idiot. The way she's reacting shouldn't surprise me, but it does because even when she's made her feeling on Josh well known, she was still supportive. She was still there for me. Right now, it feels like the complete opposite and the nervousness I've already got because of what tonight means, is being compounded with her reaction.

"I told you when we started hanging out I would always tell you the truth, didn't I?" Nodding my head, she continues. "I'm just keeping to it now, Aly. I know you don't like it, but I'm being honest. Sure, I'm kind of Josh's friend, but I'm your friend first. I know too much about him and I've seen the way things have gone with the two of you since I came to town. I really think this is a bad idea. Anyone else from our class and I swear it wouldn't be the same, but Josh is going to hurt you."

She doesn't get it.

If tonight goes the way I'm planning, neither one of us is going to hurt again.

Having sex with JJ, making love the way couples do in books and movies, it's only going to bring us even closer than we already are. It's the ultimate connection.

She really doesn't know us at all.

"I think I need to be alone."

"Come on, Aly! Don't be like this."

It's funny how she says it since I'm thinking the exact same thing about her.

I don't want her being like this. I want my friend to actually be my friend.

"You should go," I tell her emphatically before climbing off the bed and heading toward the door. Making my stance known loud and clear when I swing the door open.

"Fine!" she exclaims, jumping off the bed and grabbing her bag from off my chair. "If you don't want to hear the truth, fine! But when he fucks you and leaves again, like we all know he's going to, don't come crying to me."

Shoving her way past, her obvious anger continuing to grow as I hear her feet stomp heavier down the stairs, I release my hold on my door, kicking it closed when I hear the front door slam.

Making my way over to the bed, I throw myself down onto the mattress with Cara's final words on repeat as I become one with the silence.

Could she be right? If we sleep together will he turn his back on me, leave and never come back?

Am I willingly giving him another piece of me to break?

Joshua

She forgets how well I know her.

Four years apart may have changed us in the physical sense, but it didn't change much else.

AJ has always been an open book.

She knows this, has admitted to it numerous times, which is what makes this plan I know she has even more ludicrous.

Right from the moment she ran up the front steps at school yesterday, presenting me with tickets to her favorite movie, I've been on to her.

It also helps when not eight hours later she made a point of telling me her parents weren't going to be home tonight.

I've had idiotic moments a lot over the last few years, but this isn't one of them.

She's planning something.

Honestly, though, when is she not?

But this one, other than knowing something's up, I'm otherwise clueless about.

I'm just thankful this one doesn't seem to be taking up residence on the damn calendar of hers.

Though, what she doesn't know and I'm not going to tell her, is the last calendar she showed me, the one she kept from when we were eight, well, I stole it.

If I wasn't entirely sure before that I loved her, what she did six weeks ago, pulling out the old, half torn and faded calendar and waiting eagerly until I found the date she marked with a big red heart, I would have been sure then.

The first time I kissed her.

Every other kiss after was also marked, but it was the first one that got me. Because even with all of the time I spent away, living through the hell I did during our time apart, our first kiss was the one I always came back to.

How it felt giving in when we were probably too young to be kissing at all, let alone understanding what all those feelings we claimed to have, actually were. It was the best decision I ever made. Though, you wouldn't hear me admitting it at the time. And definitely not now, especially not around Wayne.

Her old man might be okay with the two of us together now, but at eight years old I'm pretty sure I would have seen a whole different side of him.

That's what all of this memory lane stuff is about, right? Loving her. Knowing even back then with the way in which I held on to the memory of her lips on mine, she was it for me.

I would love Alyssa Jeffries until my dying breath.

The admission of love also meaning that whatever she has planned tonight for us, before the movie, during it, or hell, even after, I'm in.

Everything I have to give, it's her to have.

Including my heart.

Which, if we're keeping score on stolen things, she was the original thief of back in 1986.

Surely this means I'm off the hook for the calendar, right?

*****

We're not even all the way through her front door when she spins around, and flashing me the brightest smile, leans in placing her lips to the corner of mine.

"I need to grab something from upstairs. I'll be right back, okay?"

Before I get the chance to so much as nod, she's turning and barreling her way quickly up the stairs, with what I'm sure if I focus enough, will be a trail of dust left in her wake.

Shutting and locking the door, I step further into the house, slipping out of my jacket and tossing it on the hook before venturing into the living room.

It's strange being here like this.

I mean, it's not strange being in her place. I've spent days—years even—in this house. I'm more comfortable here than I've been anywhere else, but being here alone, without her in the room or even her parents moving around somewhere, is a little weird.

If there's one thing to be said about the Jeffries, their house is never devoid of life. Whether it's every room filled with the sheer presence of them or the clear love they have for one another spread throughout every inch with pictures and artwork from AJ's childhood, there's just this overwhelming sense of movement.

Slipping around the sofa and through the armchairs, I make my way over to the fireplace and it's there I notice something new. A picture frame on the mantel. There's always been a lot of those over the years, but this one is different because of the players in the picture resting inside.

AJ and I.

A picture I've never seen before; don't even remember being taken, but clearly one capturing whatever the person who took it was going for.

We're both smiling and my smile especially is natural. The most real expression I've ever seen and one that as much as I've reacted, especially with AJ, I didn't realize was capable of being caught this way.

It's a faded picture despite it being new, my messy hair a dead giveaway of when it was taken. The blurriness causing the fading an obvious sign of movement on our parts.

How did I not know about this?

I can't even remember the last time I've had my picture taken other than the times when Aly would bring out the disposal camera and take snaps. She obviously didn't take it since we're both in it, our closeness evident in the way she's leaning into my arms.

Unaware I'm not alone, I jump when her voice filters across the room to where I'm standing, my fingers froze in place over her face in the picture.

"Daddy took it about a week ago." She reads my mind, crossing the room and brushing her fingers over mine, slips it down. "When he put it up a couple of days ago, I asked him why of all pictures, he chose this one. He told me it was because it was the most natural picture of the two of us he's ever seen, and would probably ever get."

He's not wrong.

Leaning over her shoulder, my breath causing her hair to stir and fall over her shoulder, I take it in again.

"I look...happy."

Turning her head into me and looking up, she smiles wistfully.

"It's because you were. We both were."

Her proximity to me, the feel of her breath on my face and the faint scent of her vanilla shampoo awakening me to the rightness of the moment we're in, I lean down and softly place my lips to hers, but not before whispering words a year and a half in the making.

"I am so in love with you, AJ."

Months I've spent driving myself insane, looking for the right moment to say these words to her. Knowing when I did finally do it, there could be no doubt for either of us of their meaning.

This is it. This is the moment I've waited forever for.

I think I've loved Alyssa Jeffries my entire life.

Slipping the picture from her hands and pulling away just long enough to place it back on the mantle, I turn back, nervous as hell for whatever is about to come next. Wanting her to say the words back, desperate for her to do it, but not wanting her to know just how much.

"I was starting to think I would never hear those words."

"I've always known how I feel about you, Aly. Without question." Pulling her to me, placing a gentle kiss to the top of her head, I sigh. "I just wanted the perfect moment to make sure you knew it too."

"I love you, Joshua Brantley Jr. Always and forever."

Alyssa

After a few minutes of just standing together in my living room, the weight of the words I've finally spoken filling me with a confidence I've never known, I slip my hand into his, our fingers locking and turn my head up to face him, finding his eyes already there and waiting.

"Do you trust me, JJ?"

"With my life."

"There's something I want to show you."

When he nods his acceptance, I lock our hands tighter and head back the way we'd come, but instead of stopping by the door, I head up the stairs.

I planned this out so well in my head. Leaving him at the bottom of the stairs and heading up in order to light the limited candles I had strewn around my room, desperate to make the mood just right. But with each step I take, him so closely on my heels, my nerves begin to rise up and Cara's words from earlier threaten everything.

A change he must sense because as we finally reach the top, he spins me around to face him, his eyes probative but concerned.

"Aly..."

"JJ," I respond in kind, quirking my lip up in an effort to throw him off the scent.

"Cute, but what's wrong?"

Come on, Aly. You're ruining it! He's here and he loves you. It's still perfect.

As great as the pep talk is, it's also the complete opposite of what comes out of my mouth in response to his question. My ability to never lie rearing its ugly head in spectacular fashion.

"I'm nervous."

"About what?"

"What comes next."

Before he can question what I mean, I pull him the rest of the way and make my way inside. Slipping my hand out of his and taking a step away, I stand by and watch. Needing to see his response to what he's witnessing more than I need air at the moment to breathe.

Candles on my dresser, the bedside tables, even on my computer desk. Six in total, illuminating the room and setting the stage.

"Aly…" he begins softly, his voice fading before he can say anything more. So, driven by the burst of nerves now threatening to overtake me, I speak before he can finish whatever his next thought would have been.

"JJ, I love you. I think I always have, and this, what comes next, despite being scared you're going to turn around and leave, I'm ready for it and I want it with you. I want all of what comes next with you."

With trepidation, I close the distance between us, finding myself directly in front of him. His eyes raising just enough to meet mine, but quickly falling when with shaky hands, I slip the first button of my shirt open. The catch of his breath enough to give me pause, but only for a second as I move to the second button, then the third. His gaze moving from my face and down to my hands, silently but intently watching.

Letting the shirt slip to the floor once the final button has popped, a chill causes me to shiver as I stand before him in my bra, waiting for him to move. Speak. To reach out to me.

Anything.

"You're…God, AJ, you're so beautiful."

Awakened by his words, emboldened, I slip my fingers down my jeans and that's when he reaches out, his hand on mine to stop me.

"Are you…" Closing his eyes and swallowing, he starts again. "Are you sure?"

"Yes, JJ. I'm positive."

The air in the room shifts then as he grabs a hold of the bottom of his t-shirt and pulls it up over his head, tossing it to the floor before pulling me to him, his lips crashing down on mine, tentative at first, but what turns heavier when as I part them, his tongue slips its way into my mouth and he deepens the kiss.

Grabbing a hold of me and lifting, he pulls me into his arms, crossing the short distance to the bed, each kiss that follows becoming more frantic, until he places me down, his hands finding their way to the edge of my jeans, making quick work of popping the button and slipping the zipper down.

"Lay back. Aly." He demands, and when I do, he slips the pants down around my butt and down my legs and I kick them to the floor. In an instant he's moving back up and over me, his lips capturing mine. His teeth nipping my bottom lip as my arms come up and around him, bringing him down to me, as close as the two of us can get.

The need to feel him, have him as close as possible, all I'm able to focus on anymore.

It's happening.

He's not turning his back and running. He's right here in the moment with me, losing himself in me as much as I am in him.

This isn't a dream anymore.

It's very real.

When he's taken his fill of my lips, he shifts and buries his face into my neck, the assault he's just laid on my lips, leaving them with the sting of his bite, he delivers to my jawline, the soothing feel of his tongue over each nip as he continues making his way down my chest, almost too much to bear.

As I call out from the overload of feeling now building, his lips give pause and its when he shifts and brings his gaze to rest on mine again that I see it.

It would be easy to miss if this was anyone else, but knowing this is him, *my JJ*, there's no mistaking it. The watery glaze in the corner of his eyelids and falling with each passing beat of our hearts.

He's crying.

"JJ..."

Shaking his head, attempting to do away with what it's too late to erase, I shift and attempt to sit up, all sense of need completely washed away.

"What is it? Why are you crying?"

Moving and sitting beside me on the bed, he takes my hand in his while using the other to wipe at his face while lowering his head down, his eyes becoming glued to the floor.

"It's stupid. I'm stupid, Aly. God, I don't know what's wrong with me!"

Squeezing his hand, letting him know I'm here and I'm not going anywhere, I wait patiently for him to continue.

"No, that's a lie. I do know what's wrong with me. I'm defective."

To use his own words back at him...

Like hell he is.

"That's not true."

"Yes, Aly, it is. I mean, what guy in his right mind finds himself in the position of having the girl of his dreams standing in front of him, telling him she wants to have sex and he completely shuts down and can't follow through?"

The answer is on the tip of my tongue but I don't say a word.

I know what this is about and it's got nothing to do with us.

It's got to do with what he's been through.

"You planned all of this out, made everything so god-damned perfect, and I ruined it."

Placing a soft kiss to the corner of his mouth, I shake my head, letting my lips linger in place, content to just stay this way forever.

If this is what's afforded to me tonight, being here this way with him, I'm okay with it.

This is what he needs from me, and the intimate way we are, me in just a bra and panties and him shirtless with just the button of his jeans popped free, it's giving me what I had gone into this entire experience assuming only sex could give.

The ultimate connection.

Which makes the words I whisper next, my own mixed with the ones from the very movie we watched earlier, the easiest and only thing I can say that will make him realize how wrong his assumptions are.

"It's okay, JJ. I'm here, and it's okay." "I'm going to fall in love with you, you know? And you don't have to love me back, but I'm going to give you my heart. It's yours."

Chapter Nineteen
Lost and Found

Joshua

Those words of hers are calculated.

She had to know the second they were uttered, the impact they would have.

The sensory overload taking place as the memory of that night explodes in vibrant color through the surface of my mind, pulling me straight out of the moment we've found ourselves in today and straight back to the night in 1996.

*****

I have no clue what to do with the outpouring of feeling I'm experiencing here on this bed with her.

She's amazing.

I've known forever, but there's this conviction in what she's telling me, the words she saying not speaking to me in the way words usually do, but speaking directly to my soul.

There's a fullness in my chest, another thing I'm unfamiliar with. The weight is heavy, but not uncomfortably so. It feels right even if I don't have the first clue why it's there, to begin with.

As weighted as it is, it brings with it a form of strength so foreign in the moment. I feel absolutely invincible. Like I can do anything. I'm also aware it's because of the girl sitting beside me.

All of this is because of her.

Turning into her, I brush my hands over her cheek, moving in as close as I can possibly get and place my lips to hers.

This kiss, it won't be the same as the ones before.

I still want her, possibly more now than I did when all of this started, but where I had relinquished control over to my raging need to just take from her before, this time, I want to take my time.

Make this moment everything she's ever dreamed of.

It's harder than I expect controlling the scene, what with the damn near manic beat of my heart slamming against my chest and the need that always just seems to push to the surface whenever we're this close.

Her soft murmurs and moans when I finally deepen the kiss, dragging it out until my body damn near wants to combust with the internal struggle, shapes what our bodies do next.

Falling back to the bed in tandem, our arms finding their way around each other, each stroke of her hand across my back, putting me at war with myself again, igniting me, while at the same time soothing the fear still prickling on the outskirts of our moment and my mind.

"JJ..." she whispers, her hands slowly running down over my back, and around, causing my abdomen to retract under the gentle brush, as she finds her way to the waistband of my jeans while her lips begin their own descent away from my own and down over my chest, each brush of her lips against my skin, like a match that any second is going to hit its mark and set me ablaze.

All traces of the earlier fear is banished the second she pulls down the zipper of my jeans and slips her hand inside, brushing softly yet confidently over my boxers and the part of me reacting most to the moment underneath.

My body springing to life, not in the ways it did in the past. This time, the touch is the right one. The only touch I ever want to feel. Should have felt.

With it erasing every touch previously in its place, the fullness in my chest, like a cup running over, spills, and despite feeling it happen as the droplets fall from my eyes and down over my cheeks, the fear of her seeing, of it, ruining the moment has also been dispelled.

Alyssa is altering history. Changing it. Making it, with just the small brush of her hands and the feel of her lips, the way it always should have been.

She is rewriting my story.

Our story.

Applying more pressure, rubbing now instead of the gentle brushing from before, my body responds, answering her question before she's even let the words fall.

"Is this okay?"

"Y—yes." I manage to choke out through the rush of blood now flooding my brain, but also the explosion of emotion just her asking me, awakens. "It's more than okay."

It's not lost on me, how the role I always played whenever I imagined being in this position with her, has been reversed. But where it should bother me, it doesn't.

It just feels right.

Releasing my hold around her and attempting to take back some semblance of control, even if only for a brief second, I slip my hands down and meet hers, slowing her movements long enough to remove the barrier between us.

Our clothing.

Sliding my way out of my pants, I'm paused when as I'm slipping the boxers off, she chooses to unclip her bra and let the minuscule bit of fabric fall to the bed with ease. Ease that with as many times as we've spent in this very bed making out, getting as close to the edge as we'd gotten, I've never seen her possess.

She's so incredibly sure of herself.

Of us.

Blushing as she catches my eyes on her, I finish with my boxers and turn on the bed, moving until her legs are trapped between mine. My eyes finding their way to hers, never wavering as my hands find their way to the waistband of her panties and I begin the slow art of slipping them off of her.

An act that will leave us in a way we've never been.

Completely open. Bare.

Discarded to the floor with the rest of our clothes, she smiles, her lips lifting in the slyest smile as her finger shoots out, pointing first, as her grin grows and then bending, as she tells me in no uncertain terms what she wants.

What I give her when I connect us again, our now naked bodies pressed together, with no barriers in between. Our lips finding their way back to one another effortlessly and our hands, now free to explore, doing exactly that. Neither of us it seems, as *our lips nip and taste one another, our hands rubbing, massaging, and exploring, able to get enough of the other.*

"JJ." she calls, her breath, like mine, labored and coming in stages. "JJ, I love you."

It's then, in those whispered words and mine, as I tell her how I feel, the easiest and truest words I've ever spoken, repeating it, like a prayer, we tear down the final wall between us and connect in the only way left possible.

*****

"JJ..."

Dear God, I'm still locked in my memory.

As clear as her voice is to me now, the deeper set of it easily recognizable as the woman I came home to reclaim, and not her younger self, there's no way this can be happening.

Her voice, the softness of it and the musical lilt, sounding exactly as it did then.

It's only when I close my eyes, sucking in a breath as she says my name again, this time stronger than before, I'm able to turn my attention to her and see I wasn't the only one affected.

Her eyes, which before I had broken down, vibrant and full of feeling, now staring back darker, her lids heavy. Her lips full and pouty, risen in the slightest trace of a smile, calling to me. Begging me to take her the way I had all those years ago and kiss her senseless.

An act I would have no regrets about, but what can't happen yet, no matter how deeply the memory we just shared affected us.

She's not there yet.

Neither of us is.

When I kiss this girl again, the first time in twenty years, she's going to feel it. She's going to know with every single breath and touch that it's forever.

I won't settle for less.

"You were so gentle with me."

"Sentiment is mutual, princess. You gave me the best night of my life."

Eyes intent as she studies me, looking for any sign I'm being dishonest or worse, telling her what I think she wants to hear, she snorts and then attempts to cover it up by jamming her hand over her mouth.

"Surely over the years, there have been better ones."

Lifting her chin up and looking her dead in the eyes, making sure she's able to witness the absolute and unequivocal truth about to follow, I give it to her straight.

"When you said what you did, I know I wasn't the only one who went back there. I wasn't the only one back in the room, on the bed, experiencing every touch, every scent, every feeling that took place. You were there too, AJ. You felt it as powerfully as I did, maybe even more so judging by the fight you're giving to hide your eyes from me. In twenty years, I have never had one instance, day or night, as powerful as our first time together. You altered my very existence that night and it had nothing to do with sex, and everything to do with who you were. The person you are and have always been. *Will always be.* There is nothing short of watching you give birth to our child that'll change it. Not one damn thing."

When her arm comes up and shoves me away, my brain working double time in order to catch myself before I fall on my ass, I realize what I've done.

In being so brutally honest and trying my damnedest to make her see the truth, I've inevitably jammed the knife in her chest and twisted it. Taking even more steps back in my fight to regain not only this woman's heart but her trust in me.

"I'm a fucking idiot." I curse the statement a blanket one.

How could I have been so thoughtless?

"Been there, done that, Joshua. But thanks, you know, for the reminder."

Her eyes narrowing, the color—the very life—draining rapidly, delivers the punch even quicker than her words do.

I need to save this somehow. I can't let what I know is going to happen actually go down.

She can't walk away from me a second time. Not when I know when she walks away this time, it'll be the end.

"I should—"

"Stay here and talk to me?" I cut her off. My mind searching for anything at the moment to make her stay. "Forget the last bit of what I said, and focus on the rest of it? Watch me actually kick my own ass? I've learned how over the years you know. I've become quite good at it."

I'm rambling more than a little girl standing in front of her idol but she's not moving, which to me is a victory, no matter how small.

"Please, AJ. As much as the words were true, the intent behind them wasn't to hurt you. It was to make you understand how I feel. How I've always felt. Please," I plead, my voice raising higher as I beg her not to go. "Don't become me. You're better than my mistakes. Don't run the way I did."

This time when the fear of losing her sets in and the tears begin to cascade down the front of my face, I make no motion to rid myself of them.

I need them as much as I need this woman in front of me to stay.

"Stay with me."

Chapter Twenty
Light the Match
March 1996

Alyssa

With shaking hands, I manage to maneuver the box from its hiding place within the plastic and become fixed on the bag as it falls to the floor.

Stalling.

Not wanting to face what happens once I pull the stick out of the box.

How everything will change based on some pink lines on a test I hadn't even bothered to study for, even though I felt I was old enough to dive straight into the subject matter head first.

I'm blowing this out of proportion, obviously. I mean, what are the odds the reason I'm late is because of our first time together?

Now who sounds stupid, Aly.

For someone who prides herself on planning everything so incredibly well, how did I not plan to bring protection into the mix?

We even talked about it afterward. Both of us, guilt overriding what had otherwise been this incredibly life-altering moment. We both felt stupid letting hormones and feelings override common sense.

How could I have been so stupid?

How could we?

When my period didn't make its appearance the day it was due, my mind didn't even go there. It's not the first time since I had the birth control talk with my folks where I've had periods of irregularity. I mean, I had them even before the talk, which is half the reason my parents wanted me on it. My mom especially.

The doctors warned me it would take time to get everything regulated, so of course, my mind didn't jump to our first time. It had no reason to.

When one day turned into four, it became harder to deny it.

It's been seven days now, though.

I can only believe the lies I've been telling myself for so long before reality has to set in.

Where I finally realize it's not late. It's just not coming.

With as much forced strength as I can manage given the state of my hands still shaking under the weight of the box in my hand, I break it open, pull the stick out and placing it ever so gently down onto the counter, begin reading the instructions.

It seems silly, putting so much focus into making sure to read those after being so callous and reckless in the first place, but I can't chance anything else going wrong.

As much as I love JJ, am one hundred percent invested in this being more than some cheesy high school romance, neither of us is in any way ready for what comes as a result of me taking this test.

Love can get us through almost anything, but it can't get us through a baby at almost sixteen years old.

Not to mention the firestorm it's going to ignite when the time comes to tell my parents.

Slow your roll, Aly. You haven't taken the test yet. This could all be in your head.

Forcing my hands to stop shaking, secure in the knowledge of what needs to be done now after reading the instructions over twice, I pluck the test from the counter and proceed to take it.

The next two minutes feel like two years as I plop myself down on the side of the bathtub, staring anywhere but at the test now laying back gingerly on the edge of the counter.

As each second passes, the fear I've been bottling and shoving down finally begins to rise, causing me to jump and call out louder than I intend when the alarm I've set on my digital watch finally sounds.

Please God, let me wake up from this nightmare.

A prayer destined to fall on deaf ears.

The shake from my hands now also present in my legs when standing from the tub, I reach out to grab the corner of the cabinet in an effort to keep myself upright and closing my eyes, not yet ready to face the reality of what's about to come, keep them closed tight as I shift my useless legs over to where the test lies.

My worst fears becoming reality when a few seconds later, after summoning every ounce of gumption I've got and opening them, I'm faced with the two lines that spell out exactly what I've known all along.

I'm pregnant.

"No, no, no. This can't be happening."

My stomach seems to drop straight down into my boots and almost as if it's adding insult to injury, the bile starts rising in my throat. Giving into the weakness in my legs, I fall to the floor, hitting my knees hard against the linoleum.

Spots begin to appear in my field of vision and in an effort to stop what I'm sure will happen if I give into it, I move swiftly, dragging myself across and swinging the lid of the toilet seat up as quickly as I can, I give in to what my body wants, spilling out not only the contents of my stomach but the fear too. Not stopping until I'm sure it's all gone.

It's only when I'm sure everything's out and I've leaned back against the wall, it all comes to a head and the fear rises worse than before.

The knock on the door and the voice quickly following it, one even from his place on the other side, I hear dripping with concern at what is taking me so long, shoving me straight back into reality.

JJ.

What do I do now?

Joshua

When after five straight minutes of me knocking, seconds before I decide I'm going to start pounding, a sick feeling in the pit of my stomach making me want to force my way in, the door opens and the sight I'm met with is one I've never seen before.

Her normal peach coloring is ashen. She's gone completely pale, devoid of all the natural coloring I'm familiar with.

Taking the rest of her in, I notice the state of her sweater, a move she catches making her immediately yank her hands into the sleeves and lift until she's making harsh rubbing motions at the corners of her lips.

"What's going on, Alyssa?"

It's when her eyes meet mine before quickly pulling away and hitting the floor, I stop wasting time, pushing my way into the small space and wrapping her up in my arms.

I have no clue what's going on, none of how she's acting or what she's doing making any sense, but I do know, especially with the way she collapses so easily into my arms once she's securely in them, she needs me.

"Talk to me, AJ, please."

My pleading is light. I don't want to push her, but I need to understand what happened from the time she made a mad dash through her front door for the washroom and what's taking place now.

"I don't feel so good," she begins and it's all the prompting I need. Scooping her off her feet, I push my way as easily as I can back through the bathroom, not stopping until I've gotten us through her bedroom door and am laying her down on her bed.

The twisting in the pit of my stomach continues, and I know this isn't like the other times I've seen her sick. It isn't like the time she ate some bad food when we all went out to eat with our friends. It's also the complete opposite of the flu she had a few months back when she could barely turn her head, much less talk or walk.

"What hurts, baby?" I ask softly, knowing full well I'm not going to be able to make it stop even if she tells me, but wanting—needing—to do something at the moment.

She's never looked this bad and the pallor of her skin is really starting to scare me.

It's like she's seen a ghost.

When no response comes, not even after waiting, I know what I've got to do.

"I'm calling Wayne."

"No!" she calls out, her hand finding mine before I can so much as turn to go, her grip tightening along with her eyes pleading when I finally meet her gaze. "Please don't. I'm fine."

"No, AJ, you're not. You're white as a sheet and until you just called out, I wasn't even sure you were able to speak. I'm scared."

"Me too," she admits softly. "But Daddy can't help with this. No one can."

Her eyes fall from me, dropping to the bed.

"What does that even mean? What aren't you telling me?"

She sniffles a few times, which quickly turns into tears, her crying raising in pitch and volume the longer I stand in confused silence.

"AJ—"

"I'm so—god, JJ. This is all my fault."

She's not making any sense and with all the stops and starts as she blames herself for god knows what, I don't know what I should do next.

Take her in my arms the way I've been wanting to since she started sniffling and hold her until whatever this is about passes, or push her to keep talking through the obvious pain she's in until I find out what could possibly be so bad, she doesn't want me telling her dad.

What she's finding so hard to tell me.

"AJ, you didn't do anything, so there's no way this is your fault."

She hiccups again as I watch more tears fall from her eyes and my decision at the moment is made.

Screw forcing her hand.

I need to hold her.

Releasing her hold of my arm, I sit on the edge of the bed and shifting her over, I climb onto the bed and pull her into my arms.

"I swear to you, everything is going to be okay, AJ. I'm here."

Attempting to soothe her, I begin stroking the top of her head, running my fingers through her hair, continuing to softly tell her I'm here and I'm not leaving. Praying with every step I take it'll make her open up.

"Promise me."

Of all the words I expected her to say when she finally spoke again, those weren't it, but with a soft kiss to the top of her head and leaning in, I do exactly what she wants.

"Whatever you need me to promise, AJ, I promise, okay? Whatever it is."

"Promise me," she repeats again. "Promise you won't leave me."

"I'm not going anywhere." I know it's not exactly what she wants, but considering the way my life has been, I can't give her anymore. I can't promise I'm going to be around forever.

In reality, no one can.

"I don't want you to hate me. I couldn't take it if you left again. I can't lose you, JJ. I just can't. Not again."

As much as I've tried over the years to find reasons to hate this girl since leaving would have been a hell of a lot easier if I had, there was never one thing that could make me do it. Same as forgetting her. I couldn't even leave her the way I thought she deserved four years ago. I had to come back. I don't see how anything could change that.

Change the way I feel about her.

Shifting my body just enough on the bed, I bring my hand down under her chin and pull her face up to mine, wanting to make sure with the move she's fully aware of what I'm going to tell her next.

Words she really needs to hear.

"There's nothing you could do to make me hate you. I promise you, AJ. I could never hate you, not when you're the sole reason I'm still here. All I can do is love you. It's what I was meant to do."

She's fighting against my grip on her face now, she wants me to let her free, to drop her eyes from mine, hide from the truth of what I'm telling her, but I can't let her. Not when every time she looks away something inside me breaks.

"JJ..."

One breath, two, straight into ten before she finally speaks again, and when she finally does, the proverbial bottom falls out.

"I'm pregnant."

Alyssa

As soon as he pushes me off him and bolts from the bed, my worst fears are confirmed. The exact reason I couldn't get the words out is staring me right in the face.

He hates me.

All of the talks of not going anywhere, never hating me, it was all crap.

He said it to make me feel better.

Running a hand over his head, pushing back his hair, he releases a heavy breath repeating the same word over and over again in quick succession as he begins to pace back and forth from one corner of my room to the other.

"No. No. No."

"JJ..."

"No! Do you hear me, AJ? No! You didn't say what I think you said. You couldn't have. It's impossible."

Only it's not, and as much as I tried talking myself into the same train of thought for the last few days, I can't do it anymore.

I can't deny the truth.

"It's not, JJ. I swear it's not. I took a test."

Watching as all color drains from his face, I realize now why he was so scared for me when I finally opened the bathroom door. He'd seen the same look on my face.

"I don't care. The damn test is wrong! You probably screwed it up."

Swallowing down the sting of his accusation, even the slight insinuation this is wrong and I'm making it up, I sit up on the bed.

The way he was when he pulled me out of the bathroom and brought me into the room, I need to do the same for him now.

With the initial shock worn off and fear in its place, I slip off the bed and make my way toward him, not at all prepared for his backing away with each step I take to get closer. His hands finally coming out in front of him when he backs up straight into my dresser with nowhere else to go.

"Don't, AJ. Just don't."

Despite not wanting to believe it, with his cowering knocking the trinkets from my dresser off in an attempt to get away, it's hard not to believe I was right earlier.

He's going to leave me and this time he won't come back.

This is too much.

"How could I have been so damn stupid?" he curses, hands now fists beating off his thighs. "Better yet, how could you?"

When his head swings up and his eyes land on mine, the absolute look of disgust with his lips curled into a snarl as he stares, has the familiar bile from earlier rising again.

He's just shocked. He doesn't mean any of this, Alyssa.

"All you've done since the moment I met you is plan. You've got everyone's life all mapped the fuck out. How could you not have planned for this?" he yells, and in the time it takes me to blink, his eyes light up and he fires even more vitriol my way. "Or was this your plan all along? Were you so fucking afraid I was going to leave that you planned this to trap me? Keep me tied to you?"

"How can you even ask me—"

"Because you're supposed to be the smart one, Aly!" he yells. "Everyone in the damn city knows what a complete fuck up I am! You're supposed to be better!"

Something in the air shifts as he continues his barrage and the sick feeling in my stomach fades as something else rises in its place.

Anger.

All I can see is red.

How dare he put this on me? Accuse me of planning this or being the only one in our first time together? I can't make myself pregnant and it's time he's reminded of the facts.

"I didn't do this on my own, Joshua. You were there too!" I cry out, no longer caring who hears me. The pain I felt in the bathroom on my own, staring at the lines on the test and all of his false promises of a few minutes ago, fueling me. "This isn't all my fault!"

"Not what you told me a few minutes ago is it, princess?" he quips and breaching the distance between us, I cross the room and don't stop until my hand connects with his face.

The sting is as harsh as the sound that follows upon connection.

"Get out."

"Aly—" his voice softens and I put my hand up again, this time in an effort to silence him. I've had enough. I can't take any more of this.

"No, JJ. Get out. Now."

I tried really hard when he first bolted not to let it get to me. I even wanted to talk him through this, make sense of it, and what we were going to do next. I wanted to figure all of this out together, but in the span of a couple of minutes with everything he's said, the hurt it's causing, I can't do it anymore.

I need space.

"I'm sor—"

"Get out," I repeat, not even letting him get the rest of his half-assed apology out.

What I really want to tell him is I'm sorry too, but right now, I know with the distrust of me in his eyes, he wouldn't believe me if I did.

"Fine. I'll go, but AJ, this isn't over."

As he grabs his coat off the back of my desk chair and stomps from the room, I finally release the breath I've been holding onto since I told him the truth.

This isn't over.

His final words haunting, but exactly what I'm afraid of.

That it is.

Chapter Twenty-One
Set Your Life on Fire

Joshua

How we got here from where we were before I broke down is a blur, a largely emotional one, but as she places the mug down in front of me and makes her way around the table to the other side, there's no denying I'm awake and aware of the magnitude of the situation I find myself in now.

"Thanks," I say, gratitude on auto-pilot.

"My pleasure."

If only she could feel the skip my heart experiences at her choice of words, along with the many places those words take me, even if the situation I'm now facing is not one for entertaining half of them.

What happened at our spot, the blank patches in time I'm experiencing because I really have no clue how we ended up back here, has happened a few times over the years, and usually, I've had the luxury of being alone and coming around myself without much changing.

Knowing what she must have witnessed when I broke down, and what she had to deal with getting us from there to here has me unable to lift my head and meet what I can feel even across the table is her probing gaze.

"What happened back there, Joshua?"

"We're back to formalities again, I see." I scoff. "Great."

I don't have the right to act like this, let alone treat her this way, but shit. After what her calling me JJ did earlier, going back to the way it was, feels wrong. "I'm sorry. I'm being an ass."

"What you're saying is, you're acting like yourself?" she laughs, and like when we were kids, my chest begins to swell.

I'll never tire of that sound.

"Yeah, pretty much," I admit with a chuckle. "I think you know better than I do what happened before."

Catching the scratch of the chair across the wooden floor as she shifts and leans across the table, I finally summon up the courage needed to lift my head and meet her halfway.

"I don't understand what you mean. How would I know more than you?"

"It's happened a few times before," I attempt to explain. "I spoke to a doctor about it five years ago when the last one happened. He suggested some breathing exercises to alleviate the impact, but since I haven't had one since, I assumed they were done."

I'm not making this any easier for her judging from her scrunched brow.

"At the moment when it happens, I tend to go into what the doctor called a dissociative fugue state and chunks of time are completely blank. It's not the same, but I used to joke about it, saying I was like a drunk who has too many and blacked out."

Murmuring her understanding, she leans across the table until the tips of her fingers are barely brushing against my hand.

"Did he tell you what causes it?"

"A lot of things can cause it, but he believes its past trauma and stress levels."

"And tonight?"

"I'm going to call it emotional overload. As prepared as I thought I was for what I was going to face when I got here, I wasn't. Not even close."

"That makes two of us."

Slipping my hand from the cup until my fingers rest lightly across hers, I release a contented sigh.

"You said the last one was five years ago." She reminds me softly and nodding, I wait for her to put the pieces together. "JJ..."

There's my girl.

"It was a week after your dad came to see me."

"What did he do?"

"He didn't do anything. You know the way he felt about me. It wasn't anything he did."

"You don't have these fugue states over nothing, Joshua."

It takes everything in me not to laugh at the no-nonsense way she says my name.

It's like she's the parent and I'm the child.

Okay, not quite. If I go down that route the creep factor is huge.

"I didn't say nothing happened. It just wasn't any specific thing. He sure did manage to say a lot, though."

Sucking in a huge gulp of air, I watch as she prepares herself for what her father could have possibly said during our last time together.

"He honestly could have said anything knowing him, so before you tell me, I need to know something."

"I'll tell you anything."

Smiling ever so slightly, another sight I'll never tire of, I motion for her to continue.

"Did he tell you I was going to marry Mark?"

Shaking my head, she visibly relaxes.

"If he had told me, maybe everything else he wanted might have actually happened. When you told me earlier about Mark, it was the first I'd heard of it. Pinkie promise."

Raising my other hand, pinkie only in the air, the room is filled with her laughter as she wastes no time hooking hers in mine.

A reminder of our childhood playing out all over again.

"Kevin didn't?"

"No. We talked a lot over the years, but he never brought it up."

"Okay, I think I'm prepared for the worst of it. What did Daddy say?"

"He told me about the baby, and let me know in no uncertain terms what he thought of me as a man. Tough love Wayne, but honestly, I needed it. Still do."

Talking about her dad this way, knowing how fresh the loss of him is, pains me. The last thing I want to do is make this day harder than I already have.

"Me too," she agrees, accepting the slight squeeze I'm delivering to her hand without complaint.

"He told me as much as he would always love me like his own, he didn't like me much. He made no bones about telling me I lost his respect the second I walked out. When I left *our bed*. His words, not mine."

"Oh, JJ...he didn't mean it. You know how he was. He was just hurting."

As much as I appreciate her going to bat for me on this, especially against her own father, I can't have it. It would be a disrespect to Wayne to allow it to continue.

"He was right to say what he did. It was true, and I knew it after I left what he called our bed. He had every right to dislike me and not respect me. I didn't respect myself much either, let alone you."

After a few beats of silence, neither of us making a move to pull away or change position, she ends the quiet.

"Today has been a lot, and I wasn't going to push you, but since you opened the door...I have another question."

The minute I showed up in town, especially when I showed up at the funeral, I knew this moment would come. Not because I came here determined to make her fall in love with me again, but because I owed it to her.

Make no mistake, there's a lot of things I need to answer for, but the question I know is about to come has to be first. Especially since she's already asked me once today.

"Where did you go?"

"North Carolina."

"Why there?"

If I'm going to answer this one, I'm going to have to bring her back to a few months before our first time together. What happened at school, and what I'd planned on telling her about when I found her pale as a ghost in the bathroom.

"You remember me playing field hockey with Kevin before he threw down the stick for the pc, right?"

"Yeah, of course."

"Then I assume you remember what happened next?"

"Ice hockey."

"What you didn't know was, our coach had scouts come in. Guys looking for players to come play in the minor leagues. We had a scout from here, a couple of different ones from New York and well, a guy from Carolina."

Searching her face, I'm looking for any sign she knew about this before today.

There's no acknowledgment to be found.

"The only reason any of it matters is because of what happened that day. Um..." I break off, still finding it incredibly difficult to speak of the day as what it actually was. "The day you told me you were pregnant." I force out, even my voice betraying me as the words fall rough and rawer than I intended.

"For what it's worth, I still have a hard time talking about it too, Joshua. Which is why I don't think it would be smart, especially with everything you told me about earlier, to get into it. I think today has been heavy enough for both of us."

"Understood. Also, agreed." Wanting to say more, but not wanting to jump the gun and assume too much, I bite my tongue and she catches it.

"Spit it out, Brantley. You never had a problem speaking your mind before. No need to change it now."

"What gave me away?"

"Besides your entire left cheek sinking in?"

She's got to be kidding me.

"Try again, AJ. I damn well know biting my tongue doesn't cause that."

"What you said about a lot of things staying the same. It's true. It's muscle memory with you for me, JJ. I just *know* things."

She knows me better than she does herself.

Same as I do her.

"You have given me far more today, AJ, than I assumed I would ever get, given our history." Pausing and looking down at our hands on the table, still connected, my lips curve into a wistful smile. "And you doing it on what has got to be one of the most unforgiving and unrelenting days of your life, is huge. It's an olive branch I'm well aware I don't deserve."

Where I expect her to argue the way she used to, she surprises me when she agrees.

"You're right."

Maybe some things don't stay the same after all.

Good. I want her to challenge me.

"Don't think this lets you off the hook for finishing your story. You're still going to tell me the rest, but you're right. Today of all days isn't about our past. It isn't about you, me or anything in between. Today is for him. And despite the fact we're sitting here talking about us, it hasn't changed anything. It's still about him."

"How do you figure?"

"Daddy would have wanted you here, and despite our history would have wanted me to welcome you back with an open mind and clear heart."

There's a pinch in my chest when she says what she does. As happy as I am she's speaking to me at all, I had hoped at least a little of it was because of her feelings and not her attempting to honor her father by doing what he would have expected of her.

"Put the scowl away, Brantley."

When it comes to this girl, I've never been able to hide a damn thing. She's always been able to see through me, but in this instance, I didn't realize my own body had betrayed me, putting my feelings on display.

"What I meant is simple. He knew how it was meant to be. He's always known. That's why he came to see you all those years ago, I'm sure. He knew as much as I cared for Mark, my heart wasn't in it. He also knew where my heart still resided. I'd like to think he went to see you in order to get it back for me, but I know better. He—"

"AJ, he did."

I feel like a heel for interrupting, but her belief, no matter how silly it might sound to anyone on the outside of our dynamic, she's right and needs to know it.

"He did come to see me in order to bring it back to you. Maybe not in the condition you would have wanted it, but he was adamant about it."

"What do you mean?"

"He demanded I come back. He spent three days in town and not once did he relent. He came back, day in and day out. Kept telling me my place was here and I needed to come back with him. No, if's, and's, or buts. Since he came home alone, I figure you can see what my response was."

"You said no."

"Pretty emphatically too, as I recall."

There's a shift in the room, both in the air and physically, as she releases her hold on my hand and the loss is immeasurable and immediate the second the breeze of her movement falls over my now empty hand.

I've done it again. Opened my damn mouth and inserted my foot.

With my mistakes.

"Don't do that, Alyssa. Don't pull away now. We're getting somewhere, at least I thought we were. Reconnecting. Please don't put up a wall."

Her silence to my pleas both spoken and silent is answer enough.

The toll of the day, the loss, my reappearance and any mention of our past, it's too much. I should have expected the breakdown a lot sooner than this.

"Finish your story from before, Joshua."

"Why? What good is it going to do?"

"Don't you mean how much more damage will it cause?"

She wants to flip the switch, go back to despising me and being all formal, fine. Two can play that game, even if just the thought of it turns my stomach.

"Cheap shot, Alyssa."

Pushing her chair back and standing, she picks her mug up and turns her back, creating as much distance as possible as she makes her way over to the sink. It's in the moment her hand reaches up to turn on the tap, my mouth opens and before she can silence me with the water, I let it all spill out. Every bit of information I can think of from back then.

"The scout from Carolina came to school. First thing in the morning, Coach pulls me out of class and tells me he wants to talk with me. He introduced himself again and then went into detail about why he was there. What he wanted from me. He was building this minor hockey team and wanted me to be a part of it. He offered me a spot right there in the hallway, AJ. It was huge. The only thing I could think about at the time was how I couldn't wait to tell you. I tried finding you at lunch, but you had yearbook and the paper to deal with, so I settled on telling you at the end of the day."

When she makes no move with what I've admitted to turn on the water, I keep going.

I won't stop talking as long as she's willing to listen.

"I stopped myself from telling you about it at your locker after school. I started thinking about what you would feel when I told you, and the fear set in. I was scared you were going to think I was leaving you again. It kept me silent. The bus ride with you was horrendous. Back and forth I went from opening my mouth to tell you and slamming the damn thing shut because I didn't want you to hate me."

"Joshua...stop."

"No. You asked me to tell you, so I'm not going to stop until you know everything, the way you should have then."

The crash of the mug into the sink alerts me quickly to this being something more, her hands attempting to latch onto the edge of the counter filling in the rest of the blanks and shoving my chair to the ground, I race around the island standing between us, barely making it to her before she collapses.

I misunderstood.

She wasn't telling me to stop because she didn't want to hear. She did it because she reached her limit.

Placing a firmer hold around her back, I lift her enough to get my hands around the back of her knees and cradling her as close as I can, I maneuver us out of the kitchen and into the living room and the waiting sofa.

Squatting down while making sure she's secure in my arms, I grab two of the throw pillows from the one end of the sofa and piling them on with the others, lay her down, releasing her from my arms before I've gotten to fully relish just how familiar it was having her there.

Getting on my knees beside her, I'm taken back in time as my hands instinctively find their way to her hair and my fingers run through it. Her vanilla scent as familiar and intoxicating as it ever was.

After a few minutes of sitting in utter silence, stroking her hair and waiting for her to come back, her body shifts and looking down, I find her watching me.

"What happened?"

"You fainted."

"Damnit. How long was I out?"

"A few minutes. Not too long."

"I'm sorry."

She's clearly still delirious if she thinks she's got anything to apologize for.

I'm the one still doing damage and we haven't even gotten deep into things yet. If she's reacting this way already, I'm afraid of what will happen next.

"Don't be. It's been a hell of a day."

"It has," she agrees easily. "but that's not what I was apologizing for."

"What else can there be?"

Raising herself up after pulling out two of the pillows and tossing them to the other end of the sofa, she turns her entire body to face me, her hand coming out and cupping my face.

"For so many years after you left, Joshua, I picked the day apart in my mind. Trying to make sense of why, besides the baby, you left. And then, where you would have gone. I was determined. I wasn't going to give up. I was going to find you and bring you home. I don't know how much Kevin has told you about the first few years after you took off, but I hounded him relentlessly. Threatened him even. I knew if anyone would know where you were, he would. He didn't budge."

If I'd screwed my damn head on straighter and done it sooner, she wouldn't have needed Kevin to find me. I would have told her myself. Saved us both the last twenty years of questions and pain.

"As time wore on, I started to believe you were the selfish bastard everyone kept claiming you were."

It doesn't take a rocket scientist to figure out who the biggest bug in her ear was.

Cara.

Sammie and Kevin, as much as I upset them, never would have said those things.

Though, considering how long I stayed away, how long I kept myself hidden, making sure there was no way to be found, it's not like she was far off the mark.

I mean, I crossed a border in order to escape.

I *was* a selfish bastard.

"I had no idea about your offer to play hockey, and all I could see were those bright pink lines on the test. How stupid we were letting it happen. How I was going to tell you. Tell my parents. How it would change everything. I've spent all these years thinking everything you ever said to me was a lie. It was all just some sick game. Never for one second did I think there might have been more going on."

"Baby—shit. I'm sorry. Old habits die hard." The laugh escaping sounding fake and out of place even to my own ears. "None of the things I said were a lie. My feelings especially, AJ. But part of what you said, at least at the time, *was* true."

"What part?"

"I loved you, but leaving you the way I did, I didn't love you enough."

Sighing heavily, her hand still cupping my face, her finger brushes against my cheek, the motion repeating and my body responds by leaning in even closer to it, craving her touch, having gone too long without it.

"Oh, JJ…"

"I didn't decide to leave because you told me you were pregnant. In that case, after we fought and you kicked me out of your room, I never would have come back."

"But you did."

"Yeah, I did. I realized pretty quickly after you told me to leave the damage I'd done. I went back to Kev's and he just reiterated the same sentiment I'd already realized and kicked me out too. Told me to be with my girl and fix it. Real bang-up job I did there."

Memories are a tricky thing because a lot of the good ones, they're buried under the vivid technicolor of the bad ones. Every wrong decision I've ever made, they blaze in high definition video, bright and enigmatic, making it damn near impossible to forget a single second, even when I did my best to dull it any way I could.

Coming back to her that night is as clear as if it had just taken place.

Getting to the door and begging an unknowing Wayne to let me in at some god-awful hour because what I needed to say couldn't wait. Slipping my way in the darkness into her room and hearing her softly sobbing into her pillow, in an excruciating amount of pain because of the things I'd said and accused her of.

The way I left things.

Her shriek when I finally made my presence known as I lay down on the bed beside her and pulled her to me, and the inevitable second slap of the day when she realized it was me in the room.

The stupid punches to my chest that only hurt because she was giving me her pain in the only way she knew how. The second she finally gave up and collapsed into me. Her arms finally, after a few minutes of just the sound of our breathing, coming to find their way around my neck the way they had every single day for the last year and a half of us being together.

Her scent enveloping me as she brought herself as close as she possibly could. Neither of us saying a word, but somehow after a time, our lips finding their way back to each other, the two of us giving in the way we'd done so many times before in the weeks leading up to what happened.

What I had gone there to do, to make things right with my girl, to make sure she knew she wasn't alone, turning into something else entirely.

Frenzied and quick, every kiss rough and needy. Every feeling as strong as it ever was, but no words being said between us. Where before, I would tell her how beautiful she was and how much I adored her, there was silence but for the sound of our bodies moving in motion together.

There was none of what made us, *us*, and it was laying in her bed after where the gravity of the situation hit me like a ton of bricks.

I had broken her with my reaction. The absolute shit I spewed at her

I had broken us.

"Come back to me, JJ."

Her voice alone wouldn't be enough to break me away from the video taking up residence in my head, but the deeper set of it, how it's aged and isn't the same lyrical tone from when we were kids does it.

Brings me away from the girl I remember so vividly and back to the woman I want to spend the rest of my life getting to know.

"We never spoke a word to each other."

"I know."

"Why didn't we talk to each other?"

"Fear. At least for me. I was petrified. We were kids. We were in no way ready for the responsibility of being parents. Hurt was another big one. I was drowning. I'd get close to the edge, freeing myself from the tidal waves of emotion that just seemed to keep barreling through, and then another one would hit and I was knocked back down again."

Resting my hand on her arm, the softness of her skin soothing the edges of my rough and callused fingers, I slide it up to rest above hers, still cradling my jaw.

"I laid awake after we slept together and I was bombarded with what I thought at the time were truths. My own words to you on repeat. Pictures of your fathers face when they found out that not only had I had sex with their daughter, but I'd also been stupid enough to do it without protecting her—"

"Stop." she interrupts, her hand pulling away, but not separating from me completely as she adjusts herself on the sofa, slipping into a sitting position and leaning forward. Bringing her other hand down to where mine rests in my lap and slipping her fingers through it, tears when our eyes meet, falling drop by drop in quick succession.

"I can't, baby, I'm sorry." I don't even bother correcting the endearment this time, driven as I am now by what needs to happen. "I told you if you gave me the chance, I would do whatever it took to make you see that my being here is for real and it's forever. The only way it happens is if we deal with the walls still erected between us."

Releasing her hand as she closes her eyes in an effort to stop the flow of tears now cascading down her face, I begin to wipe them away, catching them one by one as they continue to fall.

I don't care if it takes minutes, hours, days, months or years. I will sit in this very spot until I've wiped every single one away.

"Every image I saw was ugly. Dark. I saw the damage I would do to our child. To us. Knowing I had the opportunity in Carolina, one I hadn't even gotten around to telling you about, I started seeing it for what it was. My way out. My way to make things right. The silence between us and then the deafening sound of absolute nothingness after you passed out, was excruciating. All I could see was, in the span of an hour, I'd destroyed everything. I'd destroyed the only thing—*the only person*—I ever truly cared about. So, I slipped out of the bed, put my clothes back on…and I left."

Chapter Twenty-Two
Breathless

Joshua

"No! Get away from me!"

Jolted awake by the sound of my own voice, flying up in bed and being met head-on by the sun as the ray's blast through the sheerness of the curtains, my arm immediately comes up to block it.

The sweep of the door across the carpet as it opens alerts me quickly to the fact that my rude awakening has now become a public event.

"Is everything okay?" Aly asks, making her way to the bed. "I heard you call out."

"Yeah, I'm good. Sorry. Bad dream."

Calling my attention to her hands, she smooths them out over her robe before sitting down on the corner edge of the bed, the questions I know she has making her eyes dance.

"To answer your question, they don't happen often anymore."

"Only when you're under extreme stress?"

Remembering our talk from the night before and the information I'd given her, I nod.

"Usually these days when I'm haunted, it's for other reasons."

"And this time?"

"My mom."

Nothing else needs to be said as evidenced by the awareness in her eyes.

"Have you seen her since..."

She doesn't even have the heart to finish her statement, my mothers arrest a year after I came to stay with Kevin's parents, as powerful all these years later as it was then.

"She's dead."

As far as bombshells go, this one's definitely one of the biggest.

"When did it happen?"

"Ten years ago. Heroin overdose."

The ease at which she takes the admission is much the same as my response when I received the call from the prison. Not one ounce of a shock to be found.

As her lips part, she surprises me when she switches gears, eliminating all talk of my mother entirely.

"You'd think the genius who came up with the great idea of talking through your problems would have come up with a solution for what comes after you do it."

"Sorry to disappoint, AJ, but they did." I laugh. "It's called medication."

"Whatever." She says with a wave of her hand, which only makes me laugh harder.

"Look, I'm sorry if I woke you."

"Don't worry about it. I wasn't exactly having the best sleep myself."

An innocent admission which only makes me feel worse.

After the way last night went down, and all of the things she learned, it had come as a shock when I mentioned heading out and back to Kevin's, she'd asked me to stay.

Bringing us to where we are now.

My head and my heart having a hard time wrapping themselves around the fact that I've somehow gotten lucky enough to wake up under the same roof as her.

"What kept you up?"

"Overactive thinker." She admits with ease, tapping the side of her head. "I had a lot to think about. Some things I had to work through and figure out."

"How'd it all work out?"

"Couldn't tell you," she laughs softly. "Some guy hollering at the top of his lungs kind of pulled me away from it."

She obviously finds the situation humorous, meaning I shouldn't read so much into things, but I still can't help feeling like an ass anyway.

"I really am sorry, Aly."

Leaning across the bed, she rests her hand over mine and smiles softly.

"I can't believe I'm about to say this, but Joshua, stop apologizing for everything."

Excuse me?

"Why are you being like this?"

Now it's her turn to not fully grasp what I've said as her eyebrows furrow and her smile begins to slip.

"I don't know what you mean. What way am I being?"

"Forgiving." Running a hand over my face, I sigh. "Nice."

"I'm a nice person, Joshua. I figured you of all people know that."

"Well, yeah. I do, but that's just it. You have every reason in the world *not* to be nice, yet here you are, your damn hand on mine, soothing me like the last twenty years didn't happen."

Her hand shifts but catching her before she can move and break the connection, I lock our fingers together.

"I'm well aware the last twenty years happened. I'm also more than a little aware of what took place before them, during them, and what's happening right here in the moment. I'm not dumb to it. I haven't forgotten. But what you're expecting, much like every other time you do this, Joshua is not going to happen."

"What are you getting at?"

"Before I answer, why don't you tell me what you expected to happen when you showed up in town?"

Definitely not this.

"I expected Kevin to knock me on my ass at the airport. Then I expected when I came across your mom, she would have let me have it for what I put her daughter and husband through."

"And me?"

"See my earlier thought process on Kevin," I half-jokingly give up. "I also didn't expect to have the door opened, much less wake up in a room down the hall from you the day after we said goodbye to Wayne. The look in your eyes before you walked away from me at the cemetery was the only thing remotely close to what I imagined happening. It doesn't make sense."

"Thank you. Now to answer your question, you always do this. It's one of the ways with as much as you've grown physically, and you've clearly done a lot of that," she pauses, perusing my body while motioning with her hands to my bared chest. "your emotional growth remained the same. You always go to the worst possible scenario."

Taking in what she's saying, no matter how indignant her telling me I'm emotionally stunted makes me, there's no denial. Even seeing with my own eyes the difference in reactions, I'm still waiting for the other shoe to drop.

Anticipating the worst possible outcome so when it happens it can't hurt me.

Kevin, Helen, Wayne, and especially Alyssa.

I've seemingly forgotten even with all my talk of truly knowing them, who they are.

"Even if I wasn't too tired from the events of the last week, I still wouldn't treat you the way you've worked yourself up into believing I would. Slamming a door in your face, screaming at you for what happened twenty years ago, even reacting the way I did the night you left, wouldn't do anyone any favors. It would only cause more hurt."

But what she doesn't get is, it's a hurt I deserve.

"It's incredibly easy for me to forgive you, JJ, and it's not because of our history. I was raised to believe that holding onto pain makes the person who hurt you retain control. They continue to win because they're still controlling your responses. Daddy taught me I would find peace in forgiveness. It's why I can forgive everything from you waking me up today, to you leaving all those years ago. Because when I do, my heart and soul are at peace."

Cara wasn't wrong at the funeral yesterday.

Alyssa Jeffries was too good for me then, and by her own impassioned statement here, it's clear she's still too good for me now.

"It doesn't mean I forget. I will never forget. There's a lot of walls built that will take time to break down, especially with you and me. But in order for either of us to really grow up and move

174 | P a g e

on with our lives, we have to start forgiving. Each other *and* ourselves."

There were a lot of instances during our childhood together where I could see her fathers influence. She had taken on a lot of his mannerisms and even her attitude towards people and life, in general, was a lot like him.

Sitting here now, it appears as though she's become him. His levelheadedness. The way he looked at every situation, seeing every imaginable side before speaking his truth, along with the maturity ringing through each and every word she speaks. His heart and how deep his empathy for others ran because of it. It's all there.

She is her father's daughter.

Wherever he is now, I hope he's proud.

She's incredible.

"About those walls you mentioned..."

"What about them?"

Alright, Joshua. This is your chance. Don't screw it up.

"How do we begin to break them down? Better yet, can we break them down?"

More frightened than I've felt in years with the silence the room becomes drenched in, equally as petrified to look her in the eye, I look down at our hands, memorizing the scene, just in case this is the last time we're ever like this after today.

Every groove of our hands, every pocket of air held between them, the softness of her skin against mine, the contact at its most basic. I never want to forget how it feels.

"You're already doing it, Joshua. You're here. And despite the way I rebuffed you at the funeral, you didn't run with your tail tucked between your legs all the way back where you came from. You followed instead. You stayed and you fought."

What you should have done years ago.

She doesn't even have to say it, it's just fact.

"Please look at me," she pleads and when I do, she's quick to move. Her legs shifting on the bed until all of her weight is pressed down upon it and she's coming closer to me, stopping only when her knees are resting over the blanket directly above my lap.

"Forget what you think you know, JJ. For once, just accept what is."

"Accept wha—"

Before I can finish her arms are around me and her body is pressing into mine, bringing me close and hugging me. Knocking the sense straight out of me at the same second my body reacts to her unexpected embrace and falls back onto the bed, bringing her along for the ride.

Aware almost immediately the position I've put us in, shifting and attempting to sit up in an attempt to rectify it, she begins laughing, the pitch louder and more drawn out until she finally rolls over on her side, laughter now turning to full-on giggling.

"I—can't believe," she stops, sucking in a gulp of air. "I didn't see that coming. But god, JJ, your face!"

Another fit of laughter escapes as she rights herself on the bed and brings herself over to where, despite being struck by the absolute insanity I'm encountering watching her lose herself in laughter, I'm able to right myself again, this time with more of a grip.

"You want to try that again?"

"Can you handle me trying again?"

She's got me there.

"I think I got it."

"Good, because I was going to do it regardless." She laughs, and this time when she wraps her arms around me, I'm ready, returning the hug with as much force as I can, burying my face in her hair the second we connect and just breathing every bit of her in.

"Just accept what is."

"Mmhmm." She murmurs, slowly releasing her hold and shifting back, her eyes quickly finding mine. "Just be here in this moment, right now."

"Is it really that easy?"

"Yes, JJ, it is. It's always been."

Maybe it's the smell of her hair overtaking my senses or the sound of her laughter when we fell back onto the bed. Maybe it's the flush in her cheeks and the absolute glow illuminating in her eyes as she loses herself in mine that does it, but whether one of these things or all of them, they drive every second of what happens next.

Leaning in, close enough to feel her breath as it catches, my lips find hers.

This kiss tentative but just as powerful, if not more so, than the combination of all the others we've shared before.

My only thought as I shut my eyes and lose myself in the moment, being what I imagine she meant earlier when she spoke of the feeling of peace.

She was right all along.

This is incredibly easy.

Alyssa

So, this is what it feels like.

It wasn't at all what I intended when I made the choice to hug him, but considering how often over the years I've questioned what it would feel like to be with him again, the man and not the boy I remember, it makes sense it's happening.

The familiar current flowing just under my skin as present as it always was whenever we kissed. Only this time becoming more potent when my lips part as I release a breath and he seizes the moment, reigniting sensations in me I swore until this moment was long dead.

Deepening the kiss, he brings me closer and I allow it. Lost in the scent of him, and the feel as his arms tighten around me and bring me closer. Our bodies so closely pressed together at the exact moment his tongue slips its way into my mouth, I can feel the quickened beat of his heart through the robe still tightly wound around my body.

My only protection from him.

As our bodies begin a slow fall back to the bed again, this time, his body atop of mine, reality sets in.

The voices from the past, flooding my head and reminding me of who he is and what he's done, like a bucket of cold water rushing over what is possibly the hottest kiss I've had in years.

Jumping back and snaking my way out from under him, I crawl across the bed, attempting to catch my breath once I've created what I think is enough distance between us.

"AJ—"

"Don't say anything, okay? I just...I need a minute."

Narrowing his eyes, clearly not believing me, he thankfully does as I ask and the room is completely barren of sound, but for the incessant beating of my heart and my breath as I fight to catch and steady it.

As the minutes tick by and the silence continues, neither of us saying a word, he breaks it when he pulls back the blanket and begins shifting his weight over to the side. Completely unaware of the stabbing pain he's causing as he positions himself with his back to me.

Keeping my eyes trained on his back, he gets up, and walking over to the chair where I can now see his pants are thrown, he continues the vow of silence as he grabs them and slips them on. Never once turning around and meeting my eyes.

Probably as afraid as I am of what he'll see when he does.

"If you're trying to come up with a polite way to say we shouldn't have done that, you should know you don't have to bother. I already know." Turning, his eyes take me by surprise because where I expect to see them hardened, they're not. They're alive. "But if you want me to admit I regret it, I'm going to disappoint you."

"I don't..." I struggle to speak and get the words out, but my heads still spinning. Our kiss doing one hell of a number on what I need to say.

"God, AJ! You are so god damned gorgeous, and what's worse is you have no idea. You always were, but now, its something else. You make it so damn easy to forget. To do what you said and live in the moment. But we can't, at least not yet. You're not ready and I will not be *that* guy."

He won't be the guy taking advantage of me.

"I don't regret the kiss."

"But?"

It physically aches knowing there's a but coming. I don't want there to be, but this is the wall that's going to take the longest to crack.

I can forgive him for the past. We can talk, laugh together, be a lot of the ways we were before, but when it comes to anything more than the kiss we just shared, I can't go there.

Not yet.

We clearly have chemistry all of these years later, but the chemistry was never our problem.

Trusting him is. Being able to rely on him. His words meaning something because of the actions he puts forth to prove them true.

"I can't fall back into the past again, Joshua. As easy as it is to do with you, I can't be guided by knee jerk reactions, history or worse, dreams of a love-sick teenager who never got over her first love and spent her entire life imagining what it would be like when they found each other again."

Making his way back around the bed, he lowers himself beside me, and taking my hand in his, implores me with his eyes with the questions I see there.

"What can I do?"

"Be here."

"I am."

"Be here longer."

Leaning back just a little, he pulls me to his side and wrapping his arm around me, cradles me to him, the steady beat of his heart calming, and the words he says next wrapping themselves around my heart.

"Is forever long enough?"

Chapter Twenty-Three
Mark the Graves

Alyssa

Dissociative fugue, formerly fugue state or psychogenic fugue, is a dissociative disorder and a rare psychiatric disorder characterized by reversible amnesia for personal identity, including the memories, personality, and other identifying characteristics of individuality. The state can last days, months or longer.

Knowing the rabbit hole I'm diving into even pulling out the laptop and looking this up, I read and reread the definition, bringing up another window and defining my search even more.

Determined to read as much as I can in an effort to understand what Joshua explained has been happening to him over the last *twenty* years.

What happened at our spot when after pleading with me not to leave, his eyes had dropped all signs of life and he hit the ground, breathing thankfully, but in every other way, no longer there.

Thankfully, unlike this definition, the state didn't last days or worse, months, but his inability once I'd gotten him back to my place, to even become aware of himself again, is still too long for my liking.

Needing answers isn't the only reason I'm sitting here, though.

It's because of what's inevitably going to happen next.

The one topic we've both been putting off even though it keeps presenting itself in every confrontation we have.

It took me years to admit to my folks the ramifications of what took place back then. What the loss did to me, both physically and mentally. Emotionally, with as put off as I still am sitting here just thinking about talking it through, it's clear I'm still a wreck.

I've never truly dealt with it, even though I've done a phenomenal job of making the rest of the world believe I have.

What I didn't tell Joshua before the closeness after the kiss became too much is, he's not the only one haunted by nightmares. His of his time with his mom and all the shuffling around and abuse he suffered. Mine, the absolute bloodbath that followed it.

It's atrocious to think about, much less put a voice to, but I would honestly give anything with what I lived through to have one of those episodes Joshua experiences.

I would just want it to last longer. Not the days and months mentioned here on the page, but years. A lifetime. Giving anything not to remember.

Clicking the X on the righthand side of the screen and closing the window, I slam the lid to the laptop down and pushing the chair back, get up.

Putting as much distance as I can between me and the screen in an effort to rid myself of the self-loathing that appears almost immediately once I've put the thought of erasing the past to the forefront of my mind.

Hating myself for entertaining it at all, when it's just not what we do.

Jeffries'.

We don't run from the past. We also don't try and come up with easy solutions to what may be too painful to deal with. What we actually do is dig our heels in the dirt, stand our ground, and no matter what level of ugliness we have to stare down, we do it. Head on.

Forgetting this, even for a second, would be doing a disservice to the man who raised me to be this way.

"I'm sorry, Daddy." I look up, whispering. Praying it can be heard through all of the noise currently taking up space in my head.

The earlier conversation with JJ leaving me spent, adding even more sound to an already emotionally overstimulated body, but also leaving me with more questions about us than I anticipated.

His openness with me about the night he left, his reasoning at the time for why he made the choice he did, and then how easy it had been on the guest bed to fall back into familiar old patterns, it's got me not just questioning things, but wanting to give him the same in return.

I have no knowledge of how much my father told him when he took his secret visit almost five years ago. I also have no idea how much Kevin could have let slip, especially considering who I was with.

The overpowering scent of rusted iron wafting its way into my nose as strongly again today as it had back then, when after experiencing what at the time, I assumed was the worlds worst cramp in my abdomen, my legs went weak and I'd collapsed, hitting the floor before Sammie even had a second to react.

The sheer brightness of the blood when after coming to as she attempted to drag me to the bed, it pooled around my feet. Darkening as it seeped deeper into the peach colored carpet.

A scene that a few days later, after being released and brought home by my folks, I saw for the true bloodbath Sammie described it as. What my parents hadn't gotten to remove because of all the time they'd spent with me at the hospital.

My father, even years later, gripping my hand on his death bed and apologizing for it.

Joshua must not know the full extent of what took place. There's just no way with the way he's been, he would be able to hide it.

It scars you, what I lived through.

Knowing Joshua Brantley as well as I believe I still do, there is no way he would have come through the telling of it unscathed. Which leaves me with the lingering question of whether or not, given what I believe to be his lack of knowledge of the loss of our child, I can be the one to explain it.

I've been running from it for years.

It's another reason it took so long for things to develop with Mark. I was petrified to be intimate with someone again but also frightened of what would happen when he found out how truly damaged I was.

How can I finally explain to Joshua what happened and expect something of him I'm not ready to give myself? And worse, how can I, knowing what I do about what happens when he reaches his emotional limit, risk it happening again?

Interrupted by the knock and turning toward it, I just stand, one breath in, then out, followed quickly by another, until another knock comes, louder this time, bringing with it a sense of finality, causing me to cross the room and open the door.

The last thing my heart wants being finality with Joshua.

It's in the moment when he looks up from his place and his eyes catch mine, the decision is made.

"I need you to do something for me," I state, at the same time he asks me to go to lunch. A request he immediately drops hearing what I've said. His answer quick.

"Anything."

Joshua

When she asked me to do something for her, responding was easy.

I'd walk barefoot to the ends of the earth for this woman.

Asking me to trust her the same way she'd done twenty years ago on the night of our first time, again the response was the same. And just as immediate.

I trust her with my life.

What I didn't expect was where we are now.

Michael Garron Hospital or as it was called the last time I was here, *Toronto East General*.

The silence palpable, but a quiet she ends as she slips off the seatbelt.

"I know this doesn't make sense, and I'm sure it hasn't helped me not saying anything, but Josh—JJ," she corrects. "This, why you needed to be here with me, it had to be this way."

And despite how confused I am, my answer again is immediate.

"It's okay. You asked me to do something for you, and that's what I'm doing. Whatever way you need me to do it."

Smiling weakly, she turns toward the door and I catch it.

If I wasn't so aware of this woman, it would have gone unnoticed, but of course, nothing she does, from the smallest breath to the biggest movement, is ever out of my reach.

Her hands, they tremor. Showing me more in the smallest shake then she ever could have said in words.

Whatever she's about to do is big. Monumentally so. And it scares her.

Reaching out, I prevent her from leaving by slipping my hand around hers and squeezing. It may have no bearing or impact on what comes next, but she's going to know I'm here with her.

She's not alone for any of it.

Looking back and smiling weakly, I let her go and watch her slip out of the car, waiting until she's out to do the same, making quick work of separating the distance the car has put between us and following her once she starts heading toward the front of the building.

Pausing just off to the side of the automatic doors, she turns toward me and motioning with her hand back to the building, she begins to speak.

"June 2, 1996. I was rushed into this very hospital, though not this exact way, at 3:43 in the afternoon. And until now, I've never once come back. Not even when Daddy had his stroke and was brought here first."

"AJ..." I need to stop her. The date isn't lost on me. I might not have known the exact time it happened, but I do know what this day is. Her earlier tremor evident again as it comes up to rest in between us.

"No, JJ. I need to get this out. Not for you, though I do want you to know what happened. This is for me, because it hit me earlier today when I was sitting alone. We're not so different, you and I."

Like hell, she's anything like me.

"No, Aly. Whatever you realized today doesn't make us alike."

"But..." she pauses, pulling her hand back to her eyes and wiping at them as her body begins to shake under the weight of what she's holding onto. "We are. I'm a runner. I've been running from something for twenty years too."

Stepping forward, the urge to hold and comfort her in an attempt to take away the panic guiding me, she quickly backs up and her arm flies out between us.

"I started bleeding a little over a month from the day you left. It was such a light pink it was barely there, really, but something about it didn't feel right so I told my mom. She took me straight to the emergency room. We waited six hours to be seen, and as silly as I felt when we finally saw the doctor and he talked me off the ledge, I still felt better having gone. This baby, I had to be vigilant about it. Nothing could happen because it was the only thing left to prove you existed. That what I felt and what we shared was real."

There's no stopping the influx of tears falling now, one after the other, the flood coming so fast there's no way she can make them stop. I reach out again, but swatting my hand away as hard as she can, she keeps going.

"It happened for a couple more days after the ER visit, but given what the doctor told me, I figured it would pass, and it did. My first OB appointment was about a month away then, near the end of May sometime. The cramping came next, but since it wasn't too bad, and I'd done all of this reading at the time detailing all the pregnancy discomforts, I didn't rush to the hospital in fear. I was going to wait for the OB appointment. JJ, not paying attention to the signs nearly cost me my life..."

As she continues to detail the months after I left, what she was enduring on her own, the aura of strength I've built up in order to be there for her slips until she's not the only one crying. The first tear as it slips from my eyes singeing my skin, and what's left of me seems to shatter under the weight of all I missed.

All I walked away from.

"J—June 2, 1996. A month before I was due to turn sixteen, I could have died."

"Jesus, AJ..." Even those two words excruciating to push out, I force myself to keep going, even if what I'm going to say seems like the worst possible thing to be said at the moment. "I'm so sorry."

"Sammie and I were going to head to the mall. The week before, she'd seen this dress she really wanted to show me, she thought it would be perfect to wear to my party. Running around the room and grabbing my wallet and jacket, not even giving it a thought, the sharpest pain I've ever felt hit, and I remember my hands immediately grabbing my abdomen as another wave of pain came. I remember hitting the floor, even crying out because my knees skidding across the carpet burned so badly. Everything went black then."

Aware of the sound of footsteps coming up the path behind us, and no longer caring if she slaps me for taking a hold of her, I pull her into me and as discreetly as I can, wipe at her eyes before turning, keeping her body curved into mine and walking her toward the bench a few feet away.

What she's facing—*what she's forcing me to see*—is hard enough.

It has to be for our eyes only.

Slipping away and moving down the bench when we're seated, I ignore the ache that follows swiftly with the loss of her and just remain still as she continues.

"When I came to a few minutes later, I smelled it first. This rusted, yet tangy smell. I didn't realize what it was, but when I looked down as Sammie was dragging me to the bed, I saw it. Blood, Joshua. A big pool seeping into the carpet. I'd been around blood before, but never that much. My head was spinning from the sight and smell. Sammie ran from the room then and I heard her so clearly it was like she was in the room with me, screaming bloody murder for my parents. Screeching at them to call 911. I remember being loaded into the ambulance, but I must have passed out after because the rest is a blur until I woke up in the hospital and the doctor told me what happened."

My own head is spinning as she informs me of just how close I came to losing the girl I love. How close I came to it being her funeral bringing me back from where I spent my life hiding.

"As soon as the drowsiness wore off, the first thing I did was ask about the baby. I had to be sure what happened didn't cause anything bad to happen to him." Swallowing hard at the use of the pronoun she uses, I curse and her eyes fly up to mine. "They told me what happened then. What I had wasn't a regular pregnancy. It—it was something else. Ectopic."

Ectopic. I have no idea what that means, and before I can even question, she's filling in the blanks. Her lips hardening into a straight line and her body going rigid and straight as she shifts forward on the bench.

"To this day, I hate how I can remember verbatim the way the doctor explained it to me. He said an ectopic pregnancy is when the fertilized egg attaches itself to the fallopian tube instead of implanting in the uterus, as it does in normal pregnancies. The fallopian tubes, he said, aren't designed to handle a pregnancy, which I already knew from health class, and so it wasn't viable."

Turning to me, eyes glazed over from the tears she's clearly struggling not to free, she scoffs. "Viable. I hate that word, even still. He reduced my baby—*our baby*—to something not possible. Something that can't exist. I remember screaming at him then. Daddy had to restrain me. I was like a feral animal. I was so livid. I hadn't processed any of what he said except for the viable part and it made me see red. It was just so cold."

I'm flooded with questions, ones possibly without answers, but I have to ask them anyway, even if there's still more she has left to tell me.

"How does this happen? How do they not pick up on it immediately?"

"I hadn't gotten an ultrasound, and other than spotting in the beginning, which is a sign of it, and the cramping I didn't tell anyone else about, there was no way for them to know. But Joshua, the worst part of it was, if I had just spoken up about the cramping, they could have found this out sooner. In my head at the time, it was the hardest pill to swallow. It still is. The blame I carry over failing to keep this pregnancy safe. I lost him because I didn't tell anyone what was happening when I had the chance."

No.

There's no way I'm letting her continue to take the blame for this. I'm not even sure I fully understand what happened here or why it had to happen at all, but what I do know unequivocally is she is not to blame for it.

This is just some sort of freak occurrence. There's no way Alyssa knew what was going on with her body. Not when all the information she had at her fingertips told her she was pregnant.

"I...God, I know I don't have the right to have an opinion here, but AJ, there is no way this is your fault. There is no way you could have caused this, and even if there was some way to cause something like this, you didn't do it by ignoring the cramping. You just didn't want to make a big deal of things or make anyone worry. It's the way you've always been."

"I don't think you'll feel that way when I tell you the rest."

Sliding across the bench and wrapping my arm around her, I pull her to me and immediately bury my face in her hair, breathing her in before kissing the top of her head.

"It doesn't matter what else is left to say, Alyssa. I would still feel the way I always have about you. No, that's not true." I catch myself, quickly fixing it, while at the same repeating her words from the past back at her. "I would feel more. I would still be right where I am because it's where I always want to be."

Alyssa

Closing my eyes and attempting to control the panic causing my body to shake and my heart to beat wildly, absolutely horrified at what I've already admitted and frightened over what is still to come, I let his words settle over me.

Words from the past, spoken as kids, without any clue of what was to come in our story, but still to this very day the truest words I have ever spoken in my life.

Also, as my breathing seems to begin to steady, the most soothing.

"I didn't learn about the rest of it until a few hours later when the sedative wore off, but I'm pretty sure they should have waited to inform me. I needed more time to process, which is probably another reason talking about this now, when so many years have passed, is so damn frightening."

I can tell with the way he shifts and has been fidgeting since I started telling him everything, he's unsure of what to do next. His urge to want to hold me obvious, but the length of time it took him to finally give in and do it, surprising. His trepidation over how much he's allowed to ask, since he wasn't here the way he should have been when it happened, keeping him quiet.

"All the blood on my carpet, what I thought was me having a miscarriage, was from my fallopian tube bursting. If Sammie hadn't moved as quickly as she had and the first responders hadn't gotten to the house when they did, this story would have a whole other ending then it does."

When he doesn't say anything, but shifts backward, his face no longer buried in my hair and he begins wiping at his eyes, I realize I don't need him to speak, because he's already responding. The loss of my life, to him, as inconceivable as my own mortality was to me when it happened all those years ago.

"What happened, AJ? H—how did they stop the bleeding?" he finally manages to ask, choking up the more he tries to force out through the reality he's faced with.

My fears earlier of how he would react to this, whether or not he could handle it, rearing their ugly head as my concern turns from the absolute panic of reliving this, to whether or not he's going to be okay.

"They had to remove it. It couldn't be saved. Which was another thing I learned while still trying to deal with the fact I'd lost what I thought was our son." I answer as clear as I can, swallowing down the flood of emotion threatening to spill over at the mere mention of my belief in what our child would have been.

Pushing back on the bench and releasing a heavy breath, he reaches out, grabbing my hands in his, lifting them until I feel his lips brushing against my bitterly cold fingers, the warmth of his breath causing me to lift my head until our eyes meet.

"Does that mean—no, never mind. What I mean is, can you still...."

The unfinished questions hang in the air, and even though I want nothing more than to verbalize it for him, all I'm capable of is nodding my head slowly.

"You're still able to have children?"

When I nod my head again, his breath hiccups as a strangled sob escapes, and he starts to move, bending into himself, same as he did before, and without thought, I'm on my feet, moving until I'm lowering to my knees in front of him, forcing his head up to look at me.

"What is it? Where are you going in your head?"

Swallowing hard, his Adam's apple protruding out deeply through his skin, another garbled sound escapes as he sucks in the sharpest breath of air and begins rocking in place on the bench, slowly at first, but the more he does it, the quicker his pace becomes.

"Joshua," I lean my forehead to his and pausing him mid rock, whisper. "Come back to me or tell me where you are so I can find you."

There's no attempt to move when I release the hold I have, but after what feels like an eternity with no response, verbal or otherwise, I stand, more than ready to find someone to help, and as I get to my feet and turn to go, he does it.

He comes back.

"I thought...I thought my mistake, not protecting you that night, took away..." Swallowing, he lifts his head to me and finishes. "I thought my mistake cost you everything."

Rushing forward and falling to my knees in front of him again, I pull him into my arms, covering him with every part of me I can.

What he believes to be true doing what I wasn't sure could ever happen.

It collapses another wall.

The sickening fear he experienced believing he took away my ability to have children in the future, enough to prove he's still my JJ at his very core.

"All your mistake cost me, is you. But you kept your promise."

Muffled by my body over his, but still discernable, asking me what promise I'm speaking of, I waste no time answering.

"You told me at fifteen you never planned to stay gone forever. You were always planning on coming back for me. JJ, you kept your promise."

Pulling back and waiting until he lifts his head level to mine, his cheeks still damp from his tears and eyes mirroring the puffiness in mine, its in the softness staring back at me that I see it.

The past, present, and future.

It's all there, shining back at me. His next words serving only to drive the point home.

"I will always keep my promise, AJ."

Chapter Twenty-Four
Try Again

Joshua

The last thing I want to do when my cell starts ringing is answer it.

It's an infringement to a moment that while we've moved from our place outside the hospital and made our way back to her house, doesn't seem finished.

Sure, we've spent the last half hour eating in absolute silence apart from quiet chewing, but it's more to do with the heaviness of what we both just experienced and less about finality.

Only, the name flashing on my screen is not a person who can be or should be, put off. Especially since if the reason I'm here is meant to be believed and accepted, I'm going to have to go through her first.

Helen Jeffries.

"Are you going to answer it?" she asks when again the shrill tone of the ringing interrupts what until now had been a comfortable, albeit heavy, silence.

On the one hand, I want to tell AJ I'd rather not answer. Being here in the moment with her has to take precedence, but it's her mother. I'm pretty sure if I said that and she knew it was her mom, I'd get my balls in a sling.

The other end is, if I slip away from the table and head into the living room, taking the call from Helen and keeping it private, my balls are also going to be at risk.

When it rings again, instead of asking, she casually leans across my lap and plucks it from my hands, a move so natural it's as though she'd been doing it for years.

"Oh," she says when she catches sight of the caller. "It's my mom."

"Yeah, I know. I was going to take it, but I didn't want to…" I trail off, not sure where I'm going with this, but wanting to admit

I didn't want to stop whatever this is. Especially after what took place at the hospital.

"Didn't want to what?"

"Leave you."

Her eyes soften and she smiles. "It's okay, Joshua. You can answer the phone, even if it wasn't my mother. It's not going to change anything."

She has no clue to the full weight of those words. The hope threaded through each and every one of them.

Handing my phone back, she rests her hand over mine. Applying just the right amount of pressure, causing me to meet her eyes and find hers dancing in sync with the lift of her lips as they raise even higher.

"It doesn't?" I ask and she softly shakes her head.

"Not a single thing."

I want to jump on what she's said and when a giggle escapes, it's obvious she knows it.

"You're wondering what I mean by anything."

When I nod, she continues. "You came all the way here, Joshua, despite knowing what others would say and what you left behind. You still did it. I would have to be blind not to see the gravity of that decision or how agonizing it must have been for you to make it."

"It wasn't as agonizing as you think, other than it is long overdue. It was the first decision I'd made since taking my job back in Carolina that was the right move. Easy."

"Fair enough, but the point is, even if it was easy, you still didn't have to do it. Twenty years could have easily turned to thirty or even the rest of our lives. You could have stayed gone. You didn't. You chose not to. I'm not exactly pleased it took Daddy dying for you to make your way back, but it doesn't make me any less happy to have you here. In town and right where you're sitting."

"Are you saying..." I start, the question dying off as another one pops up. "Does this mean..." Twisting in the chair and dragging it across the wooden floor as I turn my body toward her, pulling hers to match, taking her hands in mine and holding them as I work up the courage to get to the real question I want to ask.

"Yes, JJ. As for the second question you couldn't quite finish, it's also a yes, in case it wasn't implied. It means, in twenty years my soul has never loved another the way it loved yours, and if you're willing to stay and fight, I'm with you. I want to try again."

The gravity of what she's saying in telling me how she feels, it's too good to be true.

She's giving me what I came home to reclaim.

"Um...JJ?" she softly says. "Now would probably be the time to say something."

Rising out of the chair and bringing her with me, I crush her body to mine, giving her all the answers I can as I start at the top of her head, dropping kiss after kiss, not stopping until finally, I reach her lips. Pausing long enough to take a breath and gauge her willingness after what happened when the last kiss tool place, I move in and place my lips to hers, sealing my feelings in stone.

The exact moment of impact, what I recognize as what true elation feels like. All traces of the heaviness present between us, dissipated, and the air so incredibly light, its as though we're floating.

Her ease as her lips move against mine, all traces of fear and trepidation present in the past, also dead and buried as she sinks deeper into my arms, her hands coming up around my neck, holding on as she continues to kiss me back more passionately.

Closing my eyes and losing myself in the moment, the soft moans escaping as after parting her lips, I deepen the kiss, our tongues meeting and this time tangling in one another, neither one of us wanting to stop, I'm reminded of our past and how easy it was to get swept away in the passion and it has me pulling back.

Giving us a much-needed breather.

With heavy-lidded eyes staring me down, her lips quirked up in a smirk, her tongue slips out over her bottom lip quickly before she bites down and it takes everything in me not to kiss her again.

"Why did you pull away?"

"Despite the way you feel in my arms, the way just your lips on mine seem to breathe life back into what had before felt like a body devoid of air or worse, the absolute ache and need I have to climb those stairs with you right now in an effort to experience just how far this feeling will go, I want to do things differently this time. I want *us* to be different."

As her eyes begin to lower, I'm quick to stop her.

"No, you don't, princess. You don't let yourself go there. It's a rule."

This gets her.

"We've got rules?"

"You're damn right there's rules. The first and most important one being, you've got to believe and agree with everything I say."

Snorting then rubbing her chest when it turns into a cough, clearly being choked by the level of bullshit I'm spewing, she smacks my chest.

"Like hell."

"I had a feeling you'd say that," I admit with a laugh. "There are no rules here, AJ. Just me and you. I know I still have a lot of work to do, regaining your trust and making you believe in the things I say, so I want us to take our time. It is beyond easy to move quickly, but you deserve better. We both do."

"We do." She agrees easily, leaning in and placing her lips to mine softly, but this time making no move to change it.

A reminder of our first kiss.

"I love you, JJ."

"I love you too," I tell her, repeating it again, softer the second time, even softer the third until she places a finger to my lips in an attempt to stop me, getting a word in edgewise.

Words I know by heart and I repeat with her when she finally says them.

"Always and forever."

Alyssa

"I should call Helen back."

It's not a surprise after seeing him at the funeral, my mother would be reaching out.

After heading back to their house when I hightailed it away from Joshua at Daddy's grave, he'd been all she could talk about.

How nice it was he had come all this way to see my dad laid to rest. Then, wondering how long he was going to be in town and if he'd stop by before heading back.

Wanting to bake him something for the road, quickly following it up with a stink eye when I said he thought he was too good for her cooking these days.

The grilling lasting only thirty minutes, but ending with quite the crescendo when she told me in no uncertain terms that if Joshua came knocking, I better not turn him away.

With the way we are now, all snuggled in together on my sofa, just enjoying each other's company and catching up on the least heavy parts of the last twenty years, I assume if she knew she'd be pleased.

"She probably wants to fill you up with food."

"And I wouldn't hesitate letting her." He admits with a chuckle. "There hasn't been another person in twenty years who comes close to Helen and her cooking. Especially when it comes to those breaded pork chops."

His recall all these years later is astounding. Even when it's something as basic as food my mom used to make every week of my childhood.

"All the stuff she made us and you remember the chops? Gross!"

Make no mistake, my mom should have been a master chef if they existed in her day, but her pork chops are definitely not the reason why.

"I'm telling her you said that." He teases and I punch him in the arm.

"You're such a child."

"Like you'd want me any other way."

This, the way we're being with each other, it's as though no time has passed. No pain, hurt, or drama of any kind has ever touched us.

As frightening as it was before, the idea of falling back so easily with him and old routines, it's the opposite now.

It's the way Daddy always wanted.

"Go ahead," I tell him, motioning to the coffee table where his phone is. "Call her back."

Looking from his phone to me and returning my smile with one of his own, he does what I ask. Making no further attempt after bringing the phone over to move another inch.

Damn. He really did mean what he said. He doesn't want to leave. Not even to privately speak to my mom.

My heart swelling with the care he's taking in the moves he makes, and how true they're keeping to the words he's spoken since coming home, I take a leap and get to my feet.

Looking up with the phone to his ear, the ringing I can hear as he waits for my mom to pick up, his lips part asking me what I'm doing.

"I'm going to the kitchen to give you two some privacy. When you're done, come find me and we can make something for dinner together."

Pulling a move from his handbook and leaning over and pressing my lips to his exposed forehead, I excuse myself and leave the room.

What I said to JJ before is true.

If he's staying and fighting for me, I'm doing the same. And the first way I can think of is to trust him enough to give him his space.

Before I can settle into the kitchen and come up with a plan for dinner though, he's changing things again by coming in after me.

"She asked me to come to see her." He informs once he's come to a full stop.

Knowing my mother and how many questions she had when she saw JJ again, let alone what I'm sure is a slew of things she is determined after twenty years to finally get to say, there's no way I'm keeping him from it.

With Daddy gone, my mother has now stepped into his place.

"Well, what are you waiting for?" I ask, trying my hardest to hide the grin desperately wanting to slip through. "You better not keep her waiting."

Nodding his head, he tells my mother he will be right over, ending the call and then turning, gives me a look.

"Dinner when I get back?"

"Yeah, sure. Maybe I can be talked into making those pork chops you love so much."

"Be careful, AJ. You're giving me more of a reason to stay talking that way. Never joke with a man about the chops."

"Who said I was joking?" I ask, wiggling my brow. "But I think you misunderstood me. The only way you're getting what you want is if you go to see my mom. Staying gets you nothing."

Ignoring his pout and the sad puppy dog eyes that follow, I relish the momentary softness of his lips as they brush against mine quickly before he heads out to leave.

My chest like a hot air balloon being popped when I hear the front door close quick and harsh behind him. The loss and the instantaneous rise of fear accompanying it, proof that not all the walls between us have been destroyed.

A fear he's obviously aware of when in the time it takes to walk to the fridge and pull it back, the door is opening, the screen alerting me to his presence and the glow of his smile melting me when I turn to face him.

Embracing the rise of joy, I run across the room, not stopping until my arms are around his neck and he's holding me for dear life. The traces of panic I felt when he first walked out quickly fading away to nothingness as he whispers before lowering me to the ground.

"I don't want to go anywhere unless you're coming with me."

Bringing him closer still, breathing him in, what is said next is all that can be.

"Thank you."

Releasing an unsteady breath of his own, he lifts my chin, his smile from earlier captured in time over his entire face.

"I wasn't really in the mood for pork chops anyway."

Chapter Twenty-Five
The Legacy You Leave

Joshua

When Alyssa said she wanted to try again, it was as if the entire world stopped.

I was being handed everything I ever wanted on a silver platter and all I had to do was stay true to the words I've spoken since returning and also turn them into actions she couldn't dispute.

Be here. Love her. Never leave.

Despite my rough beginnings and my penchant for running, those three things were never easier to accomplish than in the here and now.

I was more than ready to make them happen, and she was open to letting me.

Leaving the house and making it all the way to my SUV, there was this gnawing in my gut. Even after not experiencing the feeling in years, I knew enough not to ignore it. My body was clearly telling me leaving wasn't right.

It didn't take long after for me to get the reason why.

The problematic nature of our past, what I had left behind, and what she had lived through, all of those things had been talked about. I wouldn't go so far as to say they'd been worked through, but we'd spoken about them. Begun breaking down barriers to our own happiness through each event we relived and were honest in our feelings about.

Only, there was one barrier we still hadn't breached and I can't believe I didn't think about it sooner.

Leaving.

I didn't even need to see her face to know if I got in the car and made my way over to her mothers without her, I would be making it easy for her to build the wall higher.

Something I couldn't let happen.

Which is why, after slipping her boots on and locking the door behind us, we'd jumped in her car and made our way over to her mothers, this time together.

The look on Helen's face when she opened the door to both of us standing there, reinforcing my decision to go back to AJ.

Holding onto the woman when after herding us through the front door, she'd wasted no time bringing me in for a hug, it's the best part of going back in time. The smallest showing of affection this way, leaving me with a feeling of security that in all of the years since I've never again experienced. Same as the familiar humor when she follows suit with her daughter.

"Don't let the ladies down at the bingo hall get wind of him, Alyssa. He's not the little boy any of those old crows remember. He might not make it out alive."

The reference to my body embarrassing to be sure, its AJ's response giving me pause. The ease at which she solidifies her position, setting the tone for what I hope is more visits like this one in the future.

"I have no plans on sharing him with anyone, Mom. Least of all the group of gossips down at the hall."

Affirming her position as she closes the small gap between us by slipping herself into my side. What doesn't go unnoticed by her mother, or stop the smile from growing even larger on my face.

Right here, in this entryway, there can be no room for doubt. *I'm home.*

"Enough of this standing around business," Helen announces as she turns and heads straight down the hall toward the kitchen, calling out as she goes. "Now, I wasn't sure if you had eaten or not, but given the amount of food I've accumulated over the last week, you can be assured you won't go hungry."

Slipping her hand into mine with a soft smile, Aly heads toward the kitchen and just as her mother pulls out a dish from the freezer and lays it on the counter, whatever Helen's plan was, kicks into motion.

"Why don't you take care of this, Aly, while me and Joshua head into the living room. We didn't get to speak much at the cemetery and I'd love a chance to catch up on everything I've missed."

There's a hidden meaning behind her words that not even twenty years apart can erase. Helen has never been the type to mince words and something tells me Alyssa knows it the same way I do.

The two of us heading into the living room isn't so she can catch up, at least not the way she means. It's because there are twenty years of things she needs to say, and she doesn't want her daughter in the room for it.

"Will do, Mom. Good luck, JJ." She grins before turning toward the dish on the counter and beginning the slow process of removing all of the saran wrap, the sound of her little laugh all the proof I need to know she's well aware of what I'm in for.

What this entire visit is about.

"Lead the way, Mrs. J." I smile tightly, ignoring the lump in my throat that appears as a warning over what's to come.

Heading into the room and waiting as she makes herself comfortable on the living chair across from the sofa, I slip down onto the edge of it closest to her, awaiting what I'm sure is going to be the Helen Jeffries version of the Spanish Inquisition.

"Now, Joshua," *Here we go.* "I want to make something clear before we go any further."

"Sure, Mrs. J."

"By the simple fact of you sitting on my sofa, it's evident how I feel about you. How this family regards you. But I warn you, boy. You're not going to like a lot of what I have to say."

"I have no doubt."

"I'm sure you assume I'm going to go in on you over what you did to our daughter. We'll get to it, but there's something far more pressing I need to say first."

Even if I had stayed in town and never left, growing up with this family and eventually marrying their daughter and making a life together, I would never dream of interrupting this woman or telling her I don't want to hear what she has to say.

The Jeffries, both her and Wayne, taught me my first lesson in respect. Giving as well as receiving. Sure, it didn't stick at first, but it's one I've carried with me every day since, regardless.

"You should know, five years ago wasn't the first time Wayne took a little trip south of the border. It's only the one where he made his own presence known. You'll also be surprised to know, in the twenty years since you left, he's known your location for about nineteen of them."

"Excuse me?"

No way.

The Wayne Jeffries I knew wouldn't have kept something like this quiet all this time.

"I don't understand…" I admit and she merely nods.

"You weren't meant to, but it's now my job to make you."

As much as I love this woman, I don't think even giving me all the answers she has is going to be enough to get me around what she's just said.

"Your decision to leave our house that night, Joshua, not only did what I believe to be irreparable damage to Alyssa, especially given what she experienced a few short months after but also did the same to Wayne. You broke his heart."

I knew as much when AJ tried to explain away what Wayne said to me five years ago, but hearing it from the woman who knew him best, really drives the point home.

I've always known Alyssa wasn't the only one hurt by my choices, but even coming back now, it had always been Alyssa I was concerned about. Especially since I was too late for Wayne.

"When after speaking with your social worker, the authorities, and even a private investigator he later hired, and for the first year getting nowhere on your location or even if you were alive or dead, he'd all but given up. Reliving the loss of you the same way he had when Scott passed. He was already feeling helpless where his daughter was concerned, with what she had come to us and admitted about the child, but this broke him. I don't think he ever recovered."

"Helen—"

"I hold you solely responsible, Joshua." She interrupts. "My husband was never the same. Losing a child, outliving your children, it's not something I would wish on any parent, but because of your choices, my husband had to live through it twice."

"Mom," Alyssa's soft voice interrupts, and turning toward it and seeing her face etched in pain at her mothers' words, I can't look away.

"No, Aly. I appreciate your need to defend Joshua and his actions as I am sure you've had time to talk and share your feelings about it all, but the same can't be said for your father."

"It's okay, AJ." I softly tell her, turning my attention back to Helen, ready to accept the rest of what's to come. The other side of the wreck I'd left behind. "I need to hear this."

"Alyssa, sit," Helen calls when her daughter turns to leave. "You need to hear this as much as Joshua."

Looking from her mother to me and back again, she hesitates for just a second before crossing the room and taking a seat on the sofa beside me.

"Wayne received a call with your location a little over a year after you'd left. It was a dark time for him in the months leading up to the call. He had all but thought you were dead, and the people he trusted to tell him the truth of the matter, had done nothing to alter his way of thinking. The social worker keeping your location quiet while at the same time appearing as perplexed as to you taking off as the rest of us were."

I didn't think I could feel worse about the choices I made then, especially what I'd asked of the people who helped me get down to North Carolina, but what Wayne lived through, I've never felt worse or wanted to take it back more.

"Now, we both understood her position. Her very job title meant she had to protect you above all else, but it didn't change how at the time we learned of her role in your leaving, we felt betrayed."

As soon as her mother takes a breath, Alyssa, now realizing just how much had been kept from her, jumps quickly on it.

"You and Daddy knew where Joshua was all this time?"

When mother and daughters' eyes meet, where I expect there to be the faintest trace of guilt on Helen's part, there is none.

She regrets nothing.

"Yes, Alyssa. Your father and I knew where he was. Your father, under the guise of a retreat with the men of the church, flew out on the first flight after we'd been told. He located Joshua."

"Unbelievable," AJ exclaims, jumping up from the sofa at her mother's admission. "How could you keep that from me?"

"Baby," I whisper, getting to my feet and turning to her. "I know this is a lot, and you're not the only one who didn't know, but I think we need to let her finish."

Fixing a glare her mothers' way, she bites her lower lip and her eyes finally break free, lowering to the ground before she sits back down and does what both Helen and I need.

"In answer to your question, you weren't told in the beginning because we had no idea what your father would find when he got there. We had been told Joshua was alive, given his location, along with the places he worked, but not much else."

The coffee shop and video store.

Those days as easy to recall, as my life here.

I was living, but what Helen said is right. I wasn't doing much else.

I might as well have been dead with the way I felt in those first few years.

"I still don't understand why Daddy wouldn't tell me when he found out Joshua was okay." She questions, and instead of leaving it to Helen, it's me answering.

"I wasn't okay."

I had a roof over my head and my time on the ice, which honestly, kept me going until the injury sidelined me, even had food in my stomach, but not much else.

Those were some dark times.

"You were alive!" she exclaims before aiming her wrath on her mother. "You knew how much I was suffering and *not once* did either of you think to tell me he was alive?"

I hate seeing her in this much pain, the actions her parents took all of those years ago in an effort to protect her, now coming back and threatening their relationship, but I still can't help agreeing with Helen and Wayne in their decision to keep things quiet.

They'd realized what I assumed I knew as fact already.

Alyssa was better off.

"AJ, my frame of mind at the time is why they did what they did. If Wayne had stepped out and tried dragging me home, I would have run again."

The weight of what I've just admitted is enough to make her change up her position, turning her back on me and her mother and walking straight out of the room.

"There were many times over the years," Helen begins, her voice decidedly lower with her daughter's absence. "I wanted to tell her the truth, especially when we first learned where you were. As the years passed and she started to come back from the loss of you, throwing herself back into her school work, graduating and then going to work at the library straight out college, there just never seemed to be a good time."

They were looking out for her best interests. Not wanting to derail the progress they'd witnessed since I had taken off. It's understandable, though I don't think Alyssa is ever going to see it the same way.

"Parenting doesn't come with a manual, Joshua, especially when it comes to what we faced with you. Nothing, even with all our years of life lived, prepared us for what the right thing to do was."

"I get not telling her, Helen, I do. I'm not a parent, so I don't know how hard it must have been for you, but I do know what was going on with me then. Where I was in my life, the things I believed and been taught to believe. Not even the love I felt for her could conquer it. If I had stayed and we had continued the way we had been, things still would have broken down. I still would have left."

Standing from the chair, she makes her way around the coffee table, taking up residence beside her daughter's empty spot on the sofa beside me.

"We knew that, Joshua, which is why we never told her. Not even when we had the perfect opportunities to when she was older and the loss of you wasn't as evident."

Her relationship with Mark. She doesn't even need to say it and I know it's what she means.

"The choice to come home and be with her had to be yours."

Bringing us to now.

"I blamed you, son. When Wayne had the first stroke and the doctors spoke to us about the status of his heart, there was a time where I solely placed the blame for all of it on your doorstep. In a lot of ways, your leaving, and the stress you'd put Wayne under could easily be the catalyst for what took place."

"I'm sorry, Helen." I cut in. "There are no excuses for my behavior. I made a horrible choice. A decision that affected more people than just me. I'm just sorry I never got to the chance to tell Wayne as much."

"But you did, Joshua."

"Huh?" I ask, and leveling me with a look that says I should just know, it doesn't take me long to figure out what she's getting at.

The visit five years ago.

Sure, I apologized then, owning up to all of my mistakes, but speaking those words and proving them in actions are two different things.

"You're right. I did tell him, but I never got to show him."

"Seems to me, son, you're a little confused on that point as well."

Well, of course, I am when she words it the way she is. I have no idea what she means. I had my chance to show Wayne, hell, even Helen and Alyssa how sorry I was five years ago and like the coward from my past, I hadn't taken it.

"How do you figure?"

"You're showing him now, Joshua."

Alyssa

It's a hard pill to swallow, learning the last twenty years have been a lie. Everything you thought you knew, turning out to be nothing at all.

My parents, the two people I love and respect most in this world, had spent the better part of my life keeping secrets from me. I had thought it was just Daddy's visit to JJ five years ago, which after the way we've spent the last couple of days, I could easily forgive, but with what I know now, it's hard not to look at everything differently.

At him differently.

"Baby..." Josh's voice filters through my thoughts. "Your mom wants to talk to you."

"I can't."

Aware of him crossing the room, he stops at the table and pulling one of the chairs out, throws his body down into it, leaning back with a sigh.

"Can you talk to me?"

Thank god. An easy question.

"Of course."

Joshua learned the secret my parents had kept the same time I did. Even if he had sat there and agreed with the reasoning my mother used to try and justify their actions, he was still as much a victim of their choices as I was.

"What bothers you the most about what your mom said?"

Meeting his eyes and rolling my own, the answer I assume completely obvious, he doesn't bite. Instead, choosing to tap his fingers on the tabletop, waiting me out.

Making me say it.

"They kept us apart."

"No, baby, they didn't," he answers quickly. "I did."

I don't get how he can sit here and defend them this way. If Daddy had just come and told me he found Joshua, things would have turned out differently.

How can he not see it?

We could have spent the last nineteen years together.

We could've been happy.

"What did I tell you about doing that?"

"This isn't the same thing, AJ."

"How isn't it? Aren't you trying to tell me it's all your fault again, even when there's evidence they're just as guilty?"

Shaking his head, he looks down to the table and his hand still tapping, then back to me.

"They're not guilty, they're human. They made a choice."

"Yeah, exactly." I easily agree. "They made the wrong one."

Pushing away from the table and standing, he crosses the room, stopping directly in front of me, his eyes softening.

"Stop putting the blame on your parents, AJ. They made an impossible choice, but ultimately, the right one. It was never up to them to put us back together, and deep down, I think you know it."

Swallowing heavily, ready to argue, he beats me to it.

"It's always been up to me."

He's not making light of what my parents did, even hearing me out through the frustration coating every word I've said, along with the fight I've put up against the truth.

His truth.

He's just refusing to allow the past to taint more than it already has.

Opening his arms, it doesn't even take a second for me to step into them, welcoming the security found there. His face finding its way to the top of my head and the intake of breath that follows, wrapping me completely in the warmth of his feelings.

Leading me to my truth.

Joshua Brantley is here.

He came home.

He made his choice.

Me.

"You're allowed to be upset, baby, but don't let it be all there is. Don't let what you learned today twist what you know to be true. Your father loved you unequivocally and unapologetically in the purest way possible. In a way, no other love will touch. Not even mine."

Letting go of the pain following my mother's revelation and really paying attention to what he's saying, I see Joshua's words for what they are. For who is really speaking them.

My daddy.

"I know."

No matter how larger than life Wayne Jeffries appeared to me and anyone else who knew him, he spent his life making sure we all knew the truth.

He was just a man. Human. As prone to mistakes as the next person.

It's about time I remember that.

"Thank you," I whisper, and as his face brushes against mine, I feel it.

He's smiling.

"You're welcome."

His next words, a whispered I love you, awakening something inside of me I had once thought long dead but what comes alive with such a force, there's no way it can be denied.

Bringing with it the crashing down of whatever remains of the walls standing between us.

"Take me home, JJ. I want to go home."

Chapter Twenty-Six
I Swear This Time I Mean It

Alyssa

Stepping through the doorway, willingly letting Joshua slip my jacket off and place it on the hook, I waste no time heading straight into the living room and throwing myself down onto the sofa.

Between my head and my body, I'm not sure which is more tired. The weight of the admissions my mother gave doing double duty and taking the rampant burst of happy energy I'd gone there with, and tossing it straight in the trash.

Along with it, the belief I had in my parents and their willingness to always be honest.

Accepting them as humans is easy, but knowing what they kept, it's going to take longer than just a few minutes to get over. Which is what I'd told my mother when after we tried to leave, she'd stopped us mid sneak out.

I will always love and respect her, there's no question, but this, I'm going to need time with.

Being home and away from her, alone again with Joshua the way I'd wanted when I asked him to bring me here, all thoughts of what was building between us in my mothers' kitchen have faded.

Which, I can easily see as he lowers himself down beside me, his arm easily finding its way around the back of the sofa and my shoulders, bringing me to him, he's also experiencing.

We're utterly and completely drained.

Lulled into a sense of calm by the steady beat of his heart as I rest above it, I sigh and he shifts.

"Penny for your thoughts."

"They aren't even worth a penny."

"Share them with me anyway?" he asks softly, and biting down on my lip, I debate whether or not it's the right time to bring it up.

I've been thinking a lot since we left to go to my mothers, but having just given in to my feelings, allowing this to happen, it seems almost too soon for this question to be out in the world.

Joshua doesn't want to rush us this time and I don't either.

"AJ, you've never held back before, so just spit it out. I can take it."

I know *he* can take it.

The question is whether or not I can take the inevitable response.

"It can wait, JJ."

Pausing in his perusal of my hair, he shifts and bringing his other arm around, uses it to tip my head up in his direction.

"No, it can't. Spill it, Jeffries."

Placing the tiniest kiss to my nose and causing my body to shiver, he laughs and leaning in to do it again, I stop fighting and give him what he wants.

"What are your plans, you know," I swallow hard, shoving off the nerves. "for what comes next?"

Brushing his hand across my cheek, he leans in, our lips a blink apart, and whispers.

"Well, if you must know, I planned on kissing you."

His lips press against mine then, and despite how swept up I am in the feel of his kiss, the question I asked fights with me. The need to know what comes next overriding everything and keeping me grounded in the very moment I'd like nothing more than to lose myself in.

What he must feel when a second later, he breaks away, turning on the sofa until he's facing me down, his expression serious, but thankfully not grim.

"When I got on the plane, the only plan I had was being here. For Wayne's funeral, for you, god, even for Kevin, though he really didn't need me to be. All I planned to do was be here."

"And now?"

"You've given me everything I wanted, baby. Everything I've dreamed of. So, my plan now is to deal with things back in Carolina and finalize my move back home."

This time when our lips meet, it's all me and I'm holding nothing back. His answer, just words to be sure, but ones I somehow know without reason he will hold true to. Every step he's taken since coming back all the proof I need in how serious he is.

How right he wants to make all the wrongs in our past.

It's also a kiss he's unprepared for, as my body pounces on his, bridging the little bit of distance he'd placed between us and knocking him onto his back. He recovers quickly as his hands make their way around my back, bringing me even closer as my chest presses to his.

"Slow down, love." He whispers when after a few minutes of letting my hands explore his body, slipping their way under his shirt, desperate for an even closer connection, I deepen the kiss, boldly taking charge and connecting our tongues the way he had done before, only this time, not pulling away.

"JJ, I want this with you."

There's no missing the way my answer speaks to him, his eyes hooded, his breathing heavy. The pressure of his hands alone against my back, only driving the need within me more.

Despite my fears from earlier in the day, I want this. I'm ready for it.

Joshua has spent the entire day attacking my carefully constructed walls in an effort to make it so. It's time he reaps his reward.

It's time we both do.

His admittance of coming home seemingly turning me into a teenager again, my own admission doing the same as his lips fall from mine, making their way to my neck, where he wastes no time capturing my skin and marking it as his hands finally begin to shift downwards, grabbing and rubbing as he travels a delicious line down over my ass and his hands find their way under my dress.

My own breath becoming harder to catch when without much force at all, after grabbing hold of me tightly, he changes our positions, burying me easily under him and looking down, as lost in me as I am in him.

"I wanted to go slow with you, Alyssa, but you couldn't let me do it, could you?"

Bringing my face to his, I grin.

"Going slow is overrated."

Not missing a beat, he takes my attempt at getting a rise out of him and shatters it.

"Not the way I do it."

Pressing his lips to mine, he kisses me swiftly, and before I've had the chance to react, the pressure in the room changes when he grabs a hold of me and lifts himself from the sofa.

Making his way with ease around to the staircase, I ready myself to be carried up to the bedroom, but he surprises me when he stops before taking the first step.

"I waited twenty years for this, AJ, but if you're even a little unsure, I'll wait even longer. I know what you said on the sofa, but I also meant what I said. I want to take my time with you. So, love, are you sure this is what you want?"

"You're what I want, JJ. Just you."

Joshua

I've imagined this moment so many times over the years. What she would look like standing before me, all traces of awkward teenage body issues dispelled, and her voluptuous adult form in its place.

Her love for me mixing with the desire evident deep in her eyes, making those blue irises I spent years falling for, shine as bright as the moon that's glowing outside her window tonight.

It's a moment as often as I thought about it, I was also positive would never be afforded me. I'd run too fast and too far for way too long. People who do that don't get to stand before visions like AJ.

Yet here I stand. My heart in my hand, more than ready to hand it over to her forever.

No more running. No more games.

Just love, the pure kind.

What we had every moment after she first ran across the street almost thirty years ago.

I'm the luckiest son of a bitch in the world having this striking vision of a woman standing before me, giving me permission to own not only her body but her heart.

The greatest prize of all.

"Joshua," Stepping forward at the exact moment my name falls and placing a finger over her lips to silence her, I reach up with the other and sweep a tendril of fallen hair from her face before letting my finger fall away as my lips press softly to hers.

Every time I imagined this, the kiss was always slow. Tentative. Never fast or forceful the way it was when we were teenagers and lusting for each other.

Alyssa Jeffries is too good for fast and forceful. She deserves to be savored, and with the taste of our kiss marking me now, that's exactly what I plan on doing.

Savoring her for as long as time allows.

Stepping back and making my way around to stand behind her, hearing the catch in her breath as my hands brush against the small of her back, I rest it where the zipper meets the top of the dress she's wearing.

Her pulse has quickened, her heart racing as she releases a shaken breath. Her body still, a contradiction to what I can feel is taking place inside her with the closeness of my presence.

"I've spent twenty years dreaming of this exact moment," I whisper in her ear, her body quivering as I use my hand to begin the slow descent of the zipper.

"Was it," she begins, her breath catching at my touch. "like this when you dreamed of it?"

"Not exactly."

No dream could ever compare to the way it feels having her react this way to me. Giving herself over so freely as her body melts back into mine.

"Tell me," She softly pleads. "I want to know what you dreamt."

Bringing the zipper down as far it will go and placing my hands on her shoulders, reveling in the feel of her bare skin, soft and smooth underneath, I give in to what she wants, but instead of telling, I show her.

Slipping my fingers through the thin material of the straps, I slide them down slowly. The dress doing just as I want as it loosens and begins to fall. Moving closer, her bare back now pressed up against my chest, I lower my head down until my lips are barely brushing against the side of her neck.

"In my dreams, I would kiss you here," I murmur before pressing the full weight of my lips down onto her skin, tasting and breathing her in. "And I would keep kissing until I tasted every inch of your sinfully soft skin. Letting the heat that radiates whenever we're this close pull me under until I was burning from the inside out."

As her breath catches again, I follow through on my words by tracing a line with my lips, all the way down the side of her neck and across her shoulder blade, pausing just long enough to repeat the same motion on the other side. A move that earns me the slight shift of her body as she tries to turn.

"We'll get there, AJ, but not yet. Not until I've had my fill."

"J...Joshua."

Slipping my hands around her body, grabbing just tightly enough for me to lift her without fear of losing my grip, I lift her up, and taking in the surprised yet wanton look of desire I see when our eyes finally meet again, I make quick work of the distance between us and the bed, laying her down, watching as she slides herself back comfortably, taking in the vision in front of me.

The girl I love, open and ready for me to show her just how much.

My dreams finally crashing into reality.

Chapter Twenty-Seven
Simple Man

Joshua

When I slipped out of AJ's bed before the sun came up, the last thing I expected to be met with when I finally made my way back to my best friend's place was him waiting for me on the lawn.

Feet firmly planted on the ground, a mug in his hand, he was firmly seated in what looked like one of his parent's old lawn chairs, his face not fully in my view but my eyes catching enough to see he wasn't the least bit happy.

In all the years we've known each other, this sight of him is one I'm not remotely familiar with.

"What the hell are you doing out here at this hour?"

Making my way closer, I'm able to take more of him in, and there's no denying he's pissed. His rigid posture along with the scowl he's sporting are dead giveaways. What I don't get though, is why he's directing it at me.

"You know, when all this shit started a couple of weeks ago, I really thought, this is it, right? Wayne and I talked a lot over the years about it. It's like when he passed, he knew he was giving you a reason to come back. Claim what was yours. Be back where you belong, with the people who give a damn about you. Love you. It was a lot like Helen was always claiming. Wayne was a fucking saint."

I nod, not finding a bit of fault in anything he's saying.

"Then when you got here and you and Aly, you both fell into each other again, Sammie and I were both so stinking happy. It was all happening the way it needed to. The way it should have been for decades."

"Kev, buddy, I'm with you all the way here man, but why are you saying all this now?"

"Because with what's happened the last three days, it seems you haven't changed at all. You're still fucking running. You're still an idiot."

Okay, I'm willing to accept a lot when it comes to the people I care about being hurt by the things I've done, but given the fact I've spent the last three days holed up with AJ and not running anywhere, this isn't one of those times.

He's got it all wrong and there's no way in hell I'm taking it.

"When you didn't come back for the tiny ass amount of crap you brought with you, I didn't bat an eye. The last time I saw you, you were with Aly. Then one day turned into two and then three, and given your track record, it was clear as day what was going on."

"Kevin, you don't know what you're talking about. I've—"

"No, Josh. Not this time. This time, since you're magically back again, you're gonna let me finish."

Let him finish the speech he's wasting his breath on because none of it is remotely close to what actually happened?

No way in hell.

"Kev—"

"You're deaf now too, I take it? Did I not just say you're gonna let me finish?"

Knowing if I speak again it will get me absolutely nowhere, but still annoyed at having to hear this, I shove my hands out abruptly before raising them in the air, letting him continue.

"She fucking loves you, man. She always has. You may have hightailed it over the border and made some lame ass version of a life for yourself. You may have even forgotten all about us over here, you know, the family you left behind. But, brother, she never did. She tried to make us all think she did. Landing her job and working her way up until she was running the damn library herself, finding herself a new man even. She put on the show of all shows, but she never once moved on from you."

Jesus.

He thinks I left town after the first night and left AJ in the dust. I really need to put an end to this.

"I know you wanna interrupt and tell me I'm full of it or it's none of my business, but you need to hear this. I held my tongue for twenty damn years, and it ends now. If you don't see it and won't stick up for that woman, I will. Alyssa deserves better."

He's not speaking another word, especially with the way he just ended that.

"I know she does."

"Good. Then you also know that as much as I love you, there's nothing I'd like more than to smack the smug look off your face. How could you do it, huh? How could you walk away again? It took her years to get over the loss the last time you pulled this stunt. How could you put her through it again?"

Stepping out from the chair, it's then he makes his way over to me, making a point of stopping dangerously close to where I draw the line on personal space.

He's grandstanding, making a point of looking tough, and I get it, but it needs to stop. If I don't put an end to this, I've got no doubt he'll make good on the promise of knocking me into next week.

"Are you done?" I ask, matching his glare with one of my own. "Because if you're done, I think you need to be set straight on a few things."

"Yeah, I'm done."

I'll give it to him. Over the years when we talked, he would get serious, but within a couple of minutes, he'd break and laugh. Standing here, seeing him this way, it's been nothing if not eye-opening.

AJ wasn't the only one I hurt with my stunts.

"I didn't leave town, Kev. I know what my track record shows, but I'm telling you honestly, brother to brother, I didn't come back to just leave again. And when I do have to head back to deal with things back there, I wouldn't leave without telling you and Sammie."

Mulling over what I've said, his face doesn't betray what he might be feeling. He's still as rigid as he was when I pulled up, which means I've still got my work cut out for me.

"The last time you saw me, was the last time I wanted to be seen. The last time *we* wanted to be seen. I've been with AJ this entire time. At her place. Which, if you had just called over there, I'm sure she would have told you or passed the damn phone to me and I would have. Hell, you could have come barging in with all this shit you're carrying right now and you would have seen for yourself."

It takes a little longer then I would have expected, with him continuing to stare me down, but once he gets what he's after, senses it from my words, the change is immediate.

"You've been with Aly this whole time?"

"Yes! It's what I've been trying to tell you! Geez, Kev." I sigh. "You know our history. Did you really think I'd see her and we'd fall right back into old patterns? It took time." I pause again, realizing the error quickly. "It's going to take time. A lot of it. I'm only here now because while she's sleeping, I wanted to grab my stuff and fill you in on what's been going on."

"You didn't leave her?"

"No," I repeat, beginning to feel like a broken record. "I swear to you, man. I'm done hurting everyone, you and Sammie included. I mean, that's what this speech is really about, right? It's about me and you."

Stepping back, finally backing down, he throws his body down into his chair and runs a hand heavily over his face.

Taking stock of the situation, I shuffle my way around him, heading toward the side of the house, grabbing a chair and making my way back over, putting it down beside him and taking a seat.

"When you came home and you told me what went down with you and AJ, I didn't even think much of it. Hell, being married to Sammie and how often we get into it when either of our temper flares, I thought it was nothing. You'd get back with her again at school Monday if any attempt Sunday didn't work. I didn't think I'd wake up the next day and find you gone."

As much as looking back turns me inside out, I know it's needed. This is all ancient history at this point, but history at the time I'd been too selfish to care about.

"If it helps, I didn't know I was going to run until I did it."

"When did you know? Was it right after I went upstairs to bed? And what made the choice for you? Was it because she was pregnant and you didn't want to deal with it?"

For as well as Kevin knows me, it pains me to think he would believe I left because I didn't want to deal with a pregnant AJ. Shit. It was the last thing on my mind. Now, bringing a child into the mess of my life at the time, was another thing entirely.

"I didn't run from the responsibility, and you of all people know it. As stupid as I was back then, even I knew we were both responsible for what happened the night we slept together without protection."

"Then why?"

Got no issues answering the question, but I've got one of mine first.

"Why now, Kev? You've had twenty years to ask me about this. Why did you wait until now?"

"Honestly, I was a bit afraid of the answer I'd get if I asked. Whenever I did bring up Alyssa when we'd talk, it never ended well. The last few years though, I've wanted to ask on more than one occasion, but it never seemed right getting into this historic crap with you a thousand miles away."

"Your reason for not asking and mine for leaving, they're kind of the same. You know about my parents, what happened to me the four years I was gone. If you think about it, you'll get why I ran."

"Newsflash, you're not your parents. You're also not the shit you've been through."

"Thanks, doc. I think I figured it out for myself already, but back then, every time I ran was because I was trying to outrun my past. Outrun the hand I'd been dealt. I really believed everyone was better off without it in their lives. Better off without me." When he rolls his eyes when I stop to take a breath, I can't help laughing. "I get it, okay? No one said it was logical or even right, but it happened."

"Did you guys talk about what happened with that?"

"We did. One of the biggest betrayals I've ever done was leaving her alone and what she ended up facing because of it. It's one of the things I have to spend what time I've got left making up for."

"Sammie was with her when she found out what was really going on, did she tell you?"

"She did, yeah."

"You left a lot of destruction in your wake when you left, Josh, but a lot of it for me when you reached out and we started talking again, was forgiven. I'd gotten over it as the years went by and you didn't vanish on me. But man, Sammie told me what happened, every sickening detail, and it's that memory, what Alyssa went through without you I just couldn't get over. Don't know if I ever will."

What he doesn't get is it's something I don't think I'll ever get over either. The pregnancy may not have been a viable one, but it didn't matter. She never should have been with Sammie when it all came crashing down.

It should have been with me.

"Fair play, Kevin, because honestly with everything I know now, I don't think I'll ever be able to close my eyes without seeing it either. Let alone get over it."

"Look, about earlier—"

'Don't even gotta say it, brother. I deserved it, even if it was kickstarted by a misunderstanding. We're good, at least on my end."

"Same."

Looking down and catching sight of the time, realizing just how long the two of us have been sitting here, I jump up.

When I swore to her I would prove I changed, I meant it. There's no way in hell I'm even giving her an hour alone with the thoughts I know still have to be just idling beneath the surface. She's not allowed to think I bailed.

Never again.

"I need to grab my stuff and head back. I wasn't really planning on being away this long."

"Go," he motions with his hand, and with a quick slap to his back, I head straight to the door. It's only when I hear him call out as I'm about head through, I stop. "And for fuck sakes, bro, give her the damn box!"

Chapter Twenty-Eight
Here and Now

Alyssa

Shifting in the bed, pulling the blankets as I turn to the left and the hardened body I'm expecting to feel after what we'd shared the night before, I stretch my hand out and instead of being met with the feel of his skin under my fingertips, I hit air before it drops dead to the grooves in the bunched up blanket where he no longer resides.

With my breath catching when the reality of the situation hits me, I'm reminded of the dream I'd been having before I'd woken.

Standing beside my daddy, admitting my fears to the only person who would truly understand them. Listening intently as he gave his two cents, infusing me with his strength with each word spoken.

"What's troubling you, dove?"

"It's JJ, Daddy. He's back."

"And what about his being back is causing you to frown so deeply?"

"It feels too good to be true, Daddy. I'm happy—truly happy—for the first time since I woke up to find him gone. My heart is fulfilled."

"I'm not seeing the problem here, dove. How can you feeling this way be wrong?"

"It's not wrong, but when I've spent my life as the girl always having to say goodbye, how can I expect this time to be any different?"

"Alyssa Marie," he pauses. "You're the reason it's different."

"I don't understand."

With a smile, he wraps his arms around me.

"You will, dove. When the time is right, you'll understand it all."

Never one to speak in riddles, I'm perplexed by what he's said, but before I can ask him to explain, he speaks again.

"Things are not always as they appear, Alyssa. Remember that."

He faded and shortly after, I felt myself doing the same until I began to wake up.

What had been such a beautiful dream, a wish my heart had been making every day since he passed, now turning into something ugly.

My daddy's words as false sounding as the ones Josh had spoken then and now.

It's not supposed to be like this.

After breaking down the final wall between us last night, giving in to the feelings neither one of us has ever been able to deny, becoming one again, there was to be no looking back.

How could I have been so stupid?

I should be used to this with as many times as it's happened.

I'd given into Joshua and he had gone ahead and done now, the same as he had in the past.

Taking me and the heart I so willingly handed over, twisting and breaking it before turning on his heel and running before he could be held accountable.

The problem is, this time Joshua isn't the only one at fault for the outcome.

I am too.

I lied to him, but worse, I lied to myself.

Sure, I forgave him for the past, I've never stopped loving him, and I do want to spend the rest of my life with him. None of those things were lies.

My ability to forget, though, it's there where the lie resides.

My first.

I lied when I said the walls could be overtaken. We could see our way past them and get back to where we always should have been. It was a lie because this wall, the one built around the fear of him leaving, it's rebuilding as I sit beneath the sheets we made love on.

As I'm bombarded by the scent of him still lingering, and the memory of his body as it had taken mine—loved mine—I feel my heart beginning to harden as it prepares to seal over. A heavy lock and chain tightening, protecting me from the pain threatening to flood out if I give in to the loss of him.

A heart never built to hold onto something as cold and unfeeling as hate, but one with each troubling breath I attempt in an effort to calm wants nothing more than to become what it was never meant to be.

Spiteful. Angry. Filled with loathing.

Slipping from the bed, my body bare and full of shame, I numbly move toward the dresser and pulling the nightie from the drawer, lifting it over my head and sliding it on, the first threat of emotion forces its way through. A single tear slipping from my eye. Swiping at it violently, I scrub at the other one before it has the chance to do the same.

I will not do this.

I will not let him win.

A determination that threatens to crack when my head lifts at the sound of the door opening, a tray coming around it into view before being followed up by the very person at the very center of my change.

"Breakfast is served!"

Joshua

I knew slipping out of bed the way I had, there was the small chance I would find her awake when I returned. What I wasn't at all prepared for was the version of her I'm faced with.

This isn't my AJ. It's not even my Alyssa.

Following her gaze, as it falls to the tray in my hands and then to the door I've just stepped through, coming full circle and falling on me briefly before lowering to the ground, it's easy to see what's going on.

The mistake I've made.

Again.

"AJ…" I begin, but she quickly shuts me down.

"Shut up."

This is *definitely not* my AJ.

"Let me explain."

Shaking her head wildly, she widens the space between us by taking a step back and turning away from me.

"I don't want to hear anything you have to say. Put the tray down and leave."

"No."

There is no way in hell I'm walking out of this room.

Sure, in doing so, I'd be giving her what she wants, but honestly, is it really what she wants? It's clear she's reacting to my not being here. How she felt waking up alone. What I'm witnessing is what I wasn't privy to when I took off at sixteen. She's building the wall back up between us. Doing whatever it takes to preserve her heart.

She's pushing me away in an effort to protect herself.

If I do as she asks and walk out of the room, though, I'm only proving the voice in her head, the one wanting her to believe I've been lying all this time, right.

I can't do it.

I'm not giving her what she wants.

Sighing heavily, she flips around to face me and it's where I see it. Her anger. What in turning away she'd been attempting to hide, is now on full display. Her eyes hardened, her body rigid, and her lips, the soft delicate lips I'd spent hours overnight devouring, now dipped into a frown.

"Joshua, don't make this any harder than it has to be. Please just do as I ask and leave."

It's been a long time since I've heard it, but shades of the way she stood before me twenty years ago are present in her tone now.

Her voice is completely devoid of any feeling. No inflection, all signs of her musical lilt gone.

In leaving her, I've done the unthinkable.

I've turned Alyssa into the very monster I've been running from all these years.

Cold, unfeeling, and without remorse.

Something I can't stand for.

She will not become me.

"You don't want me to leave, AJ, and we both know it." Shifting on my heel, I do what she asked and I make my way over to the nightstand, placing the tray down, but once it's safely down, I waste no time crossing the room to her, not even pausing when she flinches at my touch.

"Let me explain why I wasn't here when you woke up." I plead, but again it falls on deaf ears as her head begins to shake. This time, the force of it so strong it's almost manic.

"I don't care why you weren't here, Joshua. I just want you gone."

The clipped tone is like a knife being plunged into my heart, especially given what we shared together the night before, but I can't react. If I do, I'll lose her for good.

"You don't mean that."

"I mean every word." She spits out angrily and pulling from my hold, she turns, grabbing my jacket off the chair and throwing it at me. The hit of the material against my face letting me know in no uncertain terms how far I've fallen.

"I can't believe how stupid I was. Falling right back into the same load of crap you've been spewing since we were kids. You've been telling me for years what kind of person you are, and I was just too blinded—too stupid—to see it. I get it now, okay? So, why don't you do what we both know you're going to do now that you've been caught, and leave?"

Turning away again and making her way over to the bed, she sits, running her fingers over her hair, while closing her eyes and taking and releasing a breath.

One breath. Then two. The breaths just keep coming, but she makes no move to settle.

"I'm not leaving."

"Lies." She whispers and now it's me shaking my head.

"I'm not lying to you. I understand you don't believe me, and I also get why you don't, but my god, AJ! I'm here. I may have left the bed, but I didn't leave you. Not this time. Nothing I've said to you since I came back has been a lie!"

"Actions speak louder than words, Joshua."

Does she want actions? Fine, I'll give her some godforsaken actions.

There's obviously no way I'm getting through to her standing here pleading, so if she wants some action, I'll give her the grandest one of them all.

I knew there was a reason I'd held onto the box as long as I did.

Even when she admitted to wanting to try again, I still held back.

Standing here now, the temperature in the room as frigid as an icebox, it's clear why.

It's time.

"You want me gone, fine. I'll go." This gets her attention as her head lifts just slightly. "There's one condition."

Scoffing, she lowers her eyes from mine again but thankfully doesn't shut me out completely.

"What's the condition?"

"You come for a ride with me."

"If I let you take me wherever it is you want to go, you're telling me you'll do as I ask and leave?"

I'm not planning on going anywhere, *ever*, but for the time being, she doesn't need to know that. So, even though it pains me to do so, in this instance, I paint on the most believable expression I can and give her exactly what she wants to hear.

"Yes. Come on this final drive and I'll go."

Chapter Twenty-Nine
Heart Shaped Box

Joshua

Pulling into the empty lot, I turn the key in the ignition, killing the engine, and slip myself out of the belt. Only then do I chance a look at the woman beside me.

I'm aware of the misstep I took leaving the house this morning. How stupid it was given everything we've spoken about and my actions from the past. Just as I'm aware how lucky I am having her sitting beside me, with the way everything went down earlier.

One of her biggest fears, what I've always known, has always been being left behind. I knew it at ten before I even took off the first time. I was shown again at fourteen when I came home. Not to mention my knowledge and complete disregard of it at almost seventeen.

Waking to an empty bed, her reaction, especially given our history, is understandable.

For as much as I've learned before coming back, and even in the short time I've been here, it's clearly not been enough. I've still got a lot of work to do.

"What is this, Josh? Do you need to twist the knife in a little deeper before you head out of town for another twenty years?"

The here she's talking about is the one place in the world I know she doesn't want to be, but also the only place in the world we can be for what happens next.

Wayne's grave.

Fifteen feet away from us, the final resting place of the only father I'd ever had, covered in fresh dirt and calling to me like a beacon. Helen's words from the day before, solidifying what I had already decided.

"You're showing him now, Joshua."

It may seem hokey to most, the belief that once someone you love has passed away, they're always watching over you, but growing up the way I did, being around these people, there's no other way I can see it.

Helen is right.

Wayne is up there with a front row seat to what is easily the biggest fight of my life. He's bearing witness to what he should have gotten the chance to see five years ago.

He's going to watch me give his daughter her heart back.

"You've made your feelings crystal clear, AJ, and I swear to you, I'm going to respect them. But before I do, I'm going to need you to trust me just one more time. Come with me, let me say my piece to the both of you, and after it's over I'll go."

As gut-wrenching as it is, the mere thought of walking away from this woman, my love for her, the respect I have for her choices, even if they don't include me, makes the words easy to say.

The last thing I want to do is walk away from Alyssa. Do as she accused and stay away for another twenty years. But I also can't force her into a place she's not ready to be.

She may never be able to be.

What she doesn't know, and I'm not ready to admit, is even after what I've said, I'm not going back to North Carolina. It may have taken me twenty years to realize it, but I have now. There's no going back.

I'm home.

"Fine." she concedes, sighing heavily as she unclips and slips out of the seatbelt. Opening the door and getting out, making sure to slam it behind her.

"If you've got any pull, now would be a great time to use it, Dad." I quietly plead before following suit and getting out, making quick work of grabbing the box from the backseat and following behind Aly as she slowly makes her way over the grass leading to where her father rests.

Making sure to remain a few feet behind, I pause in my step when she finally reaches her destination, forcing myself to stay planted when after a few seconds of her just standing and staring, her knees give and she falls to the ground. The only sound to be heard, the sound of her emotion as she releases the tight grip she's held and begins to sob. Her hand coming up over her lips in an effort to silence, but what seems to only make the pain flow more freely.

"Is..." she begins, turning around and leveling her gaze on me. "Is this what you wanted, Joshua? Did you want to see me break? Are you happy now?"

Shaking my head, I cross the distance between us until she's not the only one on her knees in front of Wayne's grave.

"None of this makes me happy, AJ." I choke out when after a few minutes of using the doctors breathing exercises, I'm able to settle my own emotions. The quickened beat of my heart and the sniffling, the only reminders left of my reaction to the loss.

"When I was a kid, all I ever wanted was someone to give a damn. I wanted what you had. Leaving out how I felt about you, I was jealous of the relationship you had with Wayne. How he loved you. I wanted it for myself. The stupid thing is, I had it. I had it and I threw it away."

Losing Scott at such a young age had changed Wayne, but where it might have broken another man, it seemed to make him stronger. Better. He became a father figure to every person he encountered, but with me, it was something more. I knew it then, even if I'd been too stupid to admit it.

I may have been born Joshua Brantley, but to Wayne, I was always Joshua Jeffries.

He was my father in every way that mattered, and I was his son.

"I didn't bring you here to hurt you," I admit, turning and reaching for her hand, which thankfully, after a few seconds, she slips warily into mine. "I brought you here because I didn't get to tell Wayne—tell you—what he meant to me. What you meant. I'm showing you both now. In the only way, I know how. With all I've got left. I'm making it right, even if in the end, it's too little, too late."

Twisting around and grabbing the box, which thankfully when I'd dropped to my knees hadn't fallen open, I turn back around and looking to the gravestone solemnly, hand it over to the person who deserves it most.

Looking from me to the box and back again, her eyes questioning, her confusion obvious, I give her everything I'd been holding back.

"I found this at my aunt's house when I was eight. I liked the name on it. Not really a big fan of the shoes inside, so I tossed them and hid the box under my bed. I had no idea at the time what I was going to use it for, but after we went to see The Land Before Time, I spent half the night staring at the ticket. Just holding it in my hands, staring a hole through it. Knowing it was important, but not comprehending at the time just how important. The next morning, I put the ticket in the box, and well, in the years since I've kept adding to it."

Her trembling hand falls to the lid of the box and just as she's about to crack it, pull it back and reveal all of the treasures I've kept from our time together, I reach out and stop her. My hand tightening until her eyes lift from the box to meet mine.

"Not yet." Her gaze questioning, waiting me out, I push past the fear and smile.

"Sitting here in front of both you and Wayne, I'm telling you, Alyssa Marie Jeffries, I love you. I've been in love with you since you bounced your dirty face and knees across the road when I was seven. The contents of this box, they're proof that not once in the almost thirty years since, have I ever stopped."

"JJ—"

"No, Alyssa. Don't say anything. I'm not giving you this to get back in your good graces or to try and take away from the massive screwup I did leaving our bed this morning. I'm doing it because it's time. It's time you and your old man knew what I spent twenty years afraid to show. I love you. And no matter what you decide to do after today, just know I'll never stop. The way I feel about you, it's an always and forever kind of thing. It will never end."

Slipping my hand from hers, I get to my feet and moving around her, I pause, the vanilla scent making its way in the breeze directly to me. Leaning over, breathing it in, even if it's for the final time, I brush my lips over the top of her head softly.

And with no other words spoken, I walk away.

Giving Wayne what he wanted when he came to see me, but not in the same condition I'd found and left it in. This time when she gets her heart back, it's coming back intertwined with mine.

The way it'll always be.

Alyssa

Watching him walk away, my heart begs me with the ache appearing the further away he gets, to call out. Stop him. To just throw every ounce of caution—of absolute fear—to the wind and give in to what every part of me knows I want.

Us together.

An internal war beginning when as my lips part in order to give in, my head begins to pound. A sharp stab right above the eyes, causing me to break the connection as I pull away and close them tight. The stab becoming a dull pound when after a few minutes, I open them and finding their way back to where I'd left him, he's nowhere to be seen.

He's gone.

Keeping his word just like he said he would.

After this morning's events and the things I said when he walked into the room announcing breakfast, this should make me happy. He was, after all, respecting my wishes, but staring out over this barren field, happiness is the last thing I feel.

The ache from earlier, really a hole beginning to form, is an exact replica of the hole from twenty years ago, the loss of him just as strong, but as I shift on the ground, attempting to get up from my place before my daddy's grave and catch the box fall to the ground, I'm reminded it's not at all the same.

Daddy's words from my dream pushing their way to the forefront of my mind, reminding me of what I'd been so lost in my fear, I'd forgotten.

"Things are not always as they appear, Alyssa."

Joshua leaving while I slept and going to Kevin's in order to grab his things, not wanting to spend another day apart, and worse, him coming in with the tray filled with breakfast, no clue of what he would find on the other side of the door, was what Daddy meant.

It wasn't at all how it appeared when I first woke up, and if I had just focused on what he was trying to tell me while still sleeping, I wouldn't be here alone.

With only a box of mementos to keep me company.

Picking up the box and running my hands over the lid and down the side, turning it around and catching the name, faded, but still visible, along with all the grooves and cracks from the years it remained in Joshua's possession, the ache in my heart becomes a swell.

Thirty years.

He held onto this box, filled with what he admitted were all things from our story, for almost thirty years.

Things really aren't as they appear.

Digging myself out a spot on the ground behind Daddy's gravestone, I lean back against the hard slab, making myself comfortable, all the while never letting my eyes fall away from the box. Taking a nervous breath in preparation, following it up quickly with another one as the nerves over what I'm about to uncover threaten to overtake the moment, I close my eyes and swallowing hard, pull the Band-Aid off, yanking the lid back.

Letting my eyes fall to the contents.

An array of colors and scents assaulting my senses as I take in the numbered items filling the inside. The memories following quickly after as I slip my hand down and pick up the first item number **one**.

His words from before he'd walked away, the reason this box exists in the first place, now sitting softly in the palm of my hand, bringing with it a flood of the same emotions I'd felt that night.

Eight-year-old Alyssa, smitten with the boy across the street, over the moon to be out alone at the movies together. Connecting to the boy even more as he explained without shame just what I meant to him. What I was.

His Great Valley.

Catching the tear the second it falls, careful not to stain the ticket, I swipe at my eyes while laying it down into the box as tenderly as I can, waiting for a beat, overcome with the weight of just the ticket alone, before reaching out to the item bearing the number **two**.

What I recognize immediately, but am perplexed by. Easily recalling the manic way I'd become when a few short weeks after I'd shown it to JJ, it was nowhere to be found.

Never once guessing he had been the reason it was missing.

Flipping the calendar open, I make quick work of the paper, finding the date and what is now the faded red marker circling it.

Our first kiss.

Only, that's not the only thing I find when I land on the page.

In the top righthand corner, is the number **three** and though this one confuses me for a second as I process what I'm seeing, it doesn't take long once I've popped it from the tape holding it to the page, twirling it in my hands and feeling every groove, to understand.

These two go together.

A piece of bark from a tree might not make sense to many, but flipping it over again between my fingers, remembering how it felt when he'd pressed his lips to mine after catching me, I'm warmed by the knowledge he felt the same. My own memento from then matching his perfectly.

The same way we always have.

Picking through the box, coming across the items he's listed as **four** and **five**, I'm moved at just how much care he'd taken with them.

The birthday cards—ones from our time together, as well as the ones I'd handed over when he came back at fourteen—tied with my twenty-year-old hair tie, no bends or folds to be found. The small note I'd written to him before he took off at ten, as crisp and new as the day I'd written it. Bringing with it another round of tears I have to fight off as I attempt to read the scribbled words.

You belong here, JJ. I don't want you to go. But, like Daddy always tells me, it's not about me. So, whenever you get where you're going, I hope you're happy. I hope you find what you're looking for.

Laying the note down, my hand finds its way easily to the pendant now hanging around my neck and wrapping my hand around the angel, I embrace the tightness and pull that follows when I squeeze, closing my eyes and letting the memory wash over me.

The innocence I still managed to hold onto, even after leaning the truth about the world, mixing with the maturity level I attempted to put forward when penning the note.

Recalling with ease my one biggest wish at the time. My need for Joshua to see me, not as the naïve girl I was, but something more.

Something worthy of him.

"He never realized, Daddy," I whisper to the wind. "He spent so long believing he was the only one. He never realized he wasn't alone."

He was never alone.

Closing my eyes, I revel in the stillness as the air begins to shift with each slow and even breath I take. The swift force of it in seconds picking up and rushing over me, a small comfort and reminder I'm not alone either in what comes next.

A reminder I need when upon opening my eyes and bringing the box back into my lap, I'm met with an item I never expected to see again. Much less be holding in my hands.

One mans trash really is another one's treasure.

Running my fingers over the result and swallowing hard, I'm transported back in time as my stomach bottoms out, just as it did then, when the two pink lines, now faded with time come into focus.

The pregnancy test. He's had it for the last twenty years.

But how?

Instead of fighting against the memories as they come this time, I welcome them, going through all the pictures in my mind, trying to pinpoint when it happened. How he got his hands on it. Remembering how I left it on the counter, even recalling how I'd gone back to get it in order to throw it away and how sick I felt finding it gone.

The panic I experienced then so intense it caused me to vomit again. How easily I believed my parents had already found it. How my dad acted when I told him I was pregnant all the proof I needed, to tell me he had already known.

I truly believed he'd found the test all these years.

Letting the test fall, I don't stop myself when my hands find their way to my abdomen, the hole left over from the loss a gaping one not even the passage of time could heal.

Curling over, my hands still cradling my stomach, I relive it.

The emptiness I experienced at the doctor's admission. The web of denial I found myself trapped in, never admitting to myself or anyone else what they all knew and needed me to accept. Never admitting the pregnancy wasn't real.

Viable.

Believing for as long as I could I was carrying a real child.

Our child. JJ's and mine.

A boy. One who would have my eyes, but in every other physical way, be the spitting image of his father. A child who would be wise like my daddy, a take no prisoners spitfire like my mother, but who would have the best parts of his parents.

My heart and Joshua's soul.

Landon Joshua Brantley.

Swallowing down the rush of emotion threatening to boil over just thinking of the child I wanted so badly, believed in so completely, I focus my attention again on the box. This time, given what I've already come across, petrified over what I'll find next.

Pushing all of the other items I've already seen to the side, I'm left with four more, but out of order. In reaching down and grabbing the test, I'd veered off the roadmap Joshua had attempted to create for me. A roadmap beginning in 1988, traveling an immeasurable amount of distance until it found itself here and now.

At the end.

His capturing of our first time unsurprising as I take note of the item he has listed as number **six**.

Untamed Heart tickets.

The date is illegible on the paper but alive and bright in my head.

Of course, given every other moment he's captured in our story, he would capture this one too, the item he's listed at number **eight** an even deeper reminder.

The picture of us from the mantel at my parent's house.

A copy, since to this day, the original still rests atop the fireplace. It's the reason for being in the box, given to me easily in Joshua's own words when I flip it over and catch sight of his familiar scrawl.

Photographic proof Josh Brantley is truly happy.

The ache from before presenting again, knowing just how true for him this was. Him admitting as much that night. Making the reminder of him leaving an even harder pill to swallow.

"Oh Josh," I whisper, moved by all of the items I'm seeing, fissures appearing in the wall I'd taped back together to protect myself this morning, and threatening to break altogether when reaching down, I grab hold of what he's listed as number **nine**.

Sir Wilfred Laurier Collegiate Institute – Commencement
October 9, 1999

The program from my high school graduation.

Sucking in sharply, like I've been burned, I drop the booklet. Shifting back, scooting across the grass in shock, I stare at it as it blows in the wind. Not understanding for the life of me what this has to do with us. What my graduating class has to do with our story.

He must have gotten a copy of this from Kevin...*right?*

How else would he have come across this and kept it in this good of condition? Especially since I know for a fact my parents are still in possession of their copy. It's framed right alongside the pictures I had taken earlier in the year in their foyer.

Their proudest moment.

Staring at the program, as if the answers will present themselves if I just continue to look at it, I try to understand. Every other item in the box, even the two I have yet to pull out, they're all connected and told a story. Our story.

This program, especially the position it's numbered, throws the entire story off course.

His roadmap leading straight into a ditch.

My graduation was part of my story alone, not ours.

Needing answers, I slide back over to the box and picking the fallen program off the ground and tossing it back in, I pick up the final two items.

The first, a red rose in the early stages of wilting labeled number **ten**, I accept readily. Closing my eyes when after bringing it to my nose and inhaling its scent, I succumb to the memories of the last time I'd been this close to one.

Daddy's funeral.

Eyes popping open, where this rose is from, along with what it symbolizes slams its way straight into me, knocking my breath away.

Much the way he did when he appeared seemingly out of nowhere three days ago.

His words to me before he left ringing in my ears.

The rose is here to symbolize his relationship with my father.

Placing the lid back onto the box, I get to my feet and make my way around. Brushing the petals of the flower across my lips before leaning down and placing it to the darkened dirt below.

Admitting to my daddy easily what I've been struggling to admit to myself since I told Joshua I wanted to try again.

"I love him, Daddy. I always have. I'm afraid of what might happen, but I'm even more frightened of a future without him. I forgave him a long time ago, and I hope, even though it came far too late, you can forgive him too. The same way I forgive you for keeping what you did a secret all these years. You went to your grave protecting me. But what I told you a few days ago, I meant. You can let go now, Daddy. I've got this."

Moving in closer and placing my hands to my lips, I kiss them before leaning over and placing them on the gravestone. Hoping he can feel them as easily as I know he can hear my words.

Getting back to my feet and walking around to where the shoebox lays in wait, I pull the final item marked eleven from inside. A black jewelry box, smooth to the touch with an envelope taped on top, thick black scrawl marking it from one side to the other.

READ ME FIRST

Settling back in on the grass and leaning back against the gravestone, I rip the envelope at the end and pull out the letter, doing exactly as he asked.

I read.

AJ,

This was never meant to be a part of the box, but after seeing you again and handing over the guardian angel, something needed to go in its place.

It seemed only fair it was this.

Before you open the box and see what's inside though, there are some things you need to know.

I bought this seventeen years ago.

It was just after I turned nineteen. Kevin, who I'd already reached out to at the time, called me up and begged me to come home for graduation.

It was so easy to say no.

Only, I lied.

I came back.

I was there, hidden away where I was sure no one would see me, but there none the less.

I watched as you crossed the stage, your left hand out, accepting the diploma being handed to you. I stayed long enough to see Kevin do the same, but it was in watching you, I made my decision.

It was time to come home.

Even if it took me years, I needed to fight for you.

For us.

So, riding the rush, I took things a step further and walked into the jewelry store in the mall. Determined to find the perfect ring to give to my perfect girl.

Only, like all the decisions and choices I made in my life up until that point, I never followed through.

I lost my nerve.

Alyssa, baby, I'm sorry.

Sorry for leaving, sorry for coming back and keeping it a secret, and for losing my nerve, but most of all, I'm sorry for not realizing what has been staring me in the face for the last thirty years.

You and I, we're infinite.

What I wanted then, hiding behind the tree watching you graduate, I want now. I want it even more if it's even possible.

I want you. Us. I want always and forever.

Despite the way it looks, I'm not giving up, and I'm not running away. I'm here for the long haul, baby, no matter how bumpy the road or rough the terrain.

I'm here and I'm home, this time for keeps.

So, when the time is right and you're ready to hear the question, come find me.

I promise you, no matter how long it takes, I'm still going to be here dying to ask, and desperate to hear your answer.

I love you, and it's an always and forever kind of thing.

-JJ

Chapter Thirty
Get it Right

Joshua

"Landon Joshua Brantley." She huffs out as she busts past the now open door, breezing past me, not stopping until she's almost all the way to the kitchen.

If I was surprised at how quickly she'd found me, I shouldn't have been. Even all these years later, she's still a determined spitfire when she wants something.

Focusing back on what she'd been saying when she barreled her way through the front door, I follow her to the kitchen where once I enter, I see her occupying a stool at the bar.

The ring box directly between us, resting like a time bomb.

"The name missing on this ring," she explains, popping the lid back on the ring box. "It's Landon."

Softening at her admission, her pronouns from our night at the hospital making all the more sense, I step toward her and just like before, her hand comes out, halting me.

"I have questions..."

No doubt.

With the bombshell of me being at her graduation and then my proposal on paper, I'm sure she had an endless supply of them.

"Shoot."

"You came to my graduation?"

I nod and she sighs.

"Why?"

"AJ—"

"No, don't do that." She interrupts. "You don't get to be all soft and sweet with those swoony eyes, calling me AJ and making me melt."

"Swoony eyes?" I ask, all attempts at seriousness ruined when the snort I've been trying to hold back falls out. "You think my eyes are swoony, baby?"

Hanging her head and shaking it, her hair flinging from side to side, I can't help it, I laugh. The last couple of minutes haven't turned out at all as I expected. A feeling appearing to be mutual when she looks up again a few seconds later and her cheeks are crimson.

"Yes, Alyssa, I came to your graduation." I reiterate in an attempt to get the conversation back on track.

"Why?" she repeats and this time, I give her what she's after.

"At the time, I couldn't tell you. I just needed to be there. My mind didn't settle until I boarded the flight. I see it a little differently these days." Motioning to the letter I see in her left hand, she looks down and nods.

"You wanted to come home."

"No." Eyebrows raising in surprise, I waste no time correcting her. "I *needed* to come home."

"I'm going to sound like a broken record, but why?"

Holding up my hand, I cross the room until I'm pulling out the stool at the opposite end of the bar and sitting down. Only then do I turn toward her and answer.

"You."

Picking up the ring and moving it around in her hand, her eyes never once leaving the sterling silver as it glistens under the lights, she swallows and turns to me.

"Were you really planning to propose?"

"Then or now?"

"Both."

The easiest answer I've ever had to give.

"Yes...to both."

This gives her pause. The façade she's desperately attempting to hold onto is failing her.

"Your parents knew what I didn't when I was nineteen. If I had proposed then, AJ, it would have ended badly. Because even then, I still believed everything I touched would turn to shit."

"And now?"

"Now I know the difference. The only way I can turn everything I touch to shit is by doing what I did at sixteen. Leaving and running away. Nothing is lost if I stay and fight. If I just am. I can be the creator of my destiny or the creator of my demise. I choose the first option."

"Oh, JJ..."

Her words barely register before she's off her feet and ending the divide between us, my body moving just in time to sweep her up into my arms, reveling in the feel of her as I bury my face into her neck and just breathe her in.

She's here. She's real. She's mine.

All of these facts play on repeat as she refuses to let go, using her strength instead and tightening her hold. Her body shaking under what I can only assume is the full weight of what her being here this way means.

"Waking up and finding you gone was debilitating, JJ. I physically felt like I was dying. My arms felt like noodles, my legs were rubber. My head was swimming, but my brain was numb. Broken. Even with your promise of never leaving again, I still went back there. The room as empty and cold this morning as it was then. Maybe more. It came over me like a tidal wave, the frigidness. I could physically feel my body hardening. Pushing you out. I loved you so ferociously and all I could see was you doing it to me again. You'd got me."

"AJ—" I attempt to stop her, not needing her to explain. Understanding exactly what she must have felt, especially after how many times I swore I would never leave her again.

"Let me finish."

So, as she steps back, really letting me see her for the first time since she found her way back to my arms, that's exactly what I do.

"You walked into the room carrying the tray full of food with the brightest grin on your face, and I couldn't see any of it. All I had was the cold and the fear it was wrapped in. Even knowing you hadn't left, you were standing in front of me the same way you are now, I let the fear take over. I got you before you could get me."

Leaning in, I brush my lips against her forehead softly and when she shivers, pull back and lock my irises to hers.

"I already know, AJ. I knew the minute I walked into the room."

"Then why didn't you stop me?"

"I would have invalidated your fear if I stopped you, baby. It's a valid fear, but one we both have to fight and beat. I had to let it play out, otherwise, you wouldn't be standing here now. I can keep coming back every single day for the rest of my life, but until you dealt with your own feelings about it, nothing would change."

Her fear of me leaving is a lot like my fear of ruining things. The longer I lived under the belief and let it dictate every step I took in my life, the longer I stayed away.

I had to conquer it. Face it and prove myself wrong.

Each step leading me home again changed my perception.

Admitting I wanted and needed Alyssa. Booking the flight, then getting on the plane. Landing in Toronto and going back to Kevin's place. Going to Wayne's funeral and being persistent.

It all leads me to where I am. To what I've conquered.

I'm not all the way there, and I will always have moments where I feel like Alyssa deserves better, but as long as we're together, those thoughts won't win.

We will.

"Why this house?"

I was wondering how long it would take for her to ask. Truth be told, I assumed it would have been the first question she had when she showed up on the doorstep, but I'm glad I was wrong. Her sliding back into my arms again before asking, has me feeling the rightest I've felt since we made love the night before. A gift I'm not sure I would have been afforded if the conversation had gone any other way.

"You mean besides the prime location?"

Slapping my chest, she laughs softly.

"I knew it! You did let your stomach decide."

"Maybe, but only a little. My heart did the rest."

Ten years ago, when my aunt and uncle put their house on the market, moving to Florida in some half-assed attempt to live out their glory years, I bought it. Out of sight was never out of mind for me, so when the opportunity to own this place came up, I knew I couldn't waste it.

Standing here now and witnessing all of the renovations I'd paid for over the years actually taking form, every room in the place having been remodeled and made new again, I knew it was the perfect place for what comes next.

My life coming full circle.

The house I ran from at ten now becoming the house I want to make memories in.

Marriage, pregnancy, love, and everything in between.

I want it all with her. Only ever her.

My AJ.

"Ask me." She murmurs, and tipping her head up, searching her eyes for any sign of doubt and finding none, I take the ring from her hand. Watching her eyes light up and her breath catch, she steps back and her entire face comes alive as she smiles. "Stop stalling, JJ. You heard me the first time."

"Say it again." Grinning when she rolls her eyes, she doesn't waste a beat.

"Ask me."

Dropping down to one knee, with my heart on my sleeve and the ring held out between us, I take the final mistake I made and I make it right.

"Alyssa Marie Jeffries, will you marry me?"

Epilogue
It All Begins Again
5 Years Later

Alyssa

"Joshua!" I call out across the backyard to my husband. "Come quick!"

Motioning with my hands when looking up he pauses in his raking, he tosses the rake to the ground and sprints over to me and the back door.

Placing a finger to my lips to make sure he stays silent, I make my way back through the kitchen and the entryway. Only pausing once I've swung the front door open.

"AJ, as cute as this is, and as curious as I am, those leaves out there aren't going to—"

"Look!" I whisper hiss and pointing out the door, I wait until he catches it.

Our son Jamieson is sitting on the front lawn, but where one would say it's an everyday occurrence, the other person sitting with him, pointing up to the sky, isn't.

We made a decision early on in our marriage that while we still had the ability to have our own children together, we wanted something different. We wanted more.

So, after a lot of soul searching and reaching out to the Children's Aid Society in an effort to be sure we were prepared fully, we became foster parents. After what happened with Joshua over the years, the flaws in the system, on top of the parents who weren't exactly in it for the right reasons, it seemed like the right thing to do.

The right thing for us.

We had more than enough love alone and together to give a child not only a good home, but a great life filled with love.

Jamieson, our second foster—the first having gone back to his mother after a six-month engagement—came to us a little over a year ago. Coming from a background eerily similar to the man he now calls his dad, he wasn't exactly the easiest nut to crack.

He was no match for JJ, though.

Within a few months, we'd broken down the little guys' walls and there was no looking back. He was completely and utterly ours. Our connection with him, how he took to us, both together and separately, was what I didn't even know I was missing in my life until I experienced it. Also, a connection I could never and would never want to imagine not being there.

If being with Joshua made me a stronger person, being a mom to Jamieson has made me a better one.

Today, though, the current state of our relationship, well, it changes.

Not where it matters of course, but the way we appear legally, it all changes with the papers we received.

We're adopting him.

Jamieson is officially a Brantley.

And just like his soon to be namesake, it looks as though he already has admirers.

"Is that little Ayala from next door?" Joshua asks and I merely nod and smile.

What's taking place outside on the grass, especially given the fact of Jamieson turning seven last week, is such a sweet reminder.

History repeating.

Turning into his side when after watching the two of them playing, Joshua laughs when Ayala pushes Jamie down to the ground and jumps up, ready to run, a rush of emotion hits me straight in the stomach.

"You think he's going to chase her down?" Joshua asks with a chuckle, bringing my face up to his and kissing the top of my nose softly.

Smiling wistfully, I nod.

"If he's anything like his father, he will."

"Do you think she'll let him catch her?"

Leaning in, he brushes his lips against the side of mine now, teasing yet tickling me with stubble from his five o'clock shadow.

"I think she will. Especially with the giggling she was doing when she pushed him down. She wants him to catch her."

Stroking my cheek tenderly his eyes never once leaving mine, not even to blink, his lips rise into a smirk.

"And once he catches her, what do you think he should do with her?"

Watching when much like we predicted, Jamieson is on his feet and bolting after the girl with the raven colored hair, I focus all my attention back on my husband, seizing the moment while we have it.

"Well, if he knows what's good for him, he'll give her the one thing she's been waiting for."

"And what pre-tell would that be, Mrs. Brantley?"

"Oh, I don't know," I respond with a grin and a bop of my finger to his nose. "Why don't you catch me and find out?"

Like a shot I'm on the move, knowing full well there won't be a second to lose, especially with all of the years Joshua spent training in North Carolina. Even recreating this moment from our past, knowing what the end result will be, and also watching our son do the same, nothing is going to stop me from making him work for it.

"AJ, admit defeat now!" I hear him call from what sounds like a few feet away. "You know you won't win!"

Making my way through the trees in the back of our house and heading straight through them, only one destination in mind, I laugh when just as I make my way through the brush, I'm swept up hard into my husbands' familiar arms, my breath taken as once I'm caught, he spins me around and his lips press deep to mine.

Our bodies moving as our breathing hitches in-between kisses until I feel the harshness of the bark against my back.

Recreation complete.

Hearing the laughter through the trees a few feet away from us, we pause in our kiss and listen to the children. Joshua breaking a few seconds later as the laughter we both held onto finally slips free.

"Let me go, Jamie," Ayala calls out, her own breathing labored. A request our son clearly doesn't heed when a few seconds later, we hear the sound of rustling leaves and the sound of her laughter and intake of breath. "Stop tickling me! Please!"

"I'll stop when you say it, Ayala."

Another round of laughter ensues as both Joshua and I slip our way through the trees closer to what is taking place.

"Say what?"

"What you whispered before you shoved me over."

Pausing mid-step and pulling me to a stop by bringing me into him, Joshua looks down at me.

"What do you think he's trying to get her to admit?"

For every ounce of smarts my husband has, his intelligence one of the things about him I find incredibly sexy, he sure can be slow sometimes.

"Like you don't know."

"Pretend I don't. What's so important he's got her on the ground tickling her?"

I could easily give him the answer, but while our son tickles his friend into submission, I think I'm going to try a different tactic. Lifting up on my toes, and cupping my hand to his ear, I press my lips in close and whisper.

"I like you, Joshua Brantley. I like you a lot."

This gets him. Between the sharp intake of breath and the shudder through his upper body as I spoke, there's no doubt he gets it now.

With hooded eyes he watches me as I lay back on my heels and wasting no time leans in close, our lips a breath apart, whispering his own revelation.

"I more than like you, Alyssa Brantley."

His lips touch mine at the exact moment our son gets the admission he's after.

"I like you, Jamie."

Like father like son indeed.

Joshua

"Hey, buddy," I announce, coming up behind Jamieson at the kitchen table, head bent over the thousand-piece puzzle he's determined to finish before heading to school Monday. "Can we talk?"

After ending Ayala's torture and letting her head home, we'd all done the same, with the agreement that Alyssa would grab the papers from our bedside table and meet me in the kitchen for the talk we're about to have with our son.

Because he is now. Legally.

Our son.

Kevin asked me a few weeks after we started looking into fostering if I was sure I knew what I was doing, and the answer was as easy then to say to my brother as it is to think about now.

I knew exactly what I was doing. My only mistake was not doing it sooner.

Sure, it might not have been the same, we wouldn't be sitting here with Jamieson as our son, it would have been another child. But, without a bat of a lash, whether then or now, I can guarantee it would have been the same amount of love being showered.

All the love we have to give.

AJ and I.

"Sure, Daddy. What do you want to talk about?"

Looking up at me, his eyes bright, wide and inquisitive, I attempt to start but am paused when Alyssa makes her entrance. Just like every other time this happens, I'm chopped liver as his lips curve into a smile when he sees her, jumping out of his seat and throwing his scrawny little arms around her waist, squeezing for all he's worth.

A feeling I'm all too familiar with.

If I could hold her every minute of every day, I would be doing what Jamie is now. Believe that.

Holding the papers in her hand out, I take them and she makes quick work of wrapping her arms around our son, bringing him as close to her as she can, all the while letting her smile grow larger and brighter with each passing second.

Alyssa as at home with Jamieson, as in love with him, as he is with her.

Mother and son.

The way it was always meant to be.

"Baby, your dad and I, we received some papers today and we wanted to sit down and talk to you about what they are and what they mean."

Releasing Alyssa from his hold, he takes up residence in the chair at the table he'd vacated and resting his hands on the top, taps his fingers impatiently as Alyssa and I pull up chairs on either side of him.

Laying the paperwork out, knowing he won't understand all of the legal jargon, but that he's more than equipped to understand the Petition for Adoption at the top of the page, I let his eyes filter down to the packet in front of him and wait for the response.

My body froze as he flips each page, my breath halted when he finally reaches the last page, takes the information staring back at him, in and flips the packet closed.

Both AJ and I, judging from the way she's also seemingly frozen in place across from me, unsure of how he'll feel about the finality of what is sitting in front of him, even with it being his decision to proceed in the first place.

Would he have buyer's remorse?

Are we really what he wants?

No, Joshua. Now isn't the time to go there. You're more than enough.

Try as I might not to have these doubts, I can't help it. As far as situations go, it feels like me and Wayne all over again. The man I adored wanting nothing more than to take me in and love me, and ultimately me not believing enough in him—in myself—and leaving.

This is way too close to home.

"Does this mean what I think does?" Jamieson, turning to Alyssa and meeting her now tear-filled eyes, asks softly.

"What do you think it means, son?" I cut in asking, wasting no time when his eyes flicker back to the papers, to reach over and place my hand on top of his. Alyssa easily following suit and resting her hand on top of my own.

"Am I yours now?"

Not moving my hand, but rocked to silence by the question, AJ easily gives the answer my heart wants to cry out with, but can't seem to find the words to utter.

"You have always been ours, Jamieson."

"Your mother is right, son." I finally find my voice and add. "You have always been ours. Right from the very first day."

Tapping the paper with my free hand, watching as both pairs of eyes fall to my movement, I say the rest of what my heart is screaming to release.

"This is just paper, Jamieson Jeffries-Brantley. If it disappeared right now, it would change absolutely nothing. You're ours and we're yours."

"Jamieson Jeffries-Brantley..." he repeats his name in a whisper. Over and over he says it, getting a little louder each time, Alyssa connecting the dots to what he's doing and joining in, both of their voices melding together the louder they get.

Pushing up from the chair, I move to where my son is seated and wrapping my arms around him, I hear the drag of Alyssa's chair as she also stands and curves her body around both Jamieson and me, I join them, by telling them what's in my heart.

The very truth in my soul.

What will take this particular ending and make it begin again.

"Jamieson Jeffries-Brantley, you're ours, we're yours, and it's an always and forever kind of thing."

THE END

Acknowledgments

I always say the stories I write wouldn't have been written without this guy supporting me, my co-author on this project, and while it's true, has always been true, it's never been more truthful than in this instance. This tale, more than any other, is our story. So much of our real lives put into this second chance love story it is hard to see where they end and, JM Winchester and I, begin.

So, to my co-author for this, thank you. Your friendship, love and acceptance, along with your impact, it is infinite and as everlasting as Joshua and Alyssa's love story.

From this gushy mama to the masses (or at least the masses that pick up this book), I couldn't do a section acknowledging those making these books possible, without giving out to my four amazing kids. One, who in the writing of this, became an adult. Your patience with me as a mother, along with your patience with me when I'm the "writer", means everything to me, just as the love you show me and spread to the world does. Just as you all do. I couldn't do this, wouldn't be able to do this, without you all by my side for the Winchester party ride. Caleb, Noah, Raine, and Isabella, I love you to the moon and back.

My beta readers. Pamela, Renee, and Aaron. Your input as I took on this challenge, after three years being away from it, kept me going. From the moments you found great, to the things I most definitely needed to look into and alter for the sake of Joshua and Alyssa's story, I'm so thankful, as I am grateful. This story wouldn't be half of what it is without you all. Much love and appreciation.

To anyone that has ever picked up a story by me. To those who will pick up this story, whether you love it in the end or hate it. I appreciate you all more than you'll ever know. It's all of you over the last six years who have allowed me to live my dream. I'll never forget your impact on my life.

About the Author

Melyssa Winchester is a mother of four from Toronto, Ontario, Canada.

When she's not writing, you can find her buried under the covers with her portable DVD player, watching marathons of Supernatural and Veronica Mars. When those aren't available, she can be found curled up in a corner with her e-reader and a plethora of books, falling in love with characters written so well she deems them her book boyfriends and girlfriends. If you want to find her, check Facebook or Twitter (@WinchesterBooks) as she may just have an addiction to both. If those don't work you can always keep up with her progress on her personal site.

Books by Melyssa Winchester

Series

Love United Series
Holding onto Heaven
No Surrender
Wanted
Stairway to Heaven
A Light in the Dark
My Heaven (Alternate Ending to Holding onto Heaven)

Count on Me Series
Count on Me
Hear Me Now
Take Me with You
All My Heart
Here & Now
Unbroken
What Lies Beneath

Black & Blue Series
Shades of Blue
Into the Blue
Heroine

Before the Light Series
Hold onto Me (Michael's Story)
Absence of Light (Ryan's Story)

Stand Alone Titles

The Space in Between
Remembering Sunday

www.ingramcontent.com/pod-product-compliance
Lightning Source LLC
Chambersburg PA
CBHW021235250626

47155CB00008B/3026